This book is due for return on or before the last date indicated on label. Renewals may be obtained on application.

-3 JAN 2009

**PERTH AND KINROSS COUNCIL
LIBRARIES & ARCHIVES DIVISION**

The Lonely Shore

FRANCES PAIGE

The Lonely Shore

HarperCollins*Publishers*

03980800

This novel is a work of fiction. The names,
characters and incidents portrayed in it are the work of the
author's imagination. Any resemblance to actual persons,
living or dead, or events is entirely coincidental.

HarperCollins*Publishers*
77–85 Fulham Palace Road,
Hammersmith, London W6 8JB

Published by HarperCollins*Publishers* 1999
1 3 5 7 9 8 6 4 2

A catalogue record for this book
is available from the British Library

ISBN 0 00 225757 2

Set in Sabon by
Rowland Phototypesetting Ltd,
Bury St Edmunds, Suffolk

Printed and bound in Great Britain by
Caledonian International Book Manufacturing Ltd, Glasgow

For Ann

Chapter One

July 1914

Alice and Joseph Lane did not allow the assassination
of the heir to the Austro-Hungarian throne to stop their
Annual Fair Fortnight visit to Largs. It was a pleasant
little town on the Ayrshire coast, popular with Glaswegians
because of the frequency of the steamers calling at the pier
to take them to the islands, Great Cumbrae, Bute, and further
afield.

'Anyhow, it's far enough away,' Alice said, 'that place with
the funny name.'

'Sarajevo.' Joseph hogged the *Glasgow Herald* to his wife's
detriment.

She nodded. 'I knew it was something like that. Well, it's
not going to bother us, and the girls need their holiday with
them both working now.'

'Don't be so sure.' Women didn't take the same interest in
politics. Now, that young man of Mary's, John Gibson . . .
he had his head screwed on the right way. A bit too far to
the left, but . . .

So, regardless of the trouble in the Balkans, the big trunk
with the brass studs was packed with sheets, pillowcases,
tablecloths and towels (a holiday let never included linen),
and all the other paraphernalia of a holiday 'doon the coast'.
At least the girls were past the pail and spade stage and these
rubber water-wings which nearly gave Joseph aplopexy when
he was blowing them up.

The trunk had been despatched by horse-drawn carrier to
arrive before them, the Lane family had caught the train from
Queen Street Station, and now they were installed in Mrs
Cochrane's house in Main Street which she vacated each

I

summer and let to the Glasgow Fair folk while she stayed with her married daughter in Fairlie.

In the bedroom which had been allocated to them the girls were feeling far from enthusiastic at finding themselves in this gem of the Ayrshire coast. 'It's the blinking limit.' Mary was settling her large-brimmed straw hat trimmed with daisies on her dark hair. 'My friend Ruby can go off with her pal to Blackpool, if you please! And we're still trailed round like weans. It's enough to make you spit.'

'Blackpool, England!' Sarah, in her white voile dress, gave the appearance of neatness, even of fragility. Her small features were neat, as was her fair hair, smooth and shining with constant brushing, her hands were narrow-wristed, slender-fingered, and well cared for. Miss Frobisher of Charles et Cie had given her assistants a lecture on the necessity of looking after their hands in case any rough skin caught on the fine materials which they handled daily. 'I've never been to England, far less Blackpool. I wonder what England *feels* like?'

'Foreign, daftie. Fat chance you have.' Mary was dismissive. 'But John's promised to take me for our honeymoon. Only two years to wait, thank goodness!' She peered at her face in the triple mirror of the dressing table, patted pale powder briskly on to her cheeks. She worried about her high colour.

'Maybe there will be a war before that. Pa was talking to me about it. Your John would be called up.'

'Rubbish! Pa's a pessimist, always reading that paper of his with a glum face. John says if it does start because of that duke being shot it will most likely be over by Christmas. Trust the British.'

Sarah's shyness kept her from questioning openly most statements made to her, but she compensated by indulging in an inner dialogue. 'Who said "Trust the British" anyhow? Forbye, I'm Scottish. And I wonder if John Gibson *did* say that. It sounds more like Mary putting words in his mouth. John's more like Pa. They have great talks together.'

'All the same,' she said aloud, 'I wish I had a boyfriend like John. I'm seventeen now.'

'If you had a boyfriend,' Mary said, surveying herself from all angles with the help of the hinged side mirrors, 'it would keep John from getting too . . .' she shuddered, closing her eyes and looking ecstatic, 'well, you know . . .'

'I don't know at all,' Sarah's Voice said, 'but I wouldn't mind if I did. It would explain all those funny sensations I get when I watch a sunset (like sucking a lemon), or look at a nice picture in a Sauchiehall Street window, or stroke silk cloth, and there was that funny one when I was running for a tram and a *piercing* sensation shot right through me from down below . . .'

'The trouble with you, Sarah,' her sister was saying, 'is that you don't know how to push yourself forward. You're too shy. Maybe that shop will bring you out of yourself, talking to customers, and that . . .'

'It's not a shop,' the Voice said, 'it's a Court Dressmakers.'

'Oh, I'm not allowed to talk to customers yet!' Not bloomin' likely! I'm just a glorified message girl, running for purns and pins to Coplands, making tea, delivering letters . . . Miss Frobisher exercised economy by only using postage stamps for clients outside the city confines. 'I've to work my way up.'

'Well, don't let them sit on you,' Mary said abstractedly, giving a last pat to her hair, a final tilt to her hat, then, rounding her eyes at Sarah, 'He's catching a train to Largs when he gets away from work. He'll have his good suit on under his overalls. Says he can't bear not to see me for a fortnight.' She rummaged in her Dorothy bag with its swinging tassle, 'Yes, got a hankie.' She closed it with a snap. 'Remember, it's a *school friend*, Bessie Cairney, if Ma quizzes you.'

Sarah looked at her sister, the rosy cheeks, the dark strong hair lying on them in peaks. Earlier she had shaved her armpits, saying that French women left it on. Her bright eyes looked out from under the straw brim like a robin's. No wonder John Gibson fancied her. 'Enjoy yourself,' she said, 'but don't be too late or they'll get suspicious.'

'Don't worry.' Mary was off with a swing of her white

flannel skirt, showing her white-laced shoes with their Louis heels. Sarah's Voice told her that they'd make a beeline for the whin bushes at the Broomfields where there was plenty of cover.

Later Sarah was walking along the promenade, having told her parents she was going to see if the stalls were up yet. She had brought her parasol so that she would feel like a lady of fashion taking the air. And, with any luck, look like one. Once when she was a small girl she had lingered behind her parents when they were out for a walk, attracted by the glitter of a jewellery stall lit by a naphtha flare. She had lost all sense of time, fascinated by the cheap baubles sparkling in the flickering light, and by a dark-skinned man wearing a scarf round his head and brass earrings who held up a mirror to two girls who were trying on necklaces. When he whispered in their ears they had looked shocked, put their hands to their mouths then burst into gales of laughter.

Her father's voice behind her had startled her. 'Lassie, lassie! We thought we'd lost you!' He had drawn her to his chest with such force that she had felt her head bob violently on her neck. And her mother, stern, but with tears running down her cheeks, had said, 'You deserve a good belting, ye wee rascal, frightening us out of our skins like that . . .'

How much better it had been as a child, Sarah thought now, no worries, winning first prize in the sand competition for her Burns' Cottage, seaweed for grass in front, shells for the fence, bathing in the chilly water and being rubbed down with a rough towel by Ma, then being taken for tea and cream cakes in the tearoom above the bakers. 'Ma, look at ma fingers! They're all white and wrinkled!'

And there had been the yearly visit to the photographic studio and being draped, with Mary, round a fake rock (a tall plant-stand), camouflaged by a whirl of spiky green material hopefully resembling seaweed. 'What bonny wee girls! My, this wee one's light!' Lifted by the man. Not liking where his hand went. Behind, the splendid painted panorama of Largs Bay with the tall spire of St Columba Church, so that everyone who was shown the photograph would say, 'It's Largs, isn't it? I'd recognise that spire anywhere.'

And, best of all, the walks with Pa up the hills to the Brisbane Glen because Mary always went with Ma to shop, and hearing his tales about the farm in Fifeshire where he had lived with Granny and Grandpa. She would have liked to live on a farm with chickens and cows rather than in the south side of Glasgow with its straight grey streets flanked by grey tenements or shops where the fruiterers set up wooden boxes on the pavement and where you were quite likely to tread on an orange skin or slimy pomegranate seeds (the bad boys spat them at each other), and skid on your heel . . . Sarah suddenly realised a young man was blocking her path.

'Hello, gorgeous!' he said. 'All on your ownio?' He swept off his straw boater.

Immediately the blood rushed to her face and a sense of panic threatened to overwhelm her, making her speechless. Mary said she would grow out of it in time. You had to remember that boys were just ordinary folks, like us, except for one thing . . . Here she would roll her eyes. If only Mary were here. Her bright robin's eyes would sparkle at such encounters, relishing them. 'I'm . . . I'm just having a walk,' Sarah heard herself stuttering.

'Mind if a jine ye?' He was blocking her path, smiling like that long-ago gypsy with the jewellery stall. 'A nice lassie like you disny want to be lonely.'

The difficulty was getting out of a situation like this. Miss Frobisher had reprimanded her about that. 'When you bring me an inch tape, don't hang about like a knotless thread. Say, "Excuse me," and get on with your work.' She looked at the boy, his cheap flannel blazer, tightly buttoned, short, bristly hair (a bowl cut, Pa called it), stringy tie grubby at the knot, and her training in Charles et Cie among the bales of expensive material, the perfection of the finished garments, seemed to give her courage. He was as cheap as his blazer, having the temerity to stop her as if she were a common pickup in Jamaica Street!

'Excuse me,' Sarah said, 'my friends will be waiting for me

at the Grand Hotel. We have dinner at eight.' She was as surprised at this statement as the young man appeared to be. His jaw dropped. The sight encouraged her to further flights of fancy. 'Then we're due at a reception in the Town Hall for important visitors . . .' She didn't want to stop now but the young man interrupted her, his face ugly.

'Huh! Don't let me keep ye. Yin o' the toffs, ur ye? Pardon me for breathin'!' She thought for a moment he was going to hit her, or even spit in her eye, but all he uttered was a long, 'Ach . . . !' of disgust, then he lunged away from her, letting her pass.

She walked on, legs trembling, head in the air, remembering to swing her parasol. She heard him shout after her, his courage regained, 'Hey, you! You're gawn the wrang way for the Grand!' She kept on walking, aware that he was right.

Mary came back at half-past ten, flushed and excited. Sarah was already in their bedroom, glad to have escaped the constant questioning from her mother, the contemplative look of her father over his newspaper when she repeated the lie.

'Did they give you a row?' she asked her sister. 'Ma said in her day she would never have got out on her own with a boy.'

'That was the Dark Ages. It could have been worse, though. They asked how Bessie Cairney's mother was. I said that it wasn't much, that she was on the mend.'

'She's at death's door with consumption in Strathaven.'

'Oh, God! Well, I was supposed to be meeting Bessie, not her mother.'

'Did you have a good time?'

'Great! That John Gibson! He says he soon won't be responsible for his actions. Especially if he's called up.' She sighed and rolled her eyes. Her bottom lip was swollen.

'I hope you looked at your skirt before you came in. Remember that time there were bits of grass and you said you'd been at the pictures!'

'I wasn't born yesterday. What did *you* do?'

'A boy tried to pick me up. I told him I was meeting friends at the Grand Hotel for dinner.'

'That Court Dressmakers is giving you ideas!' Mary was admiring. 'You should have said they were serving drinks in the lounge first. I've seen them sitting. Cocktails.'

'I said we were going on to a reception at the Town Hall – for important guests!' They laughed together, but even telling her Sarah felt a slow blush travelling up from her neck. She was ashamed when she thought of the boy's discomfiture only partly hidden by his sarcasm, the jibes. Maybe he had been shy too.

She had taken off her dress and now bent over to undo the suspenders of the pink elastic girdle which Ma insisted she should wear because your figure 'spread' if you didn't. It had a shiny panel of pink satin down the front which Ma said kept your stomach in, a waste of time in her case. She was as flat as a pancake. She sat down again and began to roll her white cotton stockings down over her legs, hairless, unlike Mary's. It was small consolation.

Chapter Two

1918

The girls' parents had been two of the first casualties of the influenza epidemic which hit an already weakened population at the end of a war which hadn't been over by Christmas but had developed into four years of mismanagement and slaughter.

They had taken ill in the summer of 1918, once again in Largs where they were having a week's well-deserved holiday. Joseph had worked in a munitions factory for the duration of the war and Alice had worked part-time in a canteen in the city.

The girls weren't with them. Mary had won her point and was in Blackpool with some friends from Templeton's carpet factory where she worked – it had been converted to make army blankets. Sarah had been persuaded to join them, but the raucous group in the boarding-house where they stayed, their noisy walks along the pier arm-in-arm, or visits to the music halls at night, made her feel isolated rather than one of the gang. And their frolics on the beach in their frilled bathing costumes, in which she reluctantly joined, embarrassed her. She was sure that to the onlookers she was a figure of ridicule.

She also felt guilty because she worked at Charles et Cie, not in a factory directed towards the war effort. But money was important in the Lane household, and her parents had advised her to 'stick in' where she was. They sensibly saw that she was better suited to a Court Dressmakers than the rough and tumble of factory life.

Sarah was a different person at Charles et Cie. Four years there of determined application, learning almost by osmosis from Miss Frobisher about style, colour and design (for her employer never passed on gratuitously any trade secrets), added to her own natural good taste, had turned her into a young woman with an air of elegance and a convincing veneer of sophistication.

When Jean, the salon saleswoman, left to be married, Miss Frobisher had appointed Sarah in her place, emphasising that she was extremely fortunate to be promoted to such an important position after only four years with the firm. Sarah was already popular with the clientele and, almost more important, with the work-room. She had a pleasant manner without a touch of arrogance, and her good taste as exemplified by her own dressing was reflected in the advice she gave, but only when invited to do so. Miss Frobisher congratulated herself that in Sarah she had a find.

'Lady Muck,' Mary's friends began to call her during their stay in Blackpool, some saying she should have gone to Torquay instead and the spiteful asking, 'who did she think she was any road?' Sarah, quick-witted, was well aware of their criticism, but had they known it, blamed herself entirely for not being able to 'let herself go', 'jine in', 'have a good tare', and took ruefully to a deck chair and a book whenever she could.

She was a misfit, she decided, only natural in the rarefied air of Charles et Cie, and this in spite of her faithful attendance three evenings each week at the church hall where she rolled bandages and packed parcels for the troops. The fact that Mary's friends had either boyfriends or husbands in the Forces only isolated her further. She had neither.

So, when they got a telegram from Mrs Laird in the next flat to theirs, saying that their parents were ill and they should come home right away, along with her anxiety, Sarah felt a secret relief. Apparently so did Mary. She confided to her in the train.

'I had a rare tare with some of them, but, well, some of the things they got up to was nobody's business. Although I like a good time I'm faithful to John.' They had been married on his last leave. 'I wouldn't carry on like that, picking up

9

boys in dance halls and on the pier. You've no idea . . .'

But Sarah had. Plenty of them. She had heard them giggling in their beds, knew that they had smuggled Bella, the ring leader, into the hotel more than once at three in the morning. Bella disliked Sarah which was a pity, she thought, because she liked Bella. She was a natural comic, devoid of self-consciousness. 'Ta-ta, Bella,' she would sing, walking along the pier, 'I'll no' say goodbye, I'm off to fight the Germans with the HLI.' She made her laugh.

Alice and Joseph were much worse than they had imagined, having thought that Mrs Laird had only wanted to be relieved of their care. She was of the 'I keep myself to myself' variety. 'You could have knocked me over with a feather when they came back early from Largs,' she said. 'They could hardly stand. I got the doctor right away and he told me to wire you. Two and sixpence it cost. I'm only mentioning it . . . ach, you shouldn't bother, Sarah. There was nae hurry.'

They were appalled at the drained white faces of their parents, their rambling talk, their loss of weight, in such a short time. They were both incontinent because of their fever, needed constant care, and the girls had to put them in separate bedrooms so that they wouldn't disturb each other.

'They're like John and me,' Mary said, tears in her eyes as they prepared gruel in the kitchen, 'can't see past each other.' It was true. Sarah had never thought of it before, but their concern for each other was pitiful to watch. She nearly said, 'Aye, faithful unto death,' but stopped herself in time. The doctor had been gloomy in his prognosis. They both felt the same deep fear of losing a loving mother and father whom they had regarded as immortal, and yet were afraid to voice it to each other.

On the fourth day after their return, when Sarah was bathing her father's face, he asked her to help him into the other bedroom to see his wife.

'Oh, no, Pa,' she protested, 'you're not fit. I'll get Mary.'

'Leave Mary be. Sarah,' he caught her hand, 'I'm missing her. She'll no settle without me.'

'Well, all right . . .' She helped him to sit up, swing his legs over the side of the bed, supported him as he stood. He was skin and bone, eyes sunken, hair plastered on his forehead with the fever. 'Oh, I don't know, Pa . . .' She shook her head.

'Whit are ye talkin' about?' He turned his gaunt face to her. 'See, right as rain.' She saw the pleading look in his eyes, and reluctantly, a step at a time, supported him into the next room where he collapsed on a chair. Mary would kill her.

'Take a rest,' she said. Her mother hadn't moved in her bed.

'Oh, lass,' he said, ignoring Sarah. He leant towards his wife, grasping her hand. 'Why did they always say Largs was good for your health?' Tears sprang to Sarah's eyes. He was trying to cheer Ma up. She called it 'his funny side'.

There was a faint smile on her mother's mouth, she saw the swollen eyelids open at the sound of his voice. 'Don't you run down Largs,' her voice was scarcely above a whisper, 'it always did us fine.' Mary sometimes said the two of them had a line of patter that would go down well at the Empire. Her mother's thin hand went towards her husband as she spoke.

'Aye,' he said, 'but I think it's goin' to be the death of us this time.' He slumped across her as he spoke.

Sarah's heart leapt in fear. 'Come on, Pa,' she said, terrified, and taking him by the shoulders, 'I shouldn't have given in to you. I'll get you back.'

'Is that Sarah?' Her mother raised her head feebly towards her.

'Yes. Oh, Ma, get him to go back . . .'

'Come on, Joe,' her mother said, 'I know your ploys. Tryin' to get in beside me, eh?' Her mouth went up at one corner. 'You haveny any notion what he's like.' She was stroking softly the back of her husband's head. 'Hiv they, Joe?'

'Oh, Ma, tell him . . .' Sarah's hand was over her mouth in her distress.

'You think,' her mother's voice was stronger, 'it's only you young yins that know about men. But we've been there, aye . . . you should have seen him when he was young, that handsome, that loving . . .' She was rambling now, about their early days, having his dinner ready when he came in, him giving her a right good cuddle first . . .

'Come on, Pa,' Sarah broke in. She put her hands on his shoulders. His face was still buried in the bedclothes. 'You'll be too heavy for Ma.' He was inert. The fear intensified, twisting her heart.

'Leave him be!' Her mother sounded angry. 'You girls shouldn't have separated us. You know we've always done everything together. He needs me!' Sarah took her hands away and ran for Mary, who was in the kitchen.

'You'll have to come and help me!' She burst in. Mary was bent over the kitchen sink, washing some clothes.

'What is it?' She looked up. 'You're as white as this sheet.'

'Come on! Come on! I'm awful worried. He's in Ma's room.'

'In the name of God how did he get there?'

'I . . . helped him.'

'What in God's name were you thinking of? Out o' his bed?' She took her hands out of the water, and without drying them went rushing out of the kitchen, Sarah at her heels.

Their father was dead when they reached him. Their mother died three days later, thinking her husband was still stretched across the bed. She ceaselessly stroked the bedclothes where his head had been. Then the hand became still.

The doctor said they had done everything they could. When Sarah fearfully confessed to helping her father get out of bed, he looked at her white face and said it wouldn't have made a scrap of difference. 'They've died happy,' he said. 'And if it's any consolation to you they're only two of the many, I'm sorry to say. They're going down like flies. You lassies look after yourselves now, plenty of fresh air, good food . . .'

They buried Alice and Joseph in a double grave in Ceres, the little Fifeshire village which had been Joseph's home. His family were all buried there, and although Alice came from Glasgow, they both agreed they shouldn't be parted, even in death.

'We should have one tombstone made for both of them,'

Sarah said after they got back from Fife. 'And put on it, "We did everything together".'

Mary looked at her, horrified, and laughed shortly. 'That's what I mean,' she said, 'there's something about you although you're so quiet. You say things . . . and you don't care if it's different . . .'

'Maybe I *am* different,' Sarah agreed. 'I feel it. And being twenty-one and never having had a steady boyfriend makes me different.' She felt a deep loneliness. Mary had John and a happy life to look forward to. She had always marvelled at her sister's conviction that John would come through the war safely. He would soon be demobbed, he would be home by Christmas. Mary spoke as if she'd had a special message from Lord Kitchener, or God.

'There's a Jock for every Jenny,' she said. Sarah wished she had her sister's cast-iron convictions.

'It's a funny thing, death,' Sarah said one evening when they were sitting in the kitchen having their tea. The flat still seemed desolate without their parents' presence. 'A here today and gone tomorrow sort of thing. You can't get used to it.'

'You have to believe,' Mary said, 'they did. They're probably up there singing hymns, sharing the same hymn book. Pa had a fine baritone. Remember how he boomed out in church, head up?' She pushed away the egg and chips Sarah had made. She didn't like it either. Too greasy.

'You haven't looked good ever since that journey to Fife,' Sarah said. 'Could I make you something else?' She longed for their bustling mother in the kitchen, the laden table, Pa coming in with the *Citizen* under his arm, always cheerful. 'We've got old Jerry on the run now.' Their absence still struck her every evening when she came home, an echoing, aching absence . . . this is grief, she would think.

'I'm pregnant,' Mary announced. 'You'd better know.'

'Well, that's good news!' She was surprised, pleased. It would help their sadness. 'I go out and you come in.' It was an old school playground game. Two die, one will be born. They didn't kiss as a rule, but she got up and hugged her.

13

'Don't!' Mary laughed. 'You'll make me sick.'

'When is it due?'

'Christmas or the New Year. Still, it's nice. We'll have a wee baby in the place and that'll cheer us all up. And John will be pleased. It's what he wanted.' Sarah's pleasure dimmed.

'You won't want me here then. I'll clear out. You should have the flat to yourselves.'

'You'll do no such thing!' Mary was indignant. 'We've been through all this before. And think of the help you'll be to us. You can look after the wee soul sometimes and let John and me go to the pictures. Am I glad, all the same, that we got married on his last leave! Bella, you remember at Blackpool, was five months gone then and it was a pick-up in Sauchiehall Street who vamoosed. She tried everything to get rid of it.'

'Ta-ta, Bella,' Sarah thought sadly. All that larking about at Blackpool and her pregnant. She remembered a remark she had overheard there but hadn't understood at the time. 'A slice aff the cut loaf disny matter.' 'And here was I thinking she was a bit fat,' she said. She felt lost in this new world of conception and birth around her.

She would have to make a life of her own now. Sometimes when she was fitting dresses she would listen to the conversation around her bent figure. That Mrs Hope's daughter, the lanky one who looked better in her tailored suit than the cream silk wedding dress, pearl-embroidered, was a great one for talking about books. Arnold Bennett, H. G. Wells. She decided she would enrol in literature classes at Langside Evening School, or the Mechanics' Institute in town . . . there were plenty of places which would teach you about books . . . Glasgow was full of interest if you looked for it.

And now there was Mary's news. Reassured, she said, 'I quite like the thought of a wee baby in the flat. It'll stop it feeling so empty, now that they're . . . gone.' Mary had got up and dashed to the bathroom. There were sounds of retching. She was left to weep on her own.

But it was a more hopeful kind of weeping.

Chapter Three

1919

Sarah ran for the tram through the darkness, anxious to get home as quickly as possible. It was a miserable January evening, 'dreich', as Minnie McConachie had said to her when they parted company at the Cameron Fountain. Charing Cross was its usual welter of homegoing traffic surging past the Grand Hotel, taxis hooting, trams clanking, and Sarah walked well in from the pavement edge to avoid the splashing of muddy rain from their wheels. Rising hemlines, as the French magazines were already predicting, couldn't come quickly enough. She stood impatiently at the stop waiting for the tram to come which would whisk her down Sauchiehall Street.

She was still in the family flat in Millbrae Road in spite of her doubts, and she and John had been up since midnight when Mary's pains – she had gone into labour around six in the evening – had become worse. 'She's doing fine,' the midwife said, having examined her. 'I've got a breach in Pollokshaws, I'll look back as soon as I can.'

Mary had said to Sarah in a brief respite, 'John would have been in a terrible stew without you.' We're all in a terrible stew, Sarah had thought, wiping her sister's brow. This strange, painful performance of giving birth . . . her involvement in Mary's pain had taken away any feeling of embarrassment, even with John there. He had come home in good time, justifying Mary's confidence, arriving on Christmas Eve. 'The sergeant was a family man,' he told them. 'Said I was better with my wife than hanging around the Demob Centre.'

Occasionally he had looked gratefully across Mary's bed at Sarah. Once he had said to her when Mary was resting,

'We're all novices at this game.' The laughing boy who had gone to war so willingly four years ago had come back changed, quieter. A humorous quirk had replaced the ready laughter. He never spoke of his experiences at the Front. At least, not when Sarah was there.

But sometimes in the middle of the night she would hear his footsteps in the kitchen and the tap running, then their voices in the bedroom. Making tea, she would think. Well, Mary would be able to comfort him, she told herself, and would feel again that special loneliness of the single woman, of being outside a private door. She had felt it even more strongly at four this morning when the baby was born and she had seen her sister's face which had been red and twisted with effort, change to a look of joy, smoothing her features and making her beautiful. And when she had seen John bending over her she had slipped out quietly.

The feeling was there when the midwife had joined her in the kitchen, rolling down her sleeves and saying, 'Aye, ah never get used to it, the joy, even wee tarts who had never wanted the wean in the first place.'

Once, just after John had come home, Sarah had said to him that she would find a place of her own now, but he was adamant, as his wife had been. 'The flat was left to the two of you. If anything, it's I who am the interloper. Never doubt that you belong here. You're one of us.'

She partly salved her conscience by reminding herself that girls didn't leave home until they were married. Mary had strong family feelings, was happy as a surrogate mother to her, said that Alice had asked her 'to look after Sarah'. She also was changed by the war and their parents' sudden deaths. The harum-scarum girl had become a circumspect young woman who had worked diligently in her job at Templeton's while John was away. Now, as a young mother, would she think it better if she and John had the house to themselves?

Sarah jumped off the tram at the Victoria Hospital and began to walk up the hill towards Millbrae Road. Ahead was the Langside Monument, a landmark since she was a child. She remembered her father telling her of Mary Queen of

Scots viewing the battle from Cathcart Knowe nearby. Her sympathies were all with the beleaguered Mary. She was a romantic figure, star-crossed, not like the hard-hearted English queen. 'She would be jealous of her beauty,' she remembered saying to her father, and he had smiled and said, 'Aye, looks aye win, but I bet Mary was a bit of a devil forbye.'

She reached the corner of the familiar road and hurried her steps once again to reach the flat. She was tired. She'd had little or no sleep, and Miss Frobisher didn't take into account new babies arriving. Some of the clients demanded Sarah and no one else, and they came first.

The nurse opened the door to her before she managed to find her key. 'My, my, Miss Lane!' she greeted her, 'you look right smart in that toque! And the cut o' that suit! Real toney, a sight for sore eyes on a grey January day. Away ben. You'll see a change in your sister.'

Sarah smiled and hurried to Mary's bedroom. Freshly washed, hair combed, wearing the satin bed-jacket Sarah had bought for her, Mary was sitting up in bed looking serene in her early motherhood, the tiny baby in the crook of her arm.

'What a picture!' Sarah bent to put her cheek against her sister's. She kissed the top of the baby's head. 'Wee Lachie!' This was the name agreed on by the child's parents. 'Lachlan Gibson's far too grand for a mite like this.' She straightened, sniffing. 'You both smell of lily of the valley.'

'I got it in Boots. An offer. Is yours Four Seven Eleven?'

'No, Coty. Miss Frobisher is partial to Coty.'

'She would be.'

Sarah laughed and looked down at the baby. 'Look at the wee soul. You'd think he was listening to us, wee Lachlan-for-John.'

'John's full of praise for you last night.'

'We were both terrified, to tell you the truth. But it must have been awful for you.'

'Bad enough, but worth it for this. I'll know what to expect next time.'

'So there's going to be a next time?'

'Aye, there's nothing like it. Nothing . . .' She looked down at the child nestling at her breast, looked up again at Sarah, her eyes moist. 'Remember I used to talk about our capers, me and John, at Largs?'

'When you got me to sin my soul for you?'

'We were pretty desperate. But I can tell you, Sarah, whatever we felt then is nothing to what we feel now. It's . . . deeper. I shouldn't go on like a sentimental fool, but I only hope you experience it as well. It was worth all the dreary waiting for him, the terrible anxiety . . .'

'You never showed it.'

'That was me doing my bit . . . my war effort.' She smiled. 'Now, off you go and get yourself freshened up, although you look as fresh as new paint and you up most of the night. And get out of those peerie heels and pointed toes into something more comfortable.'

'I pay a lot for comfort *and* fashion, I'll have you know. At least I get a discount when I mention Charles et Cie. But I'll slip out of this skirt in case I seat it, and then we'll have a cup of tea together.' She looked down at the baby again, and wished she knew this feeling Mary spoke about, something deep, secret, a covenant between two people sealed by a child at its mother's breast. Miss Frobisher said careers came first. Who was right? She had been inclined to believe her earlier today.

'I promoted you, Sarah, because you are good material. You have what I always look for in my girls, a lady-like appearance, in a word, *élégance*.' She pronounced it the French way. 'This does not only mean clothes, although attention to detail is important. No, it is,' she waved a hand, '*le tout ensemble*.' She was given to the occasional *bon mot* as befitted the owner of Charles et Cie.

Sarah came back to Mary's room carrying a tray with two cups of tea on it. She had taken off her skirt of fine grey marocain to reveal a black taffeta underskirt. She would change into a dress later when she began to prepare the evening meal.

'Here we are. I'll hold wee Lachie while you have a drink.'

'Right. I'm dying for a cup.' Mary surrendered the baby, and when Sarah cradled him in her arms, the little head turned to her breast with an urgent searching movement. She had a feeling of incompleteness, even of worthlessness, she was merely a dressed-up doll pandering to rich and spoiled women, real life was here in this room where the faint smell of birthing still lingered with its overlay of talcum powder, unlike the perfumed air of Charles et Cie.

'How many outfits did you sell today, then?' Mary enquired, looking over her teacup.

'Oh, two or three, I think. One client, Mrs de Vere, she was called, came all the way from Helensburgh escorted by her son, still in officer's uniform. He looked quite sheepish, poor soul. She said they were going to a regimental luncheon. You would have thought he could have found someone younger to take. I heard him say to her, "*Do* hurry, Mother." Miss Frobisher was all apologies, but Mrs de Vere was difficult to fit. I wanted her to look nice. Afterwards Miss Frobisher said she intended to send me to the homes of important clients like her. At least I'll see how the rich live . . .' The baby moved restlessly in her arms and whimpered, nuzzling.

'Here, give him to me. He knows he's gone to the wrong dairy.' Sarah laughed, handing over the infant who settled contentedly in his mother's arms. 'He's content to wait now. Had you finished your tea?'

'Yes. You have yours before it goes cold.'

Sarah looked at her pale pink polished nails, the white soft skin of her knuckles bent round the handle of the cup. Last night's experience had given her a dislike of her hands. The midwife's swollen fingers, scrubbed red, had been adroit. She was doing a worthwhile job, bringing children into the world. Here was the nagging feeling of worthlessness, Sarah thought, manifesting itself again – that she'd been an unskilled assistant, maybe a nuisance, at the birth.

Why was it that she, clever at school, had found herself working at a place like Charles et Cie . . . although occasionally there were clients like Mrs de Vere, whom she had liked.

19

She had noticed the direct gaze which rested on Miss Frobisher which seemed to imply a secret amusement. And her remark to her son, 'Don't rush me, Ronald. I'm not one of your men.'

You could tell she was intelligent. She had the self-confidence which a good education seemed to give. At Sarah's school you had left not knowing who you really were. Mrs de Vere looked as if she owned the earth, certainly Charles et Cie.

But Pa hadn't taken any account of such refinements. He had sat her down at the table the day she left school with the *Glasgow Herald* on which he had marked the jobs which he thought might suit her. Sarah wouldn't do in a factory. Mary had tossed her head at that and muttered 'Good enough for me.' A shop was one step up, an office a step above again, but that meant evening classes. When she landed the job at Charles et Cie her parents said it was 'just right for her'. Her future was settled. In any case, what was the point in educating girls? They only got married.

John came into the room, quiet as he always was nowadays, but with a sideways smile of collusion at Sarah. He had always recognised her inherent shyness, and so she was never shy with him. 'I've come to join the Admiration Society,' he said. He crossed to Mary's bedside, bent over and kissed her, then the baby. When he turned to Sarah his eyes were moist. 'I bet she's talking about getting up and dancing the Highland Fling?'

'Not yet. That was last night.' She laughed.

'Last night . . .' He shook his head. 'God knows how I'd have got on without you, Sarah.'

'You'd have got on fine.' She got up. 'I'm going to leave you lovebirds alone while I get on with the cooking.'

'And get that jacket off before you start,' her sister ordered. 'A stain on that would put the kibosh on it.'

'There she is, bossing me already. You've caught me in my deshabille, John,' she said, laughing, gesturing towards her taffeta underskirt. 'I might have known you'd get home early.'

'I like women in their petticoats.'

'I'll go before we make Mary jealous.' She went out thinking, that'll be the day.

In her own room she took a dress out of her wardrobe. Although it was old, her critical eye noticed its clever bias cutting, the swathing of the material over the hips; once it had had the semblance of a train which she had cut off. She put it on, looked in the mirror, took off the jade earrings which she had been wearing all day. She looked wrong in a domestic setting. Once, when she was dressed to go out, Mary had eyed her critically and said, 'Do you want to know why the fellas don't chase ye? They think they couldn't afford you.'

Was her face paler than usual this evening? She scanned it. Not surprising since she had lost so much sleep last night. 'Matt white', Miss Frobisher insisted on. 'I don't want my girls looking as if they'd just climbed Ben Lomond.' Hang Miss Frobisher, she thought. All Miss Frobisher has made of me is a spinster aunt.

She dipped a piece of cotton wool in a pot of Pond's cold cream and scrubbed off her makeup. Her eyes were dark-ringed with tiredness. Acknowledge it, she said to the mirror, you haven't the courage to move, you're too comfortable here in the house where you grew up. It's easier to sit gossiping in the evenings after supper's cleared away, and now with the baby you'll become involved in small domestic chores to help Mary. So easy ... you ought to be out in the evenings meeting people, enlarging your horizons. 'You're a pain in the neck,' she told the pale-faced girl in the mirror.

Chapter Four

In the spring of that year Sarah formed the habit of spending some time in Kelvingrove Park near where she worked before taking the tram to Langside. It would allow Mary to attend to Lachie, she thought, before she began to cook the evening meal.

When she walked along Park Gardens to the park gate, the Georgian terraces, so pleasing to the eye, seemed like an extension of Charles et Cie. My eye is adjusted to quality, she thought, that must be what makes me reject tawdriness in any shape or form – and there was plenty of that in some of the Glasgow streets – which might be the cause of what Mary said makes me seem 'distant' with young men.

She was learning words like 'élitist' from her extensive reading. She had made friends with Ruth Crosbie, a dark-haired, strong-featured girl at her local library, who sometimes advised her on the books to read. Ruth was a devotee of Virginia Woolf and the Bloomsbury set. She had confided to Sarah that she would have loved to have been one of them. 'We're so hidebound by convention in a place like Glasgow,' she had said.

But today Sarah had left those highbrow writers in favour of a small thick-leaved book she had bought, devoted to the tennis expertise of Suzanne Lenglen whom she greatly admired. By flicking rapidly through the pages the illusion of motion was conveyed, the long stride, the outstretched arm, that dark, forward thrusting head with the bandeau. She would love to play like her, she thought, and earlier had run up the grand granite stairway near Park Gardens to test her fleetness of foot. She was light and supple, small-boned, and felt with practice she might become a fairly good tennis player. It had the added advantage that it would take her out of the house.

She saw Minnie McConachie, one of the seamstresses, coming towards her. They had arranged to meet at the Stewart Fountain.

'Sorry, Sarah,' she said breathlessly, sitting down beside her. 'The old bitch made me unpick a hem and take it up another inch. It's the pressing to get the crease out that takes the time.'

'Never mind.' Sarah studiously didn't discuss Miss Frobisher with her. She was 'salon', Minnie was 'work-room'. The girls in the latter were prone to gossip as they sat sewing all day. 'It'll do you good to get a breath of air before you go home. If you close your eyes you can imagine you're sitting at the side of a Highland burn.'

'I wouldn't mind the real thing.' Minnie leant back on the bench in her plain navy-blue coat and skirt, sensible shoes, sailor hat. Her ankles beneath the skirt were swollen. Sarah, by contrast, was trim and smart in a blue velvet turban which matched the revers of her grey suit with its narrow skirt. 'Oh, my goodness!' Minnie laughed, 'look what I've come away with.' On her wrist was the small pincushion on a band which all the seamstresses wore. 'It was that Miss Arbuthnot and her blasted hem! "One inch makes a world of difference, Miss Frobisher, don't you agree?"' She spoke in a mincing voice. 'Fat besom! Now if she had ankles like yours!'

'How are things at home, Minnie?' Sarah said. The evening air was soft on her face, like a caress. She closed her eyes for a second and the noisy blackbird's song in a nearby tree sounded even more sweetly shrill.

'You mean, how's Ma? Just the same. You'd think now she had her wish to have me for herself, to fetch and carry, boss around, she'd be pleased, but not her.'

'Mary says I've to ask you to come to tea on Saturday, and I thought we might go to Queens Park afterwards and play tennis. It would be a change for you.'

'Oh, my, I haven't played for ages! Bill thought it was a cissy game.' Minnie paused, and a shadow crossed her face. 'I remember him saying I had a good serve.'

'*A la* Suzanne Lenglen? Look at this wee book.' Sarah

23

handed it to Minnie. 'I bought it in the paper shop at Charing Cross.'

Minnie took it and flicked through it rapidly. 'I've seen these. Hey, that's real dandy! I wouldn't mind having a shot at it again. Help to reduce my hips with all that sitting. I'll see if I can get a neighbour to sit in with Ma.'

'You could bring her with you, Mary says. She would see the baby. She'd like that.'

'No, thanks. I want to enjoy myself. She'd be that sweet with you all, butter wouldn't melt in her mouth, and then when she got home she'd be full of criticisms. She spoils everything for me. Oh, I wish . . .' She stopped suddenly. Sarah saw the bowed shoulders, the bun lying on the nape of her neck under the hard navy blue brim of her hat, the clasped hands, and was struck by the sadness of the posture. She put her hand on Minnie's shoulder.

'Isn't it getting any easier for you?'

Minnie shrugged and straightened. Her eyes were swimming, dark-ringed. 'I haven't any option, have I?' She sniffed, took out her handkerchief and blew her nose. 'It was a dirty trick that, fate, or whatever you call it, and knowing you're only one in thousands doesn't help much.' She breathed in deeply, put away her handkerchief. 'Some got their death sentence at that carnage in the Somme, Bill's was only deferred . . .' She breathed in again, straightened her shoulders.

'Mary's husband's a changed man since that. He's lost his youth, somehow. But he's alive . . .'

'It put a curse on them, sure enough. When you think of them going away that cheerful, waving, "back by Christmas . . ." At least Bill died in a clean bed instead of in all that muck and filth. His chest was always weak, and those trenches full of water, and worse, were the beginning of the end for him. Oh, I could take it, maybe, if it weren't for this terrible regret eating at me!' She turned her face to Sarah, pressing her hand to her chest, 'Eating and eating, like cancer . . .'

'Would it help to tell me, Minnie?'

24

'Oh, I couldny!' Sarah sat without speaking, heart sorry for the girl, turning over in her mind what she could say, or do, when Minnie's voice suddenly burst out. 'I've got to tell somebody! You'll no' pass it on, Sarah, promise?' Her eyes were feverish.

'I promise. You know me.'

'Aye, you're reliable. Well . . . well, it was his last leave, although I didny know it at the time. We were out together, we'd taken the train to Balloch, and we were walking in the woods there . . . ach!' She shook her head. 'You don't want to hear all this.'

'Try me.' Their eyes met.

'You're sympathetic, Sarah, did you know that? You've a rare way wi' folks. Maybe that's why you're so good at sales. Miss Frobisher puts the fear of God in them half the time. Mind you, I'd throw the thing at them wi' their tantrums. Well here goes . . .' She paused. Her voice had changed when she spoke again. 'We lay down, and he wanted me . . . to do it, you know?' She looked away.

Sarah waited. The colour which had flooded her face went away as rapidly. Well, what did you expect, you weam? A wee kiss and a cuddle from a man, desperate . . . She heard her heart beats in her ear. Don't you dare be shocked, she told herself.

'He said it would be all right.' Minnie's voice had become calm, perhaps with the familiarity of what she must have gone over and over in her mind. 'That he had one o' they . . . things . . . am I shockin' you?'

'No, no!' Sarah was trying hard. If she told the truth she was even experiencing a vicarious thrill . . . another word she had acquired from her reading.

'But do you know what stopped me, because by God I was just as keen as he was . . . oh, that feeling, I live it again and again in bed, rushing through you, wantin', cravin' for it . . . what stopped me, like a pail of cold water thrown over me, was the thought of the auld yin, ma upbringin'. I could even hear her breathin' over my shoulder. "No better than you should be, you trollop! To think that a daughter o' mine . . .

the shame o' it. Me, well-respected . . ." On and on. And I knew that if the inevitable happened, if the . . . thing . . . burst . . .' Minnie gave a snort, halfway between laughter and weeping, 'I would have been out on ma ear wi' ma bundle. "I can't," I said to Bill. "She'd bloody well kill me." He lay still for a long time, taking his hands away, and then he said, "Come here, Minnie," and he pulled me close to him. "Never mind, it's too much to ask. I should have known that." He kissed me, that lovin', strokin' ma face. "We'll get married on my next leave," he said, "it'll keep things tidy and it will be all the better for waiting." ' There was a long pause. 'And then,' Minnie said, 'he was shipped home, dying . . .'

'Oh, Minnie . . .' Any feeling of shock had faded into grief for the girl. She felt Minnie's regret as if it were her own, the everlasting quality of it. That *awful* war, she thought, wishing she knew a worse word for it, what was the point of it, all those useless deaths, all those grieving women like Minnie.

'An' I wish I *had* done it!' Minnie's voice was fierce. 'I've wished it a thousand times! If I had got pregnant at least I would have had his wean and I wouldn't have given tuppence whether the auld yin was pleased or not.'

'It would have been hard for you.'

'But, don't you see, I would have had *something*! Oh, what's the use of torturin' masel! I've just got to get on with things.'

Sarah heard the noise of the fountain in her ears, felt the pale spring sunshine warm on her face. She flicked the thick-leafed booklet between her hands, Suzanne Lenglen stretched and swung as she flicked, forever agile. She heard Minnie's noisy weeping beside her. She put an arm round her shoulders, feeling useless.

Let it go, she wanted to say, all your bitter regret, but how could she since there would be no more chances for Minnie with her Bill, warm and loving and eager. What would she have done if she had been lying in the woods above Balloch? She didn't have a mother breathing down her neck, but even Mary had waited. What had kept *her* back? That engulfing feeling that she was beginning to imagine, whose force she was beginning to understand and to long for . . . it didn't seem right that it should be denied because of fear, and carping mothers, because of society's opinion. Hadn't the suffragettes fought for the independence of women, for the vote?

She gave Minnie a hug and took away her arm. 'At least you've got it off your chest, Minnie,' she said. And, feeling she should change the subject, get on to a lighter note somehow, 'But I think tennis *à la* Suzanne Lenglen's going to seem pretty tame after that.'

Minnie looked up, wiping her eyes. 'Suzanne Lenglen! You're a queer one, right enough.' She shook her head in bewilderment, then suddenly they were both laughing helplessly, holding on to each other. 'Game and set!' she spluttered. After a long time they quietened and Minnie blew her nose, put away her handkerchief. 'That did me good. Right-oh. I'll come on Saturday. But remember, there isn't much chance of a click at Queens Park. The men are aw deid.'

Chapter Five

Minnie's visit to the flat on Saturday was an unqualified success. She had felt immediately the warmth of Mary's welcome. They were of a kind, practical, shrewd Glaswegian women, and Sarah could see how she responded to Mary's unspoken sympathy. *She* had her man. Minnie had lost hers.

They chatted amicably about Glasgow and mutual acquaintances, compared their work – Mary missed her days in Templeton's, she said, it was the camaraderie, the rare tares the girls had had, their outings in the blackout, their support for each other in the universal anxiety. It was lonely in the flat sometimes, she confessed to Minnie, even with a wee baby. He wasn't much company. Sarah listened to this with a degree of surprise.

Mary showed rare tact, not asking Minnie if she would like to hold Lachie, handing him over only when Minnie insisted, then tucking him away in his cot when he had been fed. He was a good baby, she said, the one who spoiled him was his Aunt Sarah who always wanted to lift him when he was quite happy. 'She's too soft. He just takes a rise out of her.' Sarah made a face at Minnie.

They set off for their game of tennis after tea, although Sarah got the impression that Minnie would rather have stayed where she was. John had joined them at the tea table, and his quiet, humorous manner had been a further inducement. 'That's a place where you're made to feel at home,' Minnie said when they were walking up the wide main drive of Queens Park, 'you don't know how lucky you are.'

Most of the players were young women, with the exception of two lads of about sixteen who were waiting for the singles court and showed no interest in the girls. 'We're like auld wives to they two,' Minnie remarked. To Sarah's surprise,

Ruth Crosbie, the librarian, was sitting in front of the club-house, and she greeted her with pleasure.

'I wish I'd known you were keen on tennis,' she said. 'It's my favourite form of exercise after a day stuck in the library.' When Sarah introduced her to Minnie she was cool, even condescending. Minnie confided to Sarah that she thought the girl was 'stuck-up'. After that, she seemed uneasy, and an hour later said she would have to get back. 'She'll be sending out a search party for me.' The fun had evidently gone out of the expedition for her.

'I'll come with you,' Sarah said, 'and see you on to your tram.' There was no point in waiting. There hadn't been a court vacant, and Ruth Crosbie was busy chatting with the friend who was with her. She brushed aside Minnie's protests. 'It wasn't a good idea anyhow. We'll walk down and get your tram at Victoria Road . . .'

'Hello!' someone said behind her. She turned and saw a youngish man in tennis gear, navy-blue blazer and white flannels. His hair was sleeked back, he looked with his too-white smile what Mary would have called 'flashy'. 'Saw you two beauties hovering,' he said. 'I'm the club secretary. Had a rush getting here. Could I fix you two up with a game?' He had a breathless kind of voice. Sarah noticed his chest was rounded under the tightly buttoned blazer. Also that he wasn't as young as she had at first thought.

'Not me,' Minnie said decidedly. 'I've hung about long enough.' She turned to Sarah. 'You stay. Don't mind me.'

'No, I've got to get back too. Besides, it'll soon be dark.'

'Oh, I'm in your black books.' The man put on a pathetic face. 'There's still time for a game.' He spoke to Sarah. 'What d'you say to making up a foursome?' His eyes were bold, small, bright, his mouth hung open as he waited. He's asthmatic, she thought.

'Gus! Gus!' Two girls were waving from an empty court. 'Come on, we're tired waiting!'

'Sure I couldn't tempt you?' Gus whatever-his-name-was spoke beguilingly, his eyes bright on her, admiring, ignoring Minnie. Sarah was painfully aware of her disapproving presence. She made up her mind. She had to work with Minnie.

'Sorry,' she said, and turning to Minnie, 'we'll be off then?'

'You've broken my heart,' the man said, putting his hand on his chest, smiling his too-white smile. 'By the way, I'm Gus Carmichael. I'm trying to get things running here, agreed to do it when I was drunk!' He laughed. 'Look how business-like I am.' He produced a small notebook. 'I could book a court for you on Monday, save you waiting?' He spoke to both of them.

'I'm from Maryhill,' Minnie said. 'I wilny be back here on Monday, I can tell you now.'

'How about you, then?' He looked at Sarah, smiling, licked his pencil and pretended to write in the notebook. He looked up again. His eyes were twinkling. 'Shoot.'

'Sarah Lane,' she said, making up her mind. She remembered Suzanne Lenglen.

'I like that.' He wrote her name down. 'Got a nice ring to it. Six o'clock?'

'Come on,' Minnie said, 'I've got to get back.'

'See you on Monday, then, *Miss* Lane. Six o'clock, okay?'

'All right,' Sarah agreed. 'Right, Minnie, I'm coming.'

'I wouldn't trust that one any further than I could throw him,' Minnie said, as they made their way down the main drive to the park gates. She was disgruntled, and obviously feeling let down. Sarah bit her lip, determined not to apologise. She wanted to improve her tennis, didn't she?

'Remember,' she said as she saw off Minnie on the tram, 'Mary says you've not to be long till you're back.'

I couldn't blame her, she thought, as she walked along Langside Road skirting the park, she's seen Mary happily married, as *she* might have been, and then there's me, single, no ties, free to accept any invitation which comes along. Minnie's future seemed mapped out for her, not as she had planned with her Bill, but saddled with a crotchety old mother. Probably she was right about Gus Carmichael, but at least there was no harm in a game of tennis.

John was in the kitchen when she got back to the flat, his

papers strewn about the table. He looked up as she came in.

'Mary slipped round to Pollokshaws to see Annie Baxter, her school chum. My, you look cute in your tennis togs! How did your friend Minnie enjoy herself?'

'Not much, to be honest. We didn't get a game and she didn't want to wait when we were offered one. Is Lachie all right? I could lift him . . . ?'

'I daresay you could.' His mouth quirked at her. 'No, he hasn't moved a muscle. I'd have half a dozen of his kind.'

'It isn't you who have them, John Gibson, don't forget.' She laughed, remembering. 'Would you like a cup of tea?'

'I would just. Then I'll walk round and escort Mary home. She looked sad, your friend.'

'No wonder. Her young man died of TB at Strathaven Sanatorium. He was invalided home from France. They were going to be married. It was the Somme that did for him.'

'And thousands of others. But that doesn't help *her*. And then those that are left can hardly get a job. A land fit for heroes to live in, they told us. Some hope.'

'You're lucky at least.' Sarah went to the sink and filled the kettle, staring out into the neat backyard where Mary's washing would be hung out on Monday as if by clockwork. She had to take her 'turn' of the boiler in the wash-house down there whether it rained or not. Piles of wet washing in the clothes basket made Mary's face black as thunder and no wonder. And yet she had never complained of what Sarah thought of as drudgery. Come rain or shine, sheets and table-cloths were always pristine, pressed immaculately with the iron which was connected by a snake-like flex to a jet at the side of the range.

Tea, she reminded herself, going to the range and pulling down the lifter, putting the kettle on one of the gas rings. She set a tray with cups and a plate of shortbread and brought it to the table. 'Tea'll be ready in a minute. Minnie was telling me her mother is so old-fashioned she won't even have gas for cooking and still uses the fire and a hob. Can you beat it?'

'Won't move with the times? A lot of the old ones feel safer in the past.'

31

'Could be.' She went back to the range, staring into the hot coals while she waited. How easy she felt with John, how at peace. No role playing, as there had been between her and Gus Carmichael, only a feeling of ease. And how concerned he was about other people! She *knew* that thousands had been killed in the war, women like Minnie bereaved, and many unmarried women unlikely to find anyone to marry, but she didn't become involved like John. She felt the familiar stab of guilt that she earned her wages by pandering to people who had never known deprivation, who always demanded luxury in their daily living, but she had never made any attempt to change . . . the lid of the kettle jumping up and down alerted her and she infused the tea.

'You shouldn't be working at those papers on a Saturday, John.' She handed him his cup and saucer, then held out the plate of biscuits.

'Oh, shortbread!' he said, taking one. 'My favourites.'

'Mary baked them.'

'Aye, Mary's a marvel.' They both laughed. 'Did you meet anyone exciting at the tennis?' he asked. 'Any gay Lotharios?'

'Well, if you could call him that. The club secretary. Gus Carmichael. You know that son of Annie Baxter's?'

'Aye?'

'He reminded me of him. Pigeon-chested. Mary has sometimes to throw open the window when wee Alec visits here. He has those asthmatic fits of coughing.'

'What age was this Gus?'

'Thirtyish.'

'Maybe he was exempted from the war. That could be why he's got time for tennis. Hey, that's a rotten thing to say. Sour. It's this stuff I'm working on just now.' He pushed the papers out of reach. 'Maybe you've met your fate?' He looked at her, smiling.

'Don't you get any funny ideas. It's only tennis I'm interested in. I'm trying to organise my life. Not hang around with you and Mary and Lachie all the time.'

'Don't feel that. Besides, you seem pretty busy to me. And you read a lot. I see your light on sometimes when I get up.'

'Yes, I've discovered books. You're still not sleeping?' Mary had confided in her that he sometimes had nightmares.

'It's getting better. The scars are fading, but I'm like you, I'm doing a lot of reading, catching up with what I missed. It seems to me that ever since Keir Hardie we've failed to grasp the nettle, and I've a terrible feeling that this is just a breathing space till the next one. The Allied Nations have made a muck of things, not to mention bungling the war.'

'You sound gloomy.'

'Do I? No, I'm a realist. The strike in January didn't help. The government blamed the trade unionists, wouldn't you know?'

'Mary and I were really worried that night. She said you would come home with a broken head – if you came home at all. I never saw her in such a state, even when you were away fighting.'

'I know. But we made it up.' His smile was boyish. 'And I did get a good look at Churchill before the fighting started and the Riot Act was read. That was a night and a half! History being made and I was there!'

Sarah stirred her tea thoughtfully. This was the kind of thing which should be occupying her mind, not romantic dreams. She ought to have a burning desire like John to improve conditions, stand up for ... something. 'When I think how I earn my money pandering to the rich, I feel ashamed,' she admitted.

'You remind me of Harry Lauder saying that after he heard good music he wanted to go out and lead a better life.' He smiled at her. 'Don't feel ashamed. You do your job well and you help with the economy, don't forget. People like Miss Frobisher employ people, buy expensive material, make the wheels go round.'

'Is she a capitalist, or an employee of labour?'

'Go to Glasgow Green on Sundays and ask your questions. You're a worker, Sarah. You've worked since you left school, applied yourself. Mary says you're great at your job, that Miss Frobisher couldn't do without you. You're okay. But there are the people who haven't jobs, worse luck, who have

33

a wife and family to support, who've helped to defeat an enemy and are thrown on the scrapheap at the end of it. That worries me. You have to make up your own mind if it worries you enough. I think education's the answer. Do you know what I would have liked more than anything else in the world, if I weren't married?'

'Tell me.'

'To go to the University. The numbers are up to five thousand already in Glasgow, made up mainly of soldiers lucky enough to get home safe and dying to tax their brains instead of just dying. I would have read history and politics, tried to find out what makes the wheels go round, but . . .' A rising wail from the direction of his bedroom interrupted him and he laughed, getting up. 'There's my "but". Never get married, Sarah, if you want to learn the answers.'

'I'll go!' She went hurrying to John and Mary's bedroom where the baby was in a cot beside their bed. He was kicking his legs furiously. The wail had changed to a steady keening.

'Oh, dearie, dearie me,' she said, lifting him in her arms. 'Oh, my, it's a clean nappy for you.'

'I'm away to get Mary!' John called from the kitchen.

'All right.' That would give her time to nurse Lachie, hug him, croon over him without Mary giving her an old-fashioned look.

She was sitting at the fire singing an old nursery rhyme to a bemused baby when Mary and John came in.

'"Wee chookie burdie",' Mary mimicked, as she took off her hat, sticking the hat-pin in it and laying it down on the chiffonier. 'As soon as ma back is turned she spoils that wean.'

'A wee bit spoilin' never harmed anybody,' John said. 'Look how you spoil me!'

'Away ye go, you daft soul!' Mary cried delightedly. Her cheeks were flushed with the cold air. She looked happy. She must have had a good chin-wag with Annie.

'You don't want him going bald at the back of his head with lying in that cot too long.' Sarah surrendered the drowsy baby. Her arms felt empty. 'How was Annie?'

34

Mary's look of happiness died. 'Her man's lost his job at Beardmore's. They're paying off thousands. And she needs special feeding for that poor wee Alec. Aye coughin'.'

'That's really bad. I'm sorry. Well, I'll be off. I'm as drowsy as Lachie sitting at the fire.'

In her room she sat on the side of her bed, half-undressed. Which was better? To devote your time to being married, or being educated? John implied you couldn't have both. Maybe not for the breadwinner, like himself. And look at Mary, busy with household chores all day. How could she possibly find time to educate herself? The fault lay in the fact that their education had been purely practical, leave school at fourteen, start earning.

Surely there was some alternative? She felt like a rudderless boat as she unlaced her white buckskin shoes and placed them together on the floor. Maybe the solution was to have a husband like John with whom you could exchange opinions, discuss books, life in general. Or did men have a different viewpoint and were able to divide their lives into compartments? There was that old adage about love . . . 'Tis woman's whole existence.' How true was that? She still had to find out.

She saw beside her tennis shoes the black patent pumps she had worn during the day, and got up to get some tissue paper to stuff in their toes. It flattened out the creases. There were still small pleasures to be had.

Chapter Six

Sarah went to Charles et Cie on Monday morning counting her blessings. Her talk with John had stimulated her. Of course she was lucky to have a job at all – think of those ex-servicemen begging in Argyle Street or selling trays of gee-gaws, their gaunt, hopeless faces . . . even more heart-rending, that one-legged man who did a pathetic little dance on crutches, and the buskers still in their rough khaki uniforms singing those ragtime war songs which brought back memories everyone wanted to forget.

Look at Minnie, she reasoned, left only with the prospect of her old mother to care for, her marriage hopes dashed because of the war. She, by contrast, had no ties, she was free to indulge herself in whatever she liked, her reading, now, tennis – Gus Carmichael might turn out to be all right – but most of all she was lucky to have a job which fulfilled her and gave her satisfaction, and if she thought at times it was frivolous, she must remember what John had pointed out, that it contributed to the economy, perhaps in a round-about way helping those begging ex-servicemen.

And there was Lachie. How good it had been to sit by the fire nursing him last Saturday, just the two of them, studying minutely the little features which already bore a resemblance to John, inserting a forefinger in the curled-up fist, feeling the strong grip, a masculine grip already. She was lucky to be part of a loving home. And, she reminded herself practically, her rations helped Mary to run the household.

The salon looked restful, the grey velvet curtains draped over the long windows with their view of the Crescent gardens opposite, the Louis XIV couches which Miss Frobisher favoured, 'I like the French *ambience*, Miss Lane,' the small gilt chairs where favoured clients sat when Miss Frobisher employed a few mannequins at the start of each season to show off the excellence of her garments. It was all so different from the work-room with its constant clatter of sewing machines, the accompanying chatter of the seamstresses. She'd had a brief word with Minnie as she had passed through earlier.

'Were things all right when you got home, Minnie?'

'Och aye, although there was the "where have you been that took you so long" bit. You get used to it. Still the old soul had made an effort, gone out and bought a bunch of daffodils at the street corner, stuck them in a milk bottle. She makes you mad and then she . . .'

'Disarms you?'

'Aye, well.' Minnie looked at her doubtfully. 'Be sure and thank your sister for her hospitality.' She has a sweet face, Sarah thought, like Mary with her dark Celtic colouring and fine eyes. She would have made a good wife and mother. It was her stoicism which had attracted Sarah to her when her Bill had died. Even Miss Frobisher had been impressed. 'We have a good worker in Miss McConachie. Puts the establishment first. Only one day off for the funeral. I like people who have the interests of the firm at heart.'

'You'll be back again soon. Mary liked you.'

'No' for tennis, though. It's no' for me. But we might go to a matinee at the Picture House. Have you been? It's great inside, talk about marble halls, and fountains playing, and palm trees. I think Mary Pickford's on soon.'

'I'd like that. Well, I must get on with my work.' She had gone back to the salon as Miss Frobisher emerged from her private sanctum. She was wearing a pleased smile as she raised her hand.

'Ah, Miss Lane. I'm glad I've caught you. I've just been speaking on the telephone to Mrs de Vere. She was very impressed by the attention you gave her when she and her son were in. She particularly asked me to tell you.'

'Thank you, Miss Frobisher. I'm pleased she was satisfied.' It had been difficult to decide whether the woman was pleased or not, and the look her son had given her from time to time was decidedly impatient. 'Have you any garments you wish laid out for today?' She wasn't going to enthuse too much.

'I haven't finished.' Miss Frobisher's tone was peremptory. 'I've arranged with Mrs de Vere that you will visit her residence next Wednesday for a fitting. It's the checked Otterburn.'

'I thought it would be.' The black suit which had also been under discussion had only emphasised the lumpiness of the woman's hips. She had been tactful in her advice.

'And she'd like you to bring one or two hats to try on with the suit.'

'Will the appointment be in the morning, Miss Frobisher?' Not too early, she prayed. She would have to get to the salon before the train. Miss Frobisher would never countenance an employee taking anything overnight from the shop even with a valid excuse. She had a suspicious mind. She would imagine that the employee might sally forth in the evening wearing the garment. Sarah, remembering Mrs de Vere's *embonpoint*, thought there wasn't even a remote possibility of that happening.

'Yes, ten thirty. That will give you time to get here and pick up the boxes. Of course, I'll arrange for a taxi and also at the other end. There will be no necessity for this on the way back.'

'Of course. Thank you, Miss Frobisher,' Sarah said. 'Is that all?'

'For the time being. The list of today's customers is on my desk. Kindly attend to it. I'm on my way to the hairdressers.'

'Certainly, Miss Frobisher.' She would have liked to say, '*Certainement*', a French word she had come across in her reading, but thought it might startle her. Instead she looked at her employer's coiffure. It reminded her, and always did, of a nest made by a very tidy bird who knew every twig and how they should lie. It was a complete entity. Separate hairs could not be distinguished. It was never disturbed by brush or comb except by Wanda, Miss Frobisher's hairdresser, on her weekly visit.

Sarah spent the next hour happily checking the list with

38

the garments to be tried on, a fragile mauve chiffon, bound with mauve satin on the panniers and the square neck, a blue-and-black striped blazer with a white dress daringly two inches above the ankles and with a scarlet tie on the V-neck, and a black hostess gown with chiffon wings over the shoulders and a diamanté belt, completed by a short train. On the pretext that the train was a few inches too long she summoned Minnie to a fitting room and tried it on for her.

'My, you can carry that, Sarah,' Minnie said, her mouth full of pins, 'you look a sight better than that skinny-ma-link Lady Morar who wants it for her Highland ball.'

'Her Highland fling,' Sarah said, swirling in front of the mirror. Minnie was giggling as she bore it off to the work-room.

She had a rushed tea when she got back to Millbrae Road, changed into her white skirt and blouse, white buckskin shoes. She had asked Minnie during a slack period to shorten the skirt for her, and now it was a daring four inches above her ankles, à la Suzanne Lenglen, she thought, surveying herself in the mirror. She went into the kitchen to see Mary, who was busy bathing Lachie in a zinc bath in front of the fire.

'My, that's a sight for sore eyes,' Mary exclaimed, looking up, 'talk about the cancan! You'll be driving your partner mad showing off your legs like that.'

'Skirts are getting shorter and shorter,' Sarah said, 'you'd better get used to it.'

'All right for those that can get away with it.' Mary was becoming matronly since the birth of Lachie.

Sarah bent down at the bath to splash some water over the baby's round stomach. He chortled, kicking his legs. 'You're a happy wee thing,' she said, tickling him, 'no worries lying there like a king in front of the fire.'

'Yes, it's a pity they grow up. Well, are you away?'

'Yes.' Sarah straightened, pulling a face at the thought.

'You watch out for any capers and nip them in the bud.'

'You sound just like Mother. Don't worry. I'll watch out.'

She would have liked to stay in the glow of the fire, being allowed to lift Lachie and envelop him in the warm towel. 'Well, I'll say cheerio.'

Once again she bumped into Ruth Crosbie just as she reached the tennis courts.

'Hello, Sarah,' she said, 'it seems I'm always meeting you here. Have you deserted the library these days?' There seemed to be a slight edge to her voice.

'No, but I'm only halfway through that last tome you gave me.' Sarah would have liked to say she found it heavy going.

'Was that the *Clayhanger* trilogy? He's required reading. But I'm not too fond of those provincial authors either. Why don't you . . .' Sarah saw Gus Carmichael coming towards them, hair brilliantine-sleeked, blazer-clad, swinging his racquet.

'Here's my partner,' he said, flashing his too-perfect smile. 'I wondered if you were going to turn up.'

'I always keep my promise.' It sounded prim. Ruth standing beside her somehow discomposed her. 'Do you know Ruth Crosbie?'

'Yes, but she's too good to give me a game. I can't pull rank with her.'

'Perhaps your ego wouldn't stand it.' Ruth was icy.

He turned to Sarah. 'Ready, then? Our partners are waiting.'

'Don't let *me* detain you,' Ruth said. Her eyes meeting Sarah's were darker than she remembered, hurt-looking. Why should she mind?

'Lead the way,' she said to Gus. She felt she was under a cloud, uncertain of what she had done to offend the girl.

She enjoyed the game nevertheless. The two giggling girls, Ethel and Ella, she discovered, were also good players, and her own inexpertness was bolstered by Gus Carmichael, who was a showy but competent partner. Once in an agony of inexperience she ran past the ball she was pursuing, but he only said 'Bad luck!' and as Ethel and Ella giggled more or less constantly, no one seemed to mind.

'You've got the making of a good player,' Gus assured her. 'You're light-footed, that's the main thing.'

They sat on the veranda of the tennis pavilion watching other players, and Sarah noticed again his half-open mouth as if he had difficulty in breathing. Her sympathy seemed to put her at ease with him.

'You've lost your puff,' she said. It was a favourite saying of Mary's, used when climbing stairs or carrying down loaded baskets of washing to be pegged out in the back green.

He smiled and put his arm round her shoulders. 'I know something that would cure that. How about you and me going for a drink?'

'You mean to a pub!'

He laughed at her. 'God, no. I wouldn't ask a nice girl like you to do that. I have a bottle in the car. We could drive up to Cathkin Braes, find a nice quiet spot and have a swig or two.'

She tried to hide her shock at the suggestion. 'I'm not in the habit . . . I think I've got to get back . . .' She was discomfited, miserable. Still with his arm round her his face came close to hers, and she saw the enlarged pores on either side of his nose. His mouth was wet at the corners.

'Don't tell me I've shocked you?' She decided that his teeth were false, and that she didn't really like him. Well, she quite liked him, but he was too fast for her, the kind of man Mary had warned her about.

'No, no!' she protested. 'It's just . . . well, we're quite up-to-date. We always have a bottle of wine at Christmas, and my brother-in-law likes his dram of whisky . . .'

'I get that,' Gus Carmichael said surprisingly. 'It depends how you've been brought up. We're quite well-off, though I says it as shouldn't,' he laughed, 'but hae ye ever seen a poor bookie? That's what my father is. Not your ordinary man-at-the-corner type, he has proper shops and we live in style. It's part of the game. Ma mother was a famous actress, well, I say, famous, but that's a bit of an exaggeration, but she played all the halls, not in Glasgow maybe but in smaller towns, and she likes her dram. The stage did that for her.

41

Don't think I'm an alcoholic or anything like that but that's the way I've been brung . . . brought up, and we have a good address, Newlands. Lots of folks dropping in, parties, drink flowing and so forth . . . d'you get it?'

'I get it,' Sarah said. She was beginning to regret her show of unsophistication. It was all a question of money, really. She thought of John and his constant worry about unemployment which would surely affect him as well, although he never mentioned that. She remembered the Bloomsbury set and how they never seemed to have any conversation without a glass of wine in their hand . . .

'I'll strike a bargain with you,' Gus Carmichael said. 'How about me and you takin' a run down the coast for a slap-up dinner with all the accompaniments.' His breathing had quietened, he had taken his arm away so that he could fling his blazer round his shoulders, and he looked smart, a man-about-town. Any girl would be pleased to be seen with him, wouldn't she? 'How about Saturday, six o'clock? Ah can't make it earlier. Ah have to count the takings fur ma Dad. The spondoolocks,' he added, flashing his falsely white smile. She was pleased with his use of the word. It was evident that he was an ordinary Glasgow lad in spite of his flashiness. On the other hand John wouldn't approve of unemployed men parting with their pittance at the bookie's. Or would he? John was broad-minded. It was she who had to get around a bit, see how the other half lived.

'All right,' she agreed. She had never been in a hotel for a meal in her life but she wasn't going to tell him that. Besides, Miss Frobisher had hinted at future visits accompanying her when she went on buying trips. She might as well get into practice.

'I'll pick you up in my sports job.' Gus was nonchalant. 'What's your address?' She told him but then took fright.

'Don't bother coming up,' she said. 'I'll meet you at the park gates at six. The main ones.'

'Are you sure? It might be raining.'

'I'm not likely to melt,' she said, laughing. 'And I could stand in a close.' In his free-and-easy lifestyle he wouldn't know that in hers they had you married if your boyfriend came to the house. And while she quite liked him, she didn't think that would ever happen.

Ethel and Ella came running up, red-faced. They were both plump.

'Gus! We're short of a partner! How about another game?'

'I'm busy.' He laughed, indicating Sarah. 'I'm getting off wi' this beauty.'

'But it's your *job* to make up foursomes,' Ella said, pouting. She was the prettier of the two, buxom, toothy, flashing-eyed.

'And you took it on, so you did,' Ethel said.

'Far be it from me to stop you.' Sarah smiled at the two girls. 'Take him with my blessing. I'll sit here and watch.'

'Hey, you're a real sport,' Ella said.

'Are you sure?' Gus rose to his feet and threw off his blazer as if he were going into battle. 'It's not often females fight ower me.'

'Make the most of it. I'll maybe pick up some tips.' She watched him walk away, an arm round each of the girls. He's puffed up with pride, she thought. Maybe all men were vain. John wasn't.

On the other hand, it was quite a pleasant feeling to sit here as Gus Carmichael's chosen girlfriend, and hand him over to Ethel and Ella as a favour. And wasn't her reason for being willing to go out with him for the sake of experience pretty questionable? Especially as she would much rather be in the cosy flat with Mary, John and wee Lachie.

But she had to grow out of that, learn to be independent, live her own life. She knew, without vanity, that she was worth being seen with. She was slender, dressed well, her colouring, fair hair and grey eyes, pale skin, was attractive, she had style. She had been told that often enough. Hadn't some of the mannequins Miss Frobisher hired assured her that she could make a fortune modelling clothes? Her appearance was acceptable, she told herself. But she had to *feel* right inside. She needed enough self-confidence to feel at home in public places, to be able to enter rooms without blushing, to be well-read . . .

43

'Hello,' Ruth Crosbie said, appearing from the clubhouse as if she had read Sarah's thoughts. 'Has the Queens Park heart-throb given you up?'

'Oh, no.' She turned to the girl to explain and then quickly changed her mind. 'I allowed him to make up a foursome.' She smiled benignly.

'Huh! You'll be sitting here for an hour at least.'

'I don't think so.' Her little show of defiance evaporated as a cold wind blew round the building. 'Ne'er cast a cloot till may be oot,' she remembered, shivering. She had discarded her woollen chemise for a lace-trimmed silk one which showed more becomingly through her voile blouse, and her cardigan was too lightweight.

'They're evenly matched.' Ruth was watching the mixed doubles in which Gus was playing. Sarah tried to concentrate. There was now only one court occupied. The players were intent on their game, and even Ethel's and Ella's giggles were stifled. Ruth was right. The score dipped and swung like the regular wash of waves on the shore.

Half an hour passed in desultory conversation between the two girls, then three-quarters of an hour. Sarah shivered again, moved uneasily. 'It's going on for ever,' she said.

'Tell him,' Ruth Crosbie said. 'Tell him you can't wait any longer. We can walk home together.' Sarah didn't reply. But when another ten minutes passed she got up. Gus was changing ends. This was her opportunity. She ran down the wooden steps leading from the clubhouse and walked quickly over to the netting. She spoke through it to him.

'I've waited long enough, Gus,' she said. 'I'll walk home with Ruth.'

'I'm really sorry.' He was contrite. 'I never thought it would last so long . . .'

'Come on, Gus,' Ella called. She was his partner. She sounded proprietorial.

'I've landed masel right enough. Is Saturday still on?' He was breathing quickly. He looked tired.

'Sure,' she said. 'At the park gates.'

'You're a sport, Sarah. I'll make it up to you.' He ran off.

'Was he disappointed?' Ruth asked when Sarah rejoined her.

'A bit, but I'm seeing him on Saturday. We're having a run down to the coast . . .' she nearly said 'in his sports job', but that was going too far. 'And having dinner in an hotel.'

Ruth didn't answer.

It was getting dark now, earlier than usual because it had been a grey day and the park was almost deserted. The lights of the city could be seen twinkling from the top of the main drive. It looked magical, a city of dreams, but it emphasised the dusk in the lonely park, and she was glad of Ruth's company. 'You live near Pollokshaws Cross, don't you?' she asked as they walked together.

'Yes, Minard Road.'

'Well, if you like I'll walk with you to the Pollokshaws Road entrance and leave you there. That's about halfway home for both of us.'

'I was going to see *you* home.' Ruth laughed.

'No, fair's fair.'

'Still cold?' Her voice was considerate.

'Not so bad now that I'm walking.'

'Did you enjoy the tennis tonight?' She was being very pleasant.

'Yes, I'm beginning to get the hang of it. Gus Carmichael's a good teacher.'

'You want to watch out for him.'

'What do you mean?' She was sorry she had told her about Saturday.

'Oh, they're well-known, the Carmichaels. Bookies.' There was scorn in her voice. 'You know he's well over thirty? He isn't the marrying kind but he hangs round places looking for girls.'

'I don't get that impression. He's taken on the job of running the courts. That's decent of him.' Sarah quickened her steps in her annoyance. She was too critical, this girl. She was clever, and it was good of her to take an interest in her reading, but she shouldn't interfere in what she did. To her surprise Ruth made up on her and put her arm through hers, pulling her close. It was a friendly enough gesture, but she wasn't really a friend.

Mary often linked arms with her when they were out walking, but this was different. She was a comparative stranger, and a librarian . . .

'I hope I haven't offended you, Sarah.' Ruth's voice was cajoling. 'I'm inclined to be a bit outspoken, I know. Mother used to tell me about it.'

'It's all right.' She was still stiff, and then, remembering the girl's remark, she said, 'Is your mother . . . er . . . ?'

'She died last year. She had been a widow for a long time. My father was an invalid. He had polio.'

'Oh, that's sad.' Sarah warmed towards her. 'I know how you must feel. I lost my mother and father practically together. They were among the first victims of that terrible flu. But I have my sister and her husband. The flat was left between Mary and me and they insisted that I live with them.'

'So we're both orphans?'

Now Sarah didn't mind the close linking of arms in her quick sympathy. 'Yes. Have you any brothers or sisters?'

'No, I was an only child. I live in our flat alone.'

'Oh, do you? Does it make you feel lonely at times?'

'Yes, it does. I have often thought of sharing, but you have to be careful who you share with . . .'

'That's true enough.' Sarah visualised the loneliness. 'Luckily I get on well with John, Mary's husband, and she's like a mother to me. John's so wise, and yet funny. We have great talks together.'

'You'd better watch out or you'll be falling for him. Men are all the same.'

Sarah drew away from her, again discomfited. She was strange, this girl. She was getting fed up with her lightning changes of mood. Perhaps reading a lot made you like that, seeing two sides . . . 'John's not that kind. He's absolutely faithful to Mary. They love each other.' She thought of the love noises she sometimes heard coming from their bedroom, probably stifled because of her, and her cheeks went hot. She was glad it was dark. They were passing the duck pond

46

now and the birds were silent, hiding in the reeds or the bushes. It had been a favourite place when she was small. She remembered the bag of stale bread her mother would give her to take to them, and how the sight of the ducklings in spring had touched her because of their small perfection. Like Lachie's little fists. And how the grown men sailing their toy boats had been cross when they had got in the way. I wish I had my mother and father now, she thought, with a pang of grief. It's that war, and the terrible damage it's done. A lone bird suddenly skeetered across the water, and the trees above the pond, their fresh green made grey-black in the darkness, seemed to shudder. 'We're lucky with parks in Glasgow,' she said.

'I suppose so.' Ruth was nonchalant. 'I'm a town type. I don't crave for Nature and all that, do you?'

Sarah considered. 'Yes, I think I do. I'm not really sporty. The tennis is just to get me out of the house for a change, but I like to be in the fresh air whatever I'm doing. I sometimes walk from Charles et Cie all the way to Argyle Street before I take the tram, just to feel the air on my face.'

'And the petrol fumes. Is it a dress shop?'

'A *couturier*.' Sarah remembered Miss Frobisher's word. 'Very expensive. Some of the customers are titled.'

Ruth didn't seem impressed. 'My best time is in the flat on a winter's night, the curtains drawn and a good fire going and a book to read. It's almost perfect.'

'And the band played believe it if you like,' Sarah sang out, and immediately regretted it. Ruth was silent. She didn't like jokes.

They were coming now to the Pollokshaws Road gates. If she walked quickly she would be home before it was pitch black. 'There's nobody about,' she said. The road with its long pewter-coloured terraces on the other side was deserted. 'I should have left you at the other gate.' She didn't like the idea of the walk home on her own.

'Don't worry.' Ruth squeezed her arm. 'I'll see you back to Millbrae Road. I like walking in the dark. It's exciting.'

'I don't call it exciting. I'd be frightened out of my skin.'

'You're timid, Sarah. And, do you know what I'm going to do?' Sarah waited. 'I'm going to give you a piece of advice. Your timidity sometimes lands you in situations you would rather not be in.' They were walking towards Pollokshaws Cross and there were more people about. Ahead Sarah could see the shop lights, fish and chip, she thought, and coming towards them a tram like an illuminated galleon. As it trundled past, she could see the heads of the passengers in dark silhouette against the lit interior. It was exciting, she thought, wondering who they were, what they were thinking of, were they looking at she and Ruth, were *they* wondering . . .

'I don't agree to just anything,' she said. Ruth's thinking of Gus Carmichael again, she thought, and my date with him on Saturday. But was Ruth right? Mary had warned her about men 'getting up to their capers', as she put it. I'm too young for my age, she thought, the typical younger sister. And Mary's experience working in Templeton's during the war had toughened her. Charles et Cie was a world apart from the rough and tumble of factory life, all female, velvet-lined.

'You have a quality of innocence, Sarah,' Ruth said. It was another strange remark.

Sarah answered flippantly. 'Oh, well, I'll just have to grow up, then.'

'Now I've offended you, haven't I?'

'No, you haven't.' Those discussions that she seemed to get embroiled in with Ruth were upsetting. 'Embroiled.' A new word . . . 'What's the time, Ruth?' She stopped, loosening herself from the girl's arm. She hadn't worn her watch. It was an heirloom, her mother's, with an expanding gold bracelet. Mary had insisted that she should have it. 'My hands are never out of water with one thing and another. You can wear it to your work, Sarah. You're a lady.' Warmth at the thought of Mary's generosity filled her.

'Just after nine,' Ruth said. 'That's not bad. You'll be home in another quarter of an hour.' She took Sarah's arm again as they resumed walking. 'You mustn't mind me. I expect I'm too direct at times. It's having to fend for myself. And running the library.' Sarah hadn't known she was the chief librarian. She doubted it. There was an older woman there, glasses, bossy . . . 'When we have more time you must come up and see my flat. I've made it very nice, no chintz for me, I like deep, dark, brilliant colours. And good pictures – well, prints of good pictures. I have a nude by Modigliani. I'm very interested in art. And I have beautiful heavy brocade curtains in my front room, tied back with tassels.'

'It sounds nice.' Sarah thought of her bedroom with its white simplicity, the woollen tapestry picture with its sewn writing, 'Home is where the heart is'. Mary had done it during the war, when she was sitting at the fire at night. 'Can't bear being idle . . .' Sarah was handless, she always said, and Sarah was quite content with the appellation. She disliked sewing. Still, it would be nice to have a kind of den where she could go occasionally to be alone . . . except that she would rather sit in the kitchen with Mary.

'And I have a gramophone for my classical records which I play when I'm reading poetry. I haven't introduced you to poetry yet, have I?'

'Oh, I know quite a lot of poetry. We got it at school.'

'I'm not thinking of "The Boy Stood on the Burning Deck" kind,' Ruth laughed, 'but the new poets, like Owen and Sassoon. I can order the latest books and read them before I put them on the shelves.'

'Lucky you.' She tried to be sarcastic, but it didn't come off.

'Yes, sometime you must come up to my flat and we'll read them together. They're truthful, they display ugly truths, they explode the old idea that poetry must be pretty. They expose war for what it really is.'

'John would like that. He has no illusions about the war. Maybe I'll get the name of some of these books and buy them for him.'

'I'll let you borrow a few first from the library, and then you can choose the ones you like best.' She was very kind.

They rounded the corner of Millbrae Road. They had come upon it suddenly, surprising Sarah. When Ruth talked about poetry and things like that she was really interesting. She could learn a great deal from her to make up for her lack of education.

They reached Sarah's close. 'I've enjoyed our walk, Ruth,' she said. 'I hope it wasn't too much out of your way. You've still to walk back to Minard Road.'

'That's all right. I've enjoyed it too.' They were standing at the close mouth facing each other. The street was quiet. Mother and Father had chosen it because it was a quiet neighbourhood, no rowdy gangs hanging about. 'We'll have more talks when you come to see my flat.'

'That would be nice. Well, I'll get up the stairs. We're only one up, fortunately, now Mary has Lachie and the pram.'

'Yes, well, goodnight.' Ruth touched Sarah's cheek briefly with her hand. 'You're cold. Remember, come into the library when you get a minute.'

'Okay.' Sarah turned and walked along the stone passageway. The smooth shining surface of the patterned tiles seemed to waver in the gaslight. On the half-landing she stopped for a second. The window with its leaded border of stained glass reminded her that when she was young she had liked to look through the different coloured squares. The yellow made everything look filled with sunlight, the blue, cold and eerie, the red dripping with blood ... She reached their own landing.

It struck her that those solid doors were like citadels guarding complete little lives from the outside world, and how different all those lives were. Mrs Robertson who kept an old tom-cat and how if you lifted the letterbox to stick something through it a baleful smell of old tom-cat nearly knocked you over. The Johnsons, a steady, church-going couple, who on Saturday nights couldn't get their key into the lock because of an extended visit to the pub. And their neighbour across the landing, Mrs Laird, who although she 'kept herself to herself' spent most of her time peeping from behind her lace curtains.

Sarah inserted her key into the lock, nearly blinded by the polish on the brass nameplate and the doorknob ... trust

Mary. She went into the dark lobby but saw by the chink of light under the kitchen door that they were still up. Maybe there would be a cup of tea going ... 'Okay', she had said to that strange girl, Ruth Crosbie. Miss Frobisher didn't like 'Okay'.

She pushed open the kitchen door. 'Is it okay for a cuppa?' she asked.

Chapter Seven

Sarah left Millbrae Road earlier than usual to give herself time to get to Charing Cross and pick up the Otterburn suit and hats for Mrs de Vere. There was a sense of excitement in the expedition. A change in routine was a good thing, she thought, sitting in the taxi with her boxes and being whisked through the Glasgow streets to Central Station to catch the train to Helensburgh.

What must it be like to travel like this all the time, or even in a private motor car? There was no doubt it gave you a different sense of yourself, of being apart from the mob. She chided herself for that word 'mob'. John would take a poor view of it. He was such a man for equality. But maybe you had to face up to it. There never would be equality in this world. People *were* different.

She herself was between two stools. She knew her appearance of what Miss Frobisher would call 'well-bred refinement' was a sham, that compared with, say, Mrs de Vere, she was badly educated, from a working-class background, but at the same time, equality didn't rest solely on that, surely? What breeding and education did seem to give you, however, was a sense of your own identity, a self-assurance. 'A man's a man for all that,' Burns had said. She felt she understood it for the first time.

Sarah was so pleased with her trip through the city that she gave the taxi driver a shilling when he helped her out with the boxes at Gordon Street, and he even offered to carry them to her platform, albeit with little enthusiasm.

'Oh, no,' she said, 'that's far too much bother for you,' and he agreed quickly, saying he'd get enough humpin' tae dae him for the rest of the day wi' a sore back into the

52

bargain, before jumping into his taxi with amazing alacrity and driving away.

The journey to Helensburgh was pleasurable, the train pulling away quickly from the dreary outskirts of Glasgow, past the shipyards at Clydebank and soon reaching the gently rolling countryside with an occasional glimpse of the Clyde.

She got out at the smaller station of Helensburgh and was immediately met by a porter, which pleased her. 'Where to, miss?' he said, touching his cap. The 'well-bred air of refinement' which Miss Frobisher worshipped seemed to have made an impression on him.

'Wellwood House,' she said, speaking carefully. 'I believe it's near Rhu.'

'Ach, a ken it fine. The de Veres' place. You'll be wantin' a taxi.' A satisfied Sarah followed in his wake.

She was being driven along the promenade, admiring the view from her vantage point of an old-fashioned taxi which seemed higher than the Glasgow ones. 'What's the name of this loch?' she said to the burly back of the driver, waving her hand in the direction of the water.

'That's the Gairloch,' he said. 'Hae ye never been here before?' Sarah had to admit she hadn't. She and Mary had been taken on Clyde steamers by their father, but they generally sailed from the Broomielaw.

'Rhu,' the man said after a time, 'then Shandon Hydro, and up to Gairlochead, and doon the other side to Roseneath. A bonny wee place, Roseneath.'

'So I believe.' She was even learning how to speak in a taxi, she thought. You only had to travel in them often enough.

'Here we ur, then,' he announced, swerving off the road and driving slowly up a long narrow drive bordered by rhododendrons. 'They've got a good view here once you get to the house.' She paid him with more aplomb than at Gordon Street, thanked him, she hoped graciously, and going up the short flight of stairs, lifted the heavy iron knocker on the solid front door of a grey stone mansion turreted and balconied, the projecting oriels outlined by scalloped wood. Fussy, she

53

thought, like a dress with too much trimming. A buxom, middle-aged woman with grey hair parted in the centre and pulled back in a bun opened the door.

'Good morning,' Sarah said, 'I'm from Charles et Cie.'

'Och aye,' she nodded. 'She telt me. You've to come up to the old nursery. She doesn't like clippings or anything like that on the carpet.' Sarah nodded and followed the woman's broad beam up the wide, shallow stairs, carrying her boxes.

Would they offer her a cup of tea, she wondered. She generally slipped into the work-room around this time where Minnie had a cup ready for her. The journey had made her thirsty.

The nursery was shabby but comfortable, with a good fire going in the black grate, and she was relieved to see a tray with a cup and saucer, a plate of digestive biscuits and a teapot covered by a woollen tea cosy with a singed woollen side, probably as a result of having been placed too near the fire.

'Help yourself,' the woman said, 'I'll tell madam you're here.'

'It's a nice morning,' Sarah volunteered.

'Aye, for those who have time to enjoy it,' she said, and went off.

Sarah was left in the shabby room with two well-worn easy chairs at the fire and a mangy-looking rocking horse fixing her from a corner with a wall-eyed glassy stare. She poured herself a cup of tea and sat down to wait, hitching up her grey skirt with the deft movement which had become second nature to her. You had to take care of your clothes. Mary laughed at her when she religiously put trees or tissue paper into her shoes every night, and pressed her skirt with a damp cloth. 'Miss Pernickety', she called her.

She admired her exposed ankle with its grey Milanese silk stocking and black patent leather shoe, long, narrow, elegant. She remembered with pleasure Mrs de Vere's home-spun stockings and brogues. Each to his own.

Mrs de Vere must have been in a bad mood the day she

had been at Charles et Cie, but on home ground she had a bluff heartiness which Sarah liked.

'My God, I wish I had your figure!' the lady of the house exclaimed, having divested herself of her skirt and cardigan to reveal an ample bust tightly bound in strong calico, and a rump covered with what felt to Sarah like steel girders. What must she be like when she takes them off, she thought, helping Mrs de Vere on with the tweed skirt, a plain silk blouse in a toning colour and then the jacket.

'What do you think?' Mrs de Vere asked, turning and twisting in front of the three-quarter length mirror which might have been set up to allow her to see *le tout ensemble*.

Sarah stepped back, bumping into the rocking horse which glared at her with seemingly such evil intent that she almost apologised. 'I like it,' she said, nodding slowly. 'Yes, I like it. The inset belt in the back is much better than an all-round one for you, and the patch pockets break up the front nicely.'

'Do you really think so?' Mrs de Vere's manner, which had before been so commanding, now almost grew supplicating. Sarah had noticed often how a woman's personality changed when she was being fitted. 'Putty in your hands,' Minnie had said, 'you can tell them anything when they're standing in their drawers. They're at a definite disadvantage.' Sarah agreed.

'Definitely,' Sarah now said, 'and the fit on the shoulders couldn't be better.' She smoothed the broad shoulders encased in their tawny mixture of Otterburn tweed, almost as you would stroke a horse, she thought, although she had never had occasion to do that.

'Since my husband died,' Mrs de Vere was now confidential (this often followed), 'I haven't really bothered much about clothes, but Ronald, my son, thinks I should smarten myself up a bit. This is for meetings in Helensburgh. I'm chairman of various committees.'

'Ideal,' Sarah said confidently. 'It suits you, and it's designed for the country lifestyle. And yet you could get away with it anywhere. It's really you.'

'You don't think it's a teeny little bit tight round the waist?'

55

The last wriggle of the fish on the line, Sarah thought, changing her analogy.

She took the suggestion seriously. 'Move your arms, please. There's no constriction in the arm-holes, is there? You can move freely? We're very particular at Charles et Cie about comfort. It's absolutely paramount in our house.' It might have been Miss Frobisher speaking.

Mrs de Vere shimmied inside the Otterburn tweed. 'No, you're right. It's most comfortable. "Good tailoring", my friend, Lady Colquhoun said, "Charles et Cie won't let you down when it comes to tailoring."'

'We pride ourselves on our tailoring,' Sarah corroborated. 'So you're quite happy?'

Mrs de Vere preened, pulling and smoothing. 'Quite happy, thank you, yes,' her chin rose in gracious assent, 'quite happy.'

'Now, shall we try on the hats?' Sarah smiled reassuringly at the woman and began untying the hat box. Minnie was right.

'Oh yes! Confidentially, Miss Lane, hats are a nightmare to me.'

'I think you'll change your mind when you see our selection.' Sarah reverentially lifted a confection from the black box with its gold lettering. 'Feathers are always fashionable,' she twirled the hat expertly on her left hand, 'a turned-up brim held by a discreet ostrich plume, not too elaborate, quite suited for the country house style.' ('Always show the most expensive one first,' was Miss Frobisher's dictum.) 'But you certainly won't see a copy of it even in the best houses.'

Mrs de Vere accepted the hat dubiously, put it on, looked at herself in the mirror, then laughed like a man in a club. Sarah had once delivered an outfit to a member of one in Blythswood Square (the gentleman had bought a fur piece for his wife for her birthday), and she knew what a club laugh sounded like. 'I look like the Sultan of Hyderabad in this! No, no, Miss Lane, definitely not me!' Sarah agreed with her. The feather resembled nothing so much as a flue brush.

'Your taste is impeccable, Mrs de Vere,' she said. 'It's, shall we say, too ostentatious for your costume.' (She was pleased with how newly-acquired words fell neatly into place.) 'I took the liberty of asking our milliner to make up this simple shape in the same Otterburn tweed as the coat and skirt, with a trimming of grosgrain ribbon picking up the brick weave.' She took the hat out of the box and handed it to Mrs de Vere. The older woman put it on and looked in the mirror, an expression of uncertainty on her face.

'I hate all this!' she protested, sounding like a petulant child. 'Still, it's got to be done. Mmmh . . .' She tilted her head this way and that. 'Yes, I see what you mean. It tones in beautifully, and it could be rolled up and stuck in my raincoat pocket if necessary . . .'

Sarah concealed a shudder. 'Yes,' she said bravely, 'stick it in your raincoat pocket and it would emerge as good as new, a most useful little hat.'

'That's all I can hope for in my clothes.' Mrs de Vere now sounded philosophical, 'useful.' She appealed to Sarah. 'Do you really like me in this?'

'It's most becoming,' Sarah said earnestly. 'If you looked and looked again you wouldn't find any hat which would do more for you than this one. It's just as if it was made for you.' She laughed. 'In fact it was!' It's strange, she thought, the many aspects of women. Mrs de Vere had struck her as the typical upper-class type who came to Charles et Cie, demanding, slightly aggressive, and here she was, stripped of her self-confidence as she had stripped herself of her dress and revealed herself in her underwear.

She helped Mrs de Vere to divest herself of the Otterburn outfit. 'You have the height and figure to wear an ensemble like this,' she said, 'you'll be just right in it wherever you go until it wears out, *if* it ever wears out . . .'

Mrs de Vere, back in her former tartan skirt, nodded briskly. 'I'll have it. And the hat. I feel suited, Miss Lane, and I shall tell Miss Frobisher how helpful you've been. Indeed, I intend to ask her if you would take over my wardrobe from now on. I'm in need of something in the nature of a dinner dress for all those functions. You wouldn't believe how many there are in this small place.'

'Country life,' Sarah smiled wisely, 'isn't as quiet as people believe.' She laid the suit reverentially over one of the shabby armchairs, put the hat on the seat. 'Thank you, Mrs de Vere. Now, a dinner dress, you said? Well, you can't beat black. Well-cut, simple in line . . .'

'I have Edgar's pearls . . .' Mrs de Vere looked out of the nursery window. There was a pause and then her briskness returned. 'I'll leave it with you, Miss Lane. You came in a taxi, I suppose?'

'Yes, I did.'

'And I expect they robbed you. How much did they charge?' In her tartan skirt and baggy cardigan, hands stuck in the pockets, she was again formidable.

'Five shillings. I gave him a tip, of course.' That was a stupid remark, she thought. She gave herself a bad mark.

'Didn't deserve it. I don't want to run down the Scots since I live amongst them, but they think people travelling in taxis should be fleeced.' Unfortunately, Sarah thought, it's Miss Frobisher who'll fleece *you*.

'I'll get Ronald to run you back to the station. You get your things together and I'll ask Mrs Mason to find him. He'll be in the garden somewhere.' She left the room, shoulders squared, a satisfied customer.

Sarah retied the hat box with the rejected hat inside and put on the loose travelling coat she had worn for the journey. In the mirror she wondered if its looseness made her look too thin. She sympathised with Mrs de Vere who had to gird herself so tightly, and who would see in the mirror the unwanted flesh when the restrictions were removed. Perhaps the departed Edgar had liked it.

Mrs Mason appeared in the doorway, still unsmiling. 'Are you ready?' she asked. 'Major de Vere has the car out, madam said to tell you.'

'Yes, I'm ready, thank you.' Sarah pulled on her grey kid gloves and lifted the hat box. The woman was already half-way down the stairs.

Mrs de Vere said a brief goodbye to her in the hall, but her eyes were kind. 'I'm busy with an agenda for a meeting this evening. My son will see you safely to the station. Thank you for coming.' She nodded briskly and retreated into the room behind her.

Mrs de Vere's son got out of the black motor to help Sarah in, and went back to his seat. She had thought of him in uniform, but he was now wearing shabby trousers and a cardigan over a shirt which was unbuttoned at the neck. No tie. He turned to her when she was seated. 'What time is your train?' He wasn't going to waste time on small talk, she thought.

'I'm not sure. But they run quite frequently to Central Station.' In the brief moment when she had seen him face on he reminded her of Sunny Jim in the cereal advertisement. 'High o'er the fence leapt Sunny Jim, Force was the force that raised him . . .' He had the same broad forehead and the small chin, young-looking despite being a major. She felt guilty about the comparison and added, 'If you just drop me in Helensburgh I shouldn't have long to wait.' He didn't answer, but drew on a pair of cuffed leather gloves, which looked strange with his cardigan, and busied himself with the gears. The engine roared and they darted down the driveway at a fast speed until he came near the gates where he slowed down.

'Got to watch this turn,' he said. 'Madmen on the road since I've been away.' A cart and horse slowly passed, the man sitting at the front bent over as if he were asleep.

'What make is your motor?' Sarah asked politely.

'It's a Pullman Limousine. Huge beast,' he shouted above the roar of the engine. 'It was laid up while I was over there.'

'I see.' It didn't seem right to ask him any more questions. She lapsed into silence, looking out of the window at the passing landscape with exaggerated interest while she wondered how she would like living here. Supposing this man were her husband she would have to get a dog, learn about gardens, maybe learn to shoot, and how to write an agenda. People like Mrs de Vere worked hard for charities, she knew, and they did it without payment. The idea of voluntary work was foreign to her. She worked to exist, to pay her way. Mary didn't take nearly enough from her, although she had protested frequently. 'Save it for things for your bottom drawer,' Mary said. Her ruminations were broken by Major de Vere's voice.

'Did you manage to fit up my mother all right?'

'Oh, yes,' Sarah said, 'I think she was quite pleased.'

'She never cared a rap about clothes.' He relapsed into silence again, but was soon negotiating the comparatively busy streets of the little town. He let her out at the station with a distracted air.

'Have to do some shopping while I'm in. I'll go to the bank first.' He looked up and down the street as if it were hiding from him. 'Well, er, goodbye.'

'Thank you for bringing me,' Sarah said, 'it was most kind.'

'Better than walking, eh?' His mind wasn't on her, she could see. His hands were going through his pockets, evidently looking for something. He gave her a quick smile, like Sunny Jim's, and drove off.

Chapter Eight

The kitchen at Millbrae Road was warm and inviting when Sarah got back that evening, the table set for high tea, and, unusually, John was there too, sitting at the fire while Mary completed her cooking over the range.

'You're in early,' Sarah said, sitting at the table to be out of the way.

'Aye, he is.' Mary replied for him. 'I canny get doing a thing here with his great legs spread all over the place.' Her look of contentment belied her words.

'I hope there's nothing wrong,' Sarah said.

'No, no. I had to attend a meeting for shop stewards, and there was no point in going back to the foundry. They'd be closing down.'

'Dixon's Blazes. A Glasgow landmark. I've known it since I was a wee lassie. Remember how Ma used to take us to the window to see the sky lit up, Mary?'

'Aye, fine,' Mary agreed, busy over the sizzling pan of sausages on the gas ring.

'I thought it was magic.'

'You would. If I was down in the street playing she would threaten me with it. "If you don't come up this minute you'll go to the bad fire!" And she would point to that glow in the sky!'

'When it stops it will mean that the foundry's finished, and that's us all in Queer Street,' John said.

'Come on, John!' Mary laughed at him. 'Your meeting's over.'

'It'll come, though. They'll amalgamate, or something. Nothing stays the same.'

'Is there a Mr Dixon?' Sarah asked, interested.

'Oh, aye, at least there was. Mr William Dixon. He built

his first blast furnace eighty years ago. He made steam engines. He had coal works nearby, and iron works at Coatbridge. He was an enterprising man all right, a Victorian of the old school.'

'Now we're going to get a lecture,' Mary said, looking up from the pan, face flushed with the heat, a few tendrils of hair loose. She looks younger, prettier, when John is around, Sarah thought.

'No fear. Ma stomach's rumbling with the smell of they sausages.' He laughed at her.

'You've got no soul.' Sarah laughed with him. 'All I know is that Dixon's Blazes was pure magic to me. I didn't feel the day was over until the sky lit up and then we'd gather round the fire for our tea.'

'Maybe no'.' John got up. 'What's facing us now is that the supply of hard coal is about finished and now we're on to coke. And how long is that going to last unless we get a coking plant of our own?'

'Don't ask us,' Mary said. 'All I know is that they sausages are beginning to burst out o' their skins.'

'Women!' John smiled at her. 'If we haven't any coke you won't be able to cook your sausages!'

'Why?'

'Because there would be no gas, that's why.'

'I never thought of that. Well, we'd better eat while we can.'

'There were some clever folk, all the same,' Sarah said, as John moved over to the table, 'and rich. Those big houses they built on the Clyde coast. I was at one of them today. I told you, Mary?' She looked at her sister.

'Aye, Helensburgh. What was that like?'

'A mansion. But she wasn't a dragon in her lair after all, this Mrs de Vere who owned it. She was quite nice. I liked her. I think she's the kind who'll put the fear of God into the Helensburgh women at her committee meetings, but when it comes to clothes her confidence in herself goes.'

Mary was intent on dishing up the sausages and tomatoes on to three plates. She took a great ashet of mashed potatoes out of the oven at the side of the range and put it on the table. 'Come on, John,' she said, pointing to the ashet, 'dig in. It's not much tonight. Lachie was a wee bit girny all day and missed his sleep, but I've got him over at last. He was tired out, poor wee soul.'

'I'll have a peep at him, if you like?' Sarah offered.

'Sarah and her peeps.' Mary smiled at John. 'No, let sleeping dogs lie, or weans. Come on. Wire in and then we'll get cleared up and take it easy. Are you going out, Sarah?'

'No, I'll have a bath later and have an early night. And a read in bed.'

'I'll stoke up the fire. There's mustard.' She pushed the pot towards her. 'I mixed it myself. It's fresh.'

'Do you know where your customer in Helensburgh got her money?' John asked. He accepted a cup of tea from his wife. 'Thanks.'

'No. Maybe some place like Dixon's for all I know. Although they're English.'

'Maybe her husband came to Scotland to show us how to do it. They're pretty good at that.' Mary laughed.

'They'd have to be asked first,' John said.

'Her husband is dead,' Sarah told them, 'but he must have left her pretty comfortable. Her son was there, Major de Vere. He ran me to the station.'

'Now it's coming out,' Mary exclaimed delightedly. 'What was he like?'

'Fair-haired. He hardly noticed me. I might as well have been a bag of John's coal he was delivering. He only took me because his mother asked him, maybe ordered him.'

'A major, though,' Mary said.

'He could have been a brigadier general for all that it matters.' John waved his fork. 'Even a major, commanding his troops, has still to take orders from his mother. Poor wee Lachie! He doesn't know what he's in for.'

'He speaks from bitter experience.' Mary rolled her eyes at Sarah. 'Did this Major de Vere not ask you for a date?'

'She never gives up.' Sarah sighed. 'I told you he hardly noticed me. But I did ask him what make his motor was, John. A Pullman Limousine.'

'My God! They're worth thousands. You should stick in there.'

'Are you two desperate to get rid of me?'

'Well, it would be nice to have you called Lady de Vere. It sounds quite, well, nice.' Mary looked slightly uncomfortable.

'Maybe you've forgotten I have a date on Saturday, if that's what you want.'

'We want you to be happy,' John said. He smiled his sweet smile at her, and she thought, let's get off this subject.

'You two should pop off to the pictures while you've got me. I'll keep an eye on Lachie.'

'What about it, John?' Mary's eyes were eager.

'Well, I'm home early, and I've got my good suit on . . .'

'There's a good picture on at Eglinton Toll,' Sarah said, 'I noticed it from the tram. Charlie Chaplin in *Shoulder Arms*. You'll get a great laugh.'

'That settles it. Eat up, John. Thanks, Sarah.' Her sister smiled at her. 'If you're sure you can manage . . . ?'

'I'm quite capable. I'll leave your kitchen spick and span, and I'll get my clothes ready for the morning, and I'll only have a bath if I'm sure Lachie is sound asleep. I'll probably be in bed by the time you get back.'

She enjoyed having the house to herself. She washed up, stoked the fire, and peeped in occasionally at Lachie who never stirred. She gave her black patent shoes an extra polish, rubbing Vaseline into the leather where it might develop cracks, and pressed her grey skirt. I'm getting old-maidish, she thought. She had a last look at the baby before she went to have her bath, standing at his cot for a full minute. His thumb was in his mouth, his other hand was cupped over his ear. She gently pulled up the covers.

In the steaming bathroom she thought of Major de Vere in a slightly annoyed fashion. It was typical of his class that they were only pleasant if it suited them. Was she annoyed because he hadn't paid any attention to her? Surely not. She could hardly remember him except when she thought of Sunny Jim. Now if she closed her eyes she could see Gus Carmichael quite clearly, the bold eyes, the slightly open mouth, the eager air. Major de Vere certainly hadn't been eager.

She was in bed, warm and scented, propped up on pillows with Ruth Crosbie's latest selection when she heard Mary and John come in.

'Was it a good picture?' she called.

'Aye, great!' Mary's head appeared round the door. 'We're sore laughing. We're just off to bed, Sarah. Was Lachie all right?'

'As right as rain. See you in the morning. I'm ready to drop off.'

She didn't drop off. She went on reading *Heart of Darkness*, which seemed mostly unintelligible to her – Ruth Crosbie had overestimated her intelligence there – and also, since she wasn't in her place, couldn't take into consideration the low murmur of voices which reached her from next door, and the silences, once broken by a quickly-suppressed groan. Your presence must be a damper, she thought, feeling miserable, an interloper. She put the book on her bedside table, wound her alarm and put out the light.

The strange thing was, she thought, lying wide awake in the darkness, that Mary was like two persons. There was the night Mary, loving, being loved, and the morning Mary, brisk, matter-of-fact. Somehow it would have been more apposite if she had been pale and heavy-eyed. The metamorphosis puzzled her often. 'Your breakfast's ready, Sarah. Make some fresh tea. That will be stewed. John was away at six. I'll go and lift Lachie. I'm going to the shops early to get some fresh haddock before it all goes. Or how about herrings, rolled up and done in the oven with vinegar? They're just as good cold, and they keep . . . Oh, that Charlie Chaplin, Sarah, just the sight o' him makes you laugh . . .'

It wouldn't sound much like a woman who had been in the grip of passion last night. What was that passion like, that it could be so overwhelming and then be forgotten so completely? There had been no sign of it this morning, no tenderness. 'John! You're away without your muffler! You'd forget yur heid!' That must be why they repeated the performance, because they had forgotten what it was like . . .

Chapter Nine

Gus Carmichael's 'sports job' was tucked in the curve of Queens Drive just past the gates of the park. When he saw Sarah he tooted his horn and flung open the door on her side.

'Jump in!' he said gaily. 'You're only five minutes late.'

'That's the prerogative of women,' she said, settling herself beside him, as surprised herself by her remark as he apparently was.

'Come again?'

'I read it somewhere,' she mumbled, spoiling the impact.

'Hey! I hope you're not one o' they bluestockings or whatever they're called. They don't know how to have fun.'

'Oh, no!' she protested.

But as they drove through the city southwards, past Newton Mearns, and over the rolling countryside towards the Ayrshire coast, her spirits lifted. Real country, she thought, and remembered Helensburgh. Am I maybe meant to live away from a city, in a place like Mrs de Vere's, not so big, of course, but with that grand view and a wee town to shop in, have a quiet life, walking, and watching birds, and digging in the garden or having time to stop and stare like that poem?

Once when she had asked Mary if she ever missed having a garden she had said, 'How can you miss something you never had?'

'Who's this wee mouse sitting beside me?' Gus Carmichael asked. Sarah blushed.

'Oh, I'm sorry! I was thinking.'

'That's dangerous,' he said, 'you'll do yourself an injury.'

'Don't pull my leg. I was just thinking . . . have you ever had a garden?'

'We've got one. All round the house.'

66

'Do you grow flowers and things in it?'

'We don't bother much about it. Roses, I think. She likes it kept nice. She has a man who comes in and cuts the grass. There's an old besom in the next house and if we let it grow long she's knocking at the door and saying we must think of the neighbourhood, Mrs Carmichael. It's the look o' the place. I wouldny like to tell you what ma mother says behind her back!'

Sarah laughed because it was expected. 'We have always lived up a stair, but sometimes I go to see customers on the Clyde coast, well, only once, but I'll be sent more often, and they have great big gardens, with drives.'

'Grounds,' Gus offered, 'they're called grounds.'

'I wouldn't mind having grounds. For privacy, then you don't have to bother about neighbours asking you if you've cut your grass, or in our case, it's Mrs Crawford chapping at the door and telling us it's our turn for the stairs . . .' Gus was evidently wearying of this conversation.

'Well, we've got privacy,' he said, nudging her shoulder as he drove. 'What could be nicer than in a sporty job like this driving down to Ayr?'

'Is that where we're going? You didn't say.' Or ask if it suited me.

'Yes, I know a slap-up restaurant there. I've been to it often.'

'D'you think we might have a walk before we go in?'

'Are you dressed for walking?' He glanced quickly but appreciatively. She had decided on a beige skirt and jacket with the skirt fashionably short to show a few inches of cream silk stocking and a slim foot in cream buckskin laceups (for the country) to match her silk blouse which had a soft bow at the neck. She had thought, looking in the mirror, that with her honey-coloured hair and fair skin there was at least nothing discordant in *le tout ensemble*.

'Oh, yes, we can stick to the path.'

'Well,' he considered. 'Have you ever been on the Heads of Ayr?'

'I've never been to Ayr, never mind the Heads. Is it nice?'

'Aye, you get a grand view of Arran. And it's a good spot for canoodling.'

'I thought it was only a slap-up meal we came for?' She was rapidly learning how to talk like Gus.

'Don't worry. The table's booked, but I didn't think you'd be leading me on like this, though.' He leered sideways at her. 'I thought I'd have to be content with soft lights and sweet music.' He gave her another nudge with his shoulder. She swayed sideways with the impact.

But she loved where he took her, the height of the promontory, the short grass like fur, the clear fresh air, the sea far beneath them. It was like being a bird, she thought, but when she told Gus that she felt she might fly away if she stretched out her arms, he gave her a strange look.

'Ma shoes are getting a bit mucky,' he said. They were two-tone brown-and-white 'sports jobs', she had thought when she first met him, too flashy. 'We'd better get back.' He put his arm round her waist as they turned and asked if anyone had ever told her what a wee beauty she was. She said no one ever had, but she wasn't so wee, she was five foot seven inches. He gave her another strange look.

In the hotel restaurant she relaxed even more. The cocktail he ordered for her seemed to go straight to her head, and she felt her personality change to suit his. She sat outside herself looking at this smart young woman laughing at his remarks, eyes sparkling. The restaurant, which had at first seemed too flashy, like Gus, was now softly lit, magical.

'What do you think of it here?' he asked her, looking around as if he had bought it. She noticed he never used her name.

'It's very nice,' she said. 'A lot of people.'

'It's popular, that's why. It's the very latest thing for the Glasgow folk to take a run down here for dinner, those that can afford it, of course.'

'There seem to be a lot of older men with young girls.'

'Aye, wee gold diggers.' She thought there must be some inducement. Most of their escorts looked decidedly unattractive, fat, red-faced men who leant across the table as if they couldn't see properly, or wanted to see more. She wondered what they had done with their wives.

'I wonder what excuse they make to their wives?' she asked Gus, her eyes on a heavily-jowled old man ogling a young girl sitting opposite him. Mary would have described her as 'no better than she should be'. She laughed loudly at some remark the man had made. She had straw-like hair, a scarlet mouth, and her breasts were half-exposed above her low-cut dress. She had the bony shoulders of an adolescent.

'Hey.' Gus took Sarah's hand across the table. 'Suppose you pay attention to me instead of looking at other people having a good time.'

'Sorry,' she said, withdrawing her hand to take up her fork and tackle some concoction which she hadn't as yet been able to recognise. She thought hard. 'Were you in the war, Gus?' she asked.

'No, I wasn't.' He looked annoyed. 'Did a no' tell you before? I was exempted because I'm chesty. But I did my bit,' he added darkly, 'never fear.'

'Oh, I know that. I was just asking.' She had been going to tell him about John and how his experiences in the Somme had changed him, and perhaps ask him if he had read any poems about the war, but decided against it. She had better keep off the whole subject.

'But it's over, thank God,' he said, 'and everybody's determined to have a good time. That suits our business fine. It's never been better. There's often a queue at our shops.'

'I hope they don't bet while their children go hungry . . .' The words died on her lips, seeing his face. She tackled the concoction again.

The trouble was he didn't seem to want to talk about anything. What he seemed to like, she was discovering, was a kind of heavy flirtatious banter which grew easier as he refilled her wine glass. It seemed to bring out in her a streak she had never known was there. When he asked her, taking both hands across the table, if she were going to be 'kind' to him on the way home, she made what she immediately recognised as a mistake. 'I'll see how I feel,' she said, and could have bitten out her tongue.

Was she drunk? She didn't know how one knew. Perhaps it lay in a reluctance to stand up, which she was feeling. It had to be done. After they'd had coffee she made an excuse about going to powder her nose, and although she was concentrating, she swayed when she stood up.

'Whoops!' Gus said delightedly. 'Do you want me to come wi' you and gie you a haun?' He laughed, and she didn't.

'I'll be back in a minute,' she said, lifting her chin, and that helped. For a brief second she was Miss Lane in the salon.

In the Ladies Boudoir (it said that on the door), at the risk of spoiling her makeup, she splashed some cold water on her face and felt better. In the mirror she saw standing beside her the young girl whom she had noticed before, being ogled by the older man. She was applying fresh lipstick to her wide mouth.

'Coolin' down, hen?' she said, and when Sarah smiled, she said, in between smacking her lips to spread the colour, 'Ye hae to watch these buggers!' Sarah could only nod. When she made for the door the girl called after her, 'Mind how ye go!', letting out a loud cackle. That, she thought, walking towards Gus, and feeling quite sober now, was what they called in books a salutary experience. And the joy I get out of knowing words like that is better than the actuality.

'I'm ready to go now,' she said when she reached the table, not sitting down. Gus nodded, without looking up. He was busy counting out an alarming pile of notes into the waiter's hand.

'Did you enjoy your pork à la crème?' Gus asked as they were speeding through what Sarah thought could well be called a velvety night. The sky was thick with stars, and the open sides let the soft wind blow on her cheeks, cooling the unusual colour in them. The air smelled differently from that in Glasgow, pure, untinged by the acrid smoke which generally polluted it when the foundries shut down. She would have liked to walk along the dark country road to savour it.

70

'Yes, it was very nice,' and, greatly daring, 'What was that thing we had first, the pink stuff in pots?'

'The pink stuff, she says! That was crab mousse, if you don't mind, the chef's speciality. There's no end to the trouble I go to, to please the girls I take out.'

'Are you in the habit of taking them to Ayr?' She could ask questions now without really concentrating on him. She was enjoying too much the swift rush of the night air on her face, and watching the twinkling lights on the far shore.

'Only the ones I like best,' he said. 'It's no' everybody that I'd take there, especially to that hotel. It's no' cheap.'

'Well, I'm greatly honoured,' she heard her voice say at the same time as she was thinking that one day she might live in a house where air like this could be smelled all the time, instead of the smoky stuff that filled her lungs in Glasgow, not to mention dirtying the lace trimming on her petticoat.

'There are ways of showing your appreciation.' He slowed down the motor and seemed to cruise along. The road was quiet, dark. It stretched ahead of them lit only by the beam from his headlamps. She saw an animal, slow-moving, cross, then stop as if transfixed in the middle by the headlights, and then disappear into the trees. She heard their faint rustle. She would have liked to know its name. Living in the country was an art. The phrase echoed in her mind. Had she read it somewhere, made it up? But it was. There were all kinds of signs, portents . . .

'Thank you very much, Gus.' She realised he was waiting and spoke too earnestly. 'I thought it was great, the whole thing. It was a lovely place, and that waiter . . . he was so attentive, couldn't do enough for us.'

'They're all like that if you give them a big enough tip. I'm glad you're pleased . . .' He was looking at the side of the road as he spoke, going slower and slower. He suddenly stopped. 'This'll do.' He turned into a clearing and stopped the engine. 'Aye, this'll do fine.'

'Is there something wrong with the motor?' It was pitch black now with the headlamps off and the trees behind them.

He laughed, and turning round drew her towards him with

his hands on her shoulders. 'I never know whether you're pulling my leg or no'. D'you no' mind what you said back there?'

'What was that?' She began to tremble, and bit her lip to steady it.

'You said you'd see how you felt.'

'See how I felt? Did I? I don't remember that.'

'C'mon. When I asked you if you were going to be kind to me.'

'Kind?' She laced her fingers together on her lap, thinking words would be her downfall yet.

'You're the limit.' His hands slipped from her shoulders to pull her even closer. 'On the way home.' He sounded irritated. 'I asked you if you were going to be kind to me and you said you'd see how you . . .' She interrupted him with a rush.

'Oh, that! Well, I feel fine, just *fine*. But I don't think you should have stopped all the same. Mary and John are very understanding but they wouldn't like me coming in at all hours.'

'Hours!' His exasperation was great. 'It's hardly bedtime, ten o'clock! For Pete's sake, you're a big lassie. They know you can look after yourself.' That's just it, I can't, she thought.

'Oh, I'm able to do that all right but . . .'

'But me no buts. Where's my reward, then?' He pushed at her face with his chin, hard, bony. She could feel the bristles under the skin. 'I took you for a nice run, didn't I, we had a nice dinner, and here we are . . .' She could hear him panting now, and even in the gloom of the car saw that his mouth as he raised his face to look at her was partly open.

He took one hand away from her body, and put it on her breast. She felt him fondling it, kneading, the way Mary kneaded dough, only this hurt. She stiffened, not moving, not uttering. Maybe if she closed her eyes the whole thing would go away.

'Relax, for God's sake.' His voice was thick. His mouth came down on hers, and as if acting like a magnet, held her there while one hand went to the neck of her blouse and tried to untie the bow. I'm like that animal that stopped in the glare of the headlamps, she thought, transfixed, stupid. Here I am, twenty-two, this has never happened to me before and I don't know how to deal with it. Somebody should have *told* me. She invoked Mary, her dead mother, some sixth sense, a book . . . Gus meantime was busy.

His mouth screwed down on hers like a vice, his fingers worked doggedly away at the knot which she had so securely tied early in the evening. She was almost catatonic with apprehension, could neither help him nor prevent him. Eventually he exploded with fury. 'Whit in God's name made you wear something like this fur on a night oot! Can you no gie a fella a haun?' She heard the sound of a tear, and the tiny noise galvanised her into sudden movement. Her arms shot up, her hands flapped, a flame of anger swept through her.

'Mind what you're doing!' she shouted, pulling fiercely away from him. This was the key. Sartorial outrage. 'That's pure crêpe de chine!' Miss Frobisher always laid particular emphasis on the word 'pure'. She put her hands up to the neck. Yes, the material was torn from the tie collar, the blouse was ruined. It could never be mended, even by Minnie's clever fingers in the work-room.

'Who the hell cares whit it is! Could you no' have helped me!' He was as angry as she was.

'What for?' she said. She had learned those icy tones in Charles et Cie when reprimanding the two juniors. She hadn't thought they would come in useful elsewhere.

'Whit fur!' he shouted. His city swagger had completely gone. 'Whit fur? In the name o' Goad, d'ye want some fun ur don't ye?'

'I just want to go home.' She was the little girl lost on the shore at Largs, she was swallowing her tears, but she kept her icy tones. 'Now!' she said. There was a long pause when she thought he was going to strangle her – she could hear his rapid breathing and almost prayed for it – and then he suddenly flung away from her.

'Ach,' he said, 'you're no' worth it. Leading men on and then behaving like a spiled wean. There's a name for your kind. Would you like to hear it?' She was tempted to say yes since it wasn't a word she knew. There was another long silence, broken only by his breathing, either caused by rage or shortness of breath. At last. 'You want to go home, is that it?'

'That's it,' she said skittishly, waiting for the blow, her eyes screwed shut. *Girl found murdered in car near Ayr. The contents of her stomach contained pork* à la crème *and crab mousse. Well-known hotel restaurants nearby have been questioned.* . . She heard his deep intake of breath, the phlegm rattling in his throat.

'Well, I'll bloody well take you hame. An' you're damn lucky. Thousands wouldn't.' He sat up straight and drew his hands down on either side of his face, muttering to himself. Then he started the motor, crashing the gears, still cursing.

The drive along the empty road was a nightmare. Sarah was sure he was trying to kill her, but remembered that would involve his own destruction and dismissed the idea. From that she began to feel sorry for him. He had spent a lot of money on her and had had no 'reward', as he put it, and at one stage she nearly said, 'if you stop now I'll try to make it up to you', but she wasn't that sorry.

She was to blame as much as he. He had chosen the wrong girl – much better to have had that one in the Ladies Boudoir, or similar, and she should not have accepted his invitation at the beginning, knowing that he was the wrong man. Well, it had been a salutary lesson. That was the second time that word had come to her mind. Perhaps it was a salutary lesson to her also that it was necessary to have the experience before the word.

At Queens Drive he decanted her rudely where he had picked her up, leaning across her to open the door in a gesture of dismissal. 'Here's your stop. You can walk from here.'

'Thanks,' she said and got out quickly. She attempted to lean in at the open window to apologise. 'I'm sorry . . .' she started to say but he drove away with a screech of tyres and a jerk which nearly threw her in the gutter. Just deserts, she thought.

Why on earth had she arranged to be picked up here, she wondered as she started walking. She could understand that it was chagrin which had made him drop her at the same place. It was quite far to Millbrae Road at this time of night, but when she looked at her watch she thought it could have been worse. It wasn't yet midnight.

She walked quickly, skirting the park, dark and mysterious now, turned right at the Victoria Hospital and half-ran up Langside Hill. Luckily the passers-by were all couples, too engrossed in each other to give her any more than a passing glance. She was panting when she got to their close, and could hardly manage the stairs. When she let herself in there was a small light in the lobby only and the house was quiet. Mary and John would be in bed. He had an early start.

She crept quietly to her room, not daring to use the lavatory in case the sound of flushing would disturb them. Good thing I went to the Ladies Boudoir, she thought. She sat for a long time before undressing, thinking over the evening. A fiasco of an evening. She recognised that she had gone out with Gus Carmichael under false pretences. 'A bit of fun' was *de rigueur*. All the same, he had no right to tear at her blouse like an animal. Girls like the one in the Ladies Boudoir would have known not to wear a blouse with a tie neck, like a red rag to a bull, she thought, suddenly giggling. There should be a book called *Do's and Don'ts for Dumbbells*. She had to put her hand to her mouth to stifle the noise she was making.

Some time later she took the blouse off and examined it. Yes, delicate material like that could never be repaired. In any case she would never want to wear it again. She would dump it somewhere. There were big bags of clippings in the work-room where it could be hidden.

She wasn't proud of herself. What was missing in her, she felt, was a lack of feeling, even allowing for an unsuitable companion. She remembered that time long ago at Largs when Mary had been going out to meet John, and how when she came back she seemed to fill the room with excitement, sexual excitement. And her lip had been bruised.

Did it mean that she was incapable of this feeling? It was

her detachment, she knew, which had infuriated Gus most. She didn't know whether to laugh or cry.

The following evening Sarah tried to have a frank talk with Mary when she asked her if she had enjoyed herself. 'You know I'm not cold, Mary.'

'Cold? No, you're not that. Why? Did you not hit it off with Mr Carmichael?'

'No, I'm not his type.'

'Did he try anything on?' He tried to get something *off*. She laughed and shook her head.

'I mean,' she tried to explain, 'I love children. Wee Lachie. Surely that proves I'm not cold. And I was worried and anxious all the time John was away. For you, but as well because I couldn't bear the thought of anything happening to him. And I was heart sorry for all those poor lads in the freezing mud. And there were those times when you didn't get news for a long time and you went out to your work every morning with that poor white face . . .'

'No,' Mary said, shaking her head slowly, 'you're not cold. You're not easy, shy, maybe. I think you missed Ma more than me. I had John.'

'I missed the talks I had with her. Pa too.'

'You have to grow up sometime. Don't you worry. You'll know the right man when he comes along. And believe me, you'll find it damned hard to stop him when he gets up to his capers, for they all do at first.' Sarah thought of her ruined blouse. Mary was smiling at her with her old flirty eyes. 'Anyhow,' she said, 'who wants to see you married to a bookie?'

Chapter Ten

The days wore on into summer. It seemed there was a febrile excitement in the air, the first summer there had been no grinding worry nor agony about the war. Yet many men were disillusioned, and some were out of work. There was a great discontent with the government.

They didn't realise, John said, that the trade unions were preventing a revolution. He was constantly at meetings, but as Mary pointed out, it didn't stop the cost of coal rising. Sarah insisted on paying her more each week, but she took the extra money reluctantly. She still wanted her to save towards her bottom drawer, although since the Gus Carmichael incident, she had kept quiet on the subject of Sarah finding 'a good man'.

She had enough worries of her own. She looked permanently tired, as if the anxiety of the war was now taking its toll. The doctor had said she was anaemic, and when Sarah suggested she should lower her household standards a little, she said that had nothing to do with it, it was a spot of 'woman trouble'. Sometimes when Sarah came home and Mary had reluctantly allowed her to help, they would sit afterwards at the open window on warm evenings to get some air.

Down in the street the older children would be playing, 'jinking' in and out of the closes, the girls would have chalked out their peever beds on the pavement, and the noise of their shouting would drift up to the two of them. 'If this was Bridgeton,' Mary said with some of her old humour, 'we'd put our cushions on the window ledge and have a good "hing oot".' Sarah laughed. What wouldn't we give for a garden, she would think, then we shouldn't be tied to the house. There would be the smell of flowers, not the stale used air of

77

the city, nor the smell of fat from the corner chip shop.

'What you and John need is to get off for a holiday,' she said. 'You need a change of air, and Lachie's wearing you out, bumping that pram up and down the stairs every day.' He was a stirring child, large for his age.

'Try telling that to John. He hardly takes time to eat.'

Sarah said one particularly hot day in June, 'I don't like you trailing to that special fish shop of yours in Pollokshaws.' She looked down at the breadcrumbed haddock on her plate, saw how, as usual, the table was immaculately set. Lachie, in his high chair, chortled and banged his spoon and Sarah half-rose to attend to him.

'Don't lift him!' Mary's voice was sharp. 'He's just going to get his tea.'

'Sorry.' She subsided, and went on eating her fish in silence. It's a good thing she hasn't had another one, she thought, and wondered if the 'woman trouble' her sister had mentioned might be in this connection. Were there problems, such as a miscarriage, or was it just the heat? She was tired herself. It had been a long day on her feet, and the customers had been more than usually exacting.

In her room later when she was changing, she thought again of finding somewhere else to live. If Minnie McConachie had been on her own they might have shared a flat, but she was bogged down with her mother who seemed to grow more difficult as time went on.

Ruth Crosbie had also suggested, to Sarah's surprise, that she should move in with her, but that was something she would have to think about. There was something in the girl's character which made her uncomfortable and gave her a feeling of inferiority. She was still making suggestions about books Sarah should read, and on one occasion she had seen the other assistant give them a sideways amused glance.

She had stopped playing tennis after the débâcle with Gus Carmichael, and he hadn't made any attempt to get in touch with her. The outing had been a failure from his point of view, money down the drain. She now applied herself even more obsessionally to her job at Charles et Cie. If some people were suffering from dire poverty on the dole, there were others who were making a lot of money. The employers and their wives were well able to patronise a Court Dressmakers, as much for the social cachet as its expertise.

Wearing now a cotton dress and comfortable shoes, Sarah went back to the kitchen and began clearing the dishes from the table. Mary had gone to her bedroom with Lachie to prepare him for bed. She heard the outside door opening, and looked up as John came in.

'Mary said you had a meeting!' she said. 'She intended to cook you something later.'

'It was cancelled.' He went to the sink to wash his hands.

'She'll be glad. Are things settling down with the men, John?'

'Not a hope.' He took a towel down from a hook. 'Sometimes I think we should save our breath to cool our porridge. Whatever you do the employers always win. It's the way of the world.' He smiled at her. 'I always grumble when I'm tired.'

'It's been a tiring day with the heat. You should take that wife of yours away for a holiday. She's run down.'

'You don't have to tell me that. Is there any chance of a cup of tea?' He changed the subject. I've hit a sore spot, Sarah thought. It's a private thing, a marriage thing. I shouldn't be here.

'How about some ham and eggs?' She tried to speak brightly. 'You must be hungry.' She knew Mary's opinion of her cooking skills as she spoke.

'No, I'll wait for Mary coming ben.' It was evident so did he. 'She'll be busy with Lachie.'

'A cup of tea, then.' She went to the door and called. 'Mary! John's just come in. Don't rush. I'm giving him a cup of tea.'

'I heard him. I'll be in as soon as I can. I'm trying to get Lachie to sleep.'

'He's teething, poor wee soul.' Sarah filled the kettle and put it on the gas. 'She thinks the same about my cooking as you do.' She smiled at him. 'I'm only the bottle-washer.'

79

'Tea's fine.' He smiled back. He was his usual good-tempered self again. 'What are you doing with yourself these days, Sarah?'

'Working hard. Miss Frobisher leaves a lot of the accounts to me now. I think she's getting tired. I don't know what age she is, between you and me probably over fifty now, but she holds a tight rein on the buying, still. "That's my forte," she says.'

'There's a daughter somewhere, isn't there?'

'Yes, Nessie. She goes with her mother on buying trips, but hardly ever comes into the shop. And, of course, we don't buy many ready-mades. Miss Frobisher turns up her nose at those, only when a customer has made a special request.'

'It's a queer world, the fashion trade. Miles away from a foundry. And how's your love life?' His eyes were mischievous, although heavy with fatigue.

'Well, Gus Carmichael finished me for men,' she said. 'He wanted me to pay for my dinner.' She laughed, and he laughed with her.

'We're the limit, aren't we? Ma mother used to say we were all brute beasts. Do you think she was right?' His eyes were still on her. 'Mary gey likely thinks she was.'

'I don't know. I haven't much experience.' She looked away from him, feeling the colour rise in her cheeks. She hadn't any, she thought, and it didn't take much to put the fear of death in her. But then, Mary had said she wasn't cold. 'I'll get your tea.'

'You're an exceptionally good-looking young woman, you know,' John said. He had looked up at her to take the cup. 'I wonder you're not married long ago.'

He and Mary had been talking. That was married couples. They shared everything. 'It's not the only thing I think about.' Sarah raised her chin. 'There's my career.'

'Oh, aye. There's your career.' She could feel his eyes searching her face, and tried to dowse the annoyance she felt sure would be showing. 'Would you like me to give you some advice?'

'Do you think I need it?' She fiddled with the sugar basin.

'Oh, nobody thinks they do,' he said. 'You'll be no exception. Sit down, Sarah, and stop fiddling. I want to talk to you.' She sat. 'You've a good brain. There's something special in you, a potential, an extra sensitivity, and if you have it in one way, excelling at your job, you'll have it in others. Why don't you take some of the courses in the Mechanics' Institute? Give yourself something else to think about than dressing rich women. We're living in exciting times, times of transition. You could study social history, philosophy . . . the Scots are great philosophers. I would go with you if I had the time. Maybe this is just me putting on to you what I'd like to do myself. I've got a terrible thirst for education. And here I am, trapped . . .'

'Who's trapped?' Mary asked, coming into the kitchen, rolling down her sleeves. But, in spite of her tiredness, her eyes brightened, Sarah noticed, as they always did, at the sight of him.

'Everybody's trapped in some way or the other.'

'Oh, aye?' She didn't answer but went over to the fire and put the frying pan on the gas ring. 'I thought you weren't coming in?' she said.

'A couldny keep away from you, dearie,' he said.

'Although you're trapped?' She crossed to the larder to bring out the plate of fish, golden-crumbed.

'Aye, trapped by a complaining wife and a greetin' wean. That's what you want me to say.' He got up and put his arms round her waist from the back, laughing.

'Stop your nonsense.' She turned, shaking him off, but Sarah saw the love in her eyes. She turned back to her cooking. 'Do you want this haddie in your face or in the pan?' Sarah smiled, feeling an outsider in this close-knit world of marriage.

She said, subconsciously trying to break the bond, 'Do you know what he's telling me to do, Mary? To give up a good job and study at the Mechanics' Institute. And maybe go to the University. Because that's what he'd like to do.'

'Well, he shouldn't have got married,' Mary said, moving the fish about in the pan with a knife. 'Don't pay any attention to him, Sarah, you've a good job, you have made the most of yourself, and in any case whoever heard of a woman going to the University! That's for toffs . . . like that woman you go to at Helensburgh . . . what's her name?'

'Mrs de Vere. I don't know about her. Maybe if she'd had a daughter, but there's only a son. He would probably go to that famous one at Oxford. I think he'll soon be going back to his regiment. He had some shrapnel in his thigh.'

'You seem to know a lot about him.' John was teasing her again.

'Only because his mother asked him to run me to the station. But his words were dispensed like gold, few and far between.'

'Maybe his passion had rendered him speechless.'

'For goodness' sake, John!'

'Your fish is ready,' Mary said, lifting it from the sizzling pan on to a plate.

'That'll stop him talking nonsense.' Sarah made up her mind. 'I think I'll take the tram over to Maryhill and see Minnie. I'm bound to get her in.'

'You do that,' Mary said. 'She'll be glad of a visit.'

She got ready with her usual care, changing once again into a light linen dress with a white sailor collar. You spend too much money on clothes, she thought, looking at her reflection in the glass. She would have liked to go out without a hat, but you could only do that in the country. She pulled on her white gloves.

'I'm ready,' she called from the lobby, but they didn't hear her.

It was still hot even at seven in the evening, and she climbed up to the top of the tram. She remembered coming back from Ayr in Gus Carmichael's motor, and how lovely the fresh air had been on her cheeks. The only good thing about that expedition, she thought now. Once had been enough for him too.

Did he see her as John saw her, different in some way, a bluestocking, he had suggested, but that wasn't true. Blue-stockings, she understood, had stringy hair, not heavy fair hair like hers, and they wore dowdy clothes and steel-framed spectacles. Although there was a lot of pleasure to be had in reading. It would be nice to go to some of those classes with John and then come home and have long discussions about life, and what was the meaning of it all, and why people went on fighting useless wars and vowing it would be the last and then going on making guns and planning for the next one.

The thought struck her forcibly that she was one of the casualties of the last war. There were no men left, or hardly any of her age except those like Gus Carmichael and the few worthwhile ones like John who came home to their wives. I am of a deprived generation, she thought, getting off the tram near Minnie's flat and walking past children playing in the street, dirty children with ragged clothes, some with bare feet. Did they have to go like that in winter to school, poor things?

Minnie welcomed her with her sweet smile. 'Sarah! You're a godsend! Come in. Ma's been driving me batty. Say hello to her anyway.' She led her along the dark lobby to the kitchen. It was a room and kitchen flat, much smaller than theirs. The old woman was sitting in front of the fire with a thin poker in her hands which she was inserting between the ribs.

'Who's this, Minnie?' she asked, turning.

'It's Sarah from the shop. Come to see you.'

'Some hope. Come to have a crack with you, more likely. Nobody ever comes to see me.'

'How are you feeling today, Mrs McConachie?' Sarah said. The woman looked her up and down.

'Fine feathers make fine birds. Did Miss Whatever-she's-called give you that cheap?'

'Oh, no!' Sarah laughed. 'I can't afford her prices, even with a reduction. But I know the Glasgow shops pretty well.'

'I never get anywhere. I used to go into Glasgow myself but I'm no' fit now, and Minnie's always saying she'll take me to Argyle Street, but she never does.'

'You say you don't like the crowds, Ma.'

'When did I ever say that? I never said anything of the

83

kind!' She turned to Minnie. 'You're only saying that to look good in front of your fine friend . . .'

'You wouldn't like it just now,' Sarah volunteered. 'The sales are on and it's pandemonium.'

'Chance would be a fine thing.' Minnie exchanged glances with Sarah. She gave an imperceptible nod.

'We're going to take a turn out, Ma,' Minnie said, 'before it gets dark. Will you be all right there?'

'How do you think I get on all day when you urny here?'

'We won't be long.' She motioned to Sarah to get out of the room.

'Well, it's been nice seeing you again, Mrs McConachie,' Sarah said. 'I'll say cheerio, then.' She got no reply.

'Cheerio!' Minnie repeated, banging the door behind them when they were safely out on the landing. 'She's been going on like that since I got in the night. Nothing pleases her. Mind you, she suffers a lot.' Sarah looked at her. Minnie wasn't much older than her but her youth was gone.

And I'm complaining, she thought, linking arms with Minnie at the top of the stairs. 'What do you say if we go to the Tally's for a double nougat? My treat.'

'Suits me. What do you say if we run doon the stairs two at a time?'

Chapter Eleven

Sarah looked forward to her visits to Mrs de Vere in Helensburgh. She had already gone twice to fit the black dinner dress, and on this occasion Mrs de Vere had asked her into the drawing room for tea, a large room where the table was set in the oriel window giving an extensive view of the Gairloch with its pretty border of white houses like lace on the opposite shore.

'You've been such a help to me over clothes, Miss Lane,' Mrs de Vere said, sitting majestically behind her Rockingham china. 'You've taken all the fear out of it. If you have a figure like mine it's such a trial to get undressed before supercilious saleswomen.' You're seeing a reflection of your own attitude, Sarah would have liked to tell her. 'Your idea of wearing stud pearl earrings to match my pearls has just given it the right air of simple sophistication which I strive for. Cream or lemon, Miss Lane?'

But Mrs de Vere's mind was not really on clothes. How could they be, Sarah thought sympathetically, when all one could do with a figure like hers was cover it to its best advantage. It was her dead husband and son who occupied her thoughts.

'I'm sure Ronald misses Edgar,' she confided over their teacups – Sarah was surprised that she wasn't offered anything to eat, thinking of Mary's overloaded plates of scones and fruitcake when a neighbour looked in. And it was tea of the rich Indian variety that Mary poured, not this golden brew with its foreign flavour which Miss Frobisher also served to her customers.

'A son depends on his father,' Sarah agreed. 'I see that in my little nephew. Boys like a bit of rough handling. Women are too gentle,' although she wondered about that looking at Mrs de Vere's strong features, her large capable hands. 'John throws him up in the air and he laughs and laughs.' She saw her hostess's horrified look.

'Is that safe?'

'Oh, yes, John's gentle although he's strong. That's what sons want from fathers, gentleness and strength.'

'Well, of course, Edgar wasn't much with us when Ronald was a baby, and in any case he was confined to the nursery. Then he was away at school most of the time.' It sounded a cold upbringing, Sarah thought, thinking of the love and warmth which surrounded Lachie.

'I'm sure he's enjoying being here with you now. Those boys had a terrible time.' Somehow 'boys' was the wrong word to use in connection with Major Ronald de Vere.

'Yes, that *frightful* anxiety . . . he likes the garden, that's true. After the ugliness of war, such a solace. He spends a lot of his time there. Of course, he's going back to his regiment soon. He's been declared fit.' Her large face took on a pathetic air. 'I shall miss him . . .'

'Any mother would,' Sarah said. I'll miss him myself, she thought. She had found him no more communicative on the subsequent occasions when he had run her to the station, but since that first time she had built round him a dreamlike scenario in which she lived in the de Vere house, gardened, picked flowers with a trug over her arm, and was occasionally taken to Helensburgh by him either for shopping, meetings, or going up to town.

She hadn't decided on their relationship. Sometimes she cast him as the gardener, sometimes the son of the house who was secretly in love with her but wouldn't dream of marrying beneath him, or her devoted husband. She wouldn't have indulged in this dream elsewhere. It was the ambience of Helensburgh she had fallen in love with, the fresh air so different from that of smoky Glasgow, and the beautiful wide-open view of the loch.

The comparison between him and Gus Carmichael was odious. Major de Vere was not eager, far from it. He was polite, but showed no interest in her. She couldn't imagine him wanting to untie her pure crêpe de chine blouse, which, of course, no longer existed. It had been consigned long ago to the clippings bag in the work-room. However, he was grateful to her, so he told her one afternoon when they were travelling to the station in the Pullman Limousine.

'You have given my mother a new interest in clothes,' he said. 'She rather let herself go to seed after my father's death, poor old thing.' It seemed a funny way to refer to your mother.

'Ronald is in the garden,' Mrs de Vere now said to Sarah when she got up to leave. 'Ask him to run you in. I have some ladies coming for a meeting of the WI Local History. A little talk. I read history at Girton, you know.' Sarah nodded as if she did.

'It's very kind of him,' she said.

'Nonsense, he's not doing anything else.'

She found the major in the vegetable garden which lay behind the stone wall with a small gate set in it. She knew her way about the grounds now. She remembered Gus Carmichael using that word. He should see this, its rockeries, its rosebeds, its lawns and even a tennis court. This was what you called grounds!

He had his sleeves rolled up and was digging furiously, head bare – the September sun wasn't strong – a bandana handkerchief round his neck, quite like a gypsy. 'Hello, Miss Lane,' he said. 'Ready to go?'

'Yes. Your mother said . . .'

'Would you sit down for a minute, please?' He indicated an old wooden bench. 'I just have this row to finish and then I'll know where I've stopped.'

'Do you like growing vegetables?' she asked him, sitting down only after passing her hand swiftly over the surface of the bench. Her skirt was pale grey and showed every mark.

'Oh, yes,' he said. You could say the sun was golden, she thought, feeling content under its warm rays. And the trees were beginning to turn. She wished she knew their names. 'What do you call . . . ?' but he cut in.

'Just as much as flowers. I gathered a basket of carrots, onions and turnips for Cook the other day. Thought it made a good still life. Carravaggio. Are you interested in art, Miss Lane?' She was as equally surprised at the volume of words as at the question itself.

'I've been to the Art Galleries at Kelvingrove,' she offered.

'You should see the London galleries. Do you ever go there?'

'I hope to. Buying.' Miss Frobisher had decided to take her. The work-room was buzzing with the news that Nessie, her daughter, had got married suddenly. Mrs Donaldson, the charwoman, had overheard Miss Frobisher on the telephone. She had been giving Nessie a piece of her mind and no mistake. There had been no confidence offered to Sarah beyond the command to be ready to accompany her next time, but she had noticed her employer's haggard appearance and distraught air. She saw by Major de Vere's concentration on his task that it would have been a waste of time to tell him why she was going.

He suddenly looked up as if the penny had dropped. 'If and when you do go, be sure and take the opportunity to pay a visit to the National Gallery.'

'I will if I get the time,' she said. 'But when you have different shows to go to . . .'

Major de Vere put down his spade and wiped his hands on a rag. 'Oh, do you intend to go to others? Courtaulds, maybe?'

'No, I mean, fashion shows . . . ?'

He looked at her, then nodded. 'I see. Well, that'll do for the time being. Want to get it finished before I go off. Job well done. I'll take you to the station now and finish the patch when I get back. Ready?'

'Yes, thank you.' She got up. She would have liked to stay here in the autumn sunlight, looking round at the rows of tidy vegetables, the stone walls, those trees turning gold at the edges, the smell of the dug earth. She would have liked to ask him if they could grow peaches on those walls, and what were those earth mounds with green feather stuff on the top. If things had been different she would like to live in a house like this and then there would have been no need to ask questions.

Away from the garden Major de Vere lapsed into his usual

taciturnity. The gentry were peculiar. Mother had always told the girls that they had to make conversation, even if they only spoke about the weather. The weather's vagaries were a godsend – Mother hadn't used the word vagaries but then she didn't read books, although she knew you were never short of a topic of conversation in a place like Glasgow where the Lost Property Office in Bath Street was *stacked* with umbrellas. Silences were to be feared, she had implied. Sarah now wondered if that was why Glasgow folk chattered so much. They feared silences.

Halfway to the station she ventured to break this one. 'How is your leg, Major de Vere?' she said.

He looked up, mystified. 'My leg? Oh, you mean the shrapnel in my thigh? That's completely better now.'

'I thought it must be when I watched you digging.'

He drove for another half-mile and then said, 'Yes, quite better. I'm going back to Salisbury in another week.' Salisbury, she thought, what's Salisbury? 'The regiment's going overseas after Christmas. Got to get myself and the men licked into shape before that.' You would have thought they'd had enough of war to last them all their lives, but she supposed if you were officially in the army you couldn't get out.

That was why he was still called 'Major', John had said. He knew all about the army, and no wonder. 'Your mother will miss you,' Sarah said. He didn't reply for another half-mile.

'She's fairly settled now, getting into things. She's a good organiser. My father retired here for the sailing. He was in the navy. Father always kept a yacht on the Clyde. He loved Scotland.'

'Do you like Salisbury?' she asked, seeing him and the house and grounds recede in her dreams. Navy, yachts. Salisbury, overseas . . .

'I go where I'm sent,' he said. 'Can't imagine settling down for long. It's been a bit of a trial passing the time here. If it hadn't been for the garden . . .'

Well, that's that, Sarah thought, smoothing her kid gloves on her lap. Not that she had been thinking of Major de Vere in *that* way. He should only have been a necessary adjunct to the house and grounds, but she had enjoyed Mary and John teasing her when she got home from Helensburgh. 'Well, has he popped the question yet?' Like him, it was the garden she was really interested in.

He got out at the station and shook hands formally with her. 'Glad you sorted the old girl out,' he said, 'keep it up.' She didn't know how to reply to that.

'Thank you for taking me to the station,' she said. 'It saved taxis.'

'Yes, there's that.' Already he was looking over his shoulder, anxious to get away. 'Well, good luck . . .'

'Good luck to you, Major de Vere.' He smiled directly at her for once and gave her a half salute. He's really a soldier, she thought, not an ordinary man.

On the way back in the train she remembered what he had said about the art galleries in London. If she could get away from Miss Frobisher she would go. It depended where their hotel was. And she would look for what Major de Vere had called 'still lives', although so far she didn't know much about art. What she preferred was a picture of the Highlands, with space and sky and water, giving you the feeling of flying into it, free as a bird.

Gus Carmichael had laughed at her when she had said she would like to fly when she had been on the Heads of Ayr. Now a feeling of sadness was creeping over her, perhaps because it was autumn, things dying . . . it would be better in winter. There were the cosy evenings in the kitchen to look forward to with Mary and John.

Or perhaps by that time she would have decided to share with Ruth Crosbie. 'My offer is still open,' she had said to Sarah the last time she had gone to the library. She had been stamping *Sons and Lovers* for her. 'That will be an eye-opener for you,' she had said. 'I think you're ready for it.' I'm ready for a lot of things, Sarah thought now, which still haven't happened. Time was passing. People swam into her life and swam out again, like Gus Carmichael and Major de Vere. It was September 1919, and she was twenty-three years of age.

Chapter Twelve

1920

The visit to London early in the spring compensated for the feeling that life was over for her before it had begun. She hadn't followed John's advice and gone to classes at the Mechanics' Institute, the bad weather seemed to drain her energy, and even more, Mary's. Sarah got into the habit of doing the shopping for her before she got home, and it was after eight o'clock at night before they were tidied up.

John said it was a pity she hadn't managed to enrol, but on the other hand he was rarely home before eight o'clock himself. 'The best-laid plans o' mice and men gang aft agley,' he quoted. 'Keep up with your reading at least.' He gave her a list of books and she worked through them slowly with the help of Ruth Crosbie. 'You should come to my flat in the evenings,' she said, 'and we could go into them in depth.' This was a favourite expression of hers, but the idea of venturing forth into the dark, drab streets later on was not appealing. Sarah sometimes thought that the only bit of colour was the red glow of Dixon's Blazes lighting the evening sky.

'At least I'm growing familiar with Robert Owen's ideas,' she told John. 'You're making a socialist of me.'

'How could you be anything else?' he asked her.

When the visit to the shows grew closer, she was closeted with Miss Frobisher more than once in her private sanctum, occasionally being offered tea (the same brand as Mrs de Vere's). 'I wish to speak to you confidentially, Sarah' she said on this particular morning. Sarah looked up in involuntary surprise at the use of her first name. But there would be no reciprocal arrangement, she thought with an inward smile. 'Miss A. Frobisher' appeared on most of the office

91

correspondence, and being curious she had made a few inspired guesses. 'Annie', 'Agatha', 'Abigail'?

Miss Frobisher went on majestically, although Sarah noticed her lip was trembling. 'I use your Christian name to make it easier to confide in you.' Sarah waited. 'I know rumours fly about in our establishment.' At that, Sarah remembered Mrs Donaldson's glee at being able to repeat the telephone conversation she had overheard. She murmured something non-committal. 'Nessie, my daughter . . .' Her employer stopped there as if the effort had been too much for her.

'Yes, Miss Frobisher?' Sarah said encouragingly.

'I followed the wishes of Mr Freitzel, that was my dear husband's name, and no expense was spared in her education. I imagined with her elegance and the knowledge of languages she would acquire at her finishing school she would be a decided asset to the House, in due course.' She stopped again, looking unusually distressed. 'I had high hopes, as any mother would.'

'Isn't she . . . ?' Sarah began, but was interrupted by Miss Frobisher. Her voice had lost its refined tones. It was loud, even strident.

'She's run off and got married!' Her hand went to her mouth, pressed it, as if she regretted the outburst. 'To someone she met in Montreaux, when she was in a café with her friends! You would have thought they would have been properly chaperoned, wouldn't you?' You would have thought no expensively educated girl would run off and get married to someone she met in a café, Sarah thought.

'Well, yes . . .'

'We had discussed it often.' Miss Frobisher was calmer now. 'When she came home she would join me here, appear from time to time in the salon to deputise for me, assist in the buying. She would have been able to converse with my clients in any language.' Her voice rose again as if she could hardly bear the disappointment. She put a handkerchief to her lips. 'I could see her adding a definite cachet to our House.' She shook her head in agonised bewilderment, raising haggard eyes to Sarah. She looked ten years older. Her skin had an unhealthy pallor. 'It's driving me out of my mind with anxiety. I had to tell someone.' Sarah was touched at the change in her formidable employer.

'Young girls . . .' she said, feeling inadequate as she was fairly young herself. 'Try not to distress yourself. Perhaps later on she'll . . .'

Miss Frobisher seemed suddenly to take command of herself. 'As you say, perhaps later . . .' She raised her chin, took a deep breath. 'The subject is now closed. I only take you into my confidence because it means that for the time being you will be promoted to assistant buyer, but, of course, one never knows. It might be only temporary.'

Sarah knew better than to proffer further sympathy. 'I appreciate your trust in me, Miss Frobisher,' she said. She put down her cup and lifted the sheet of paper she had brought with her. 'I've done what you asked, inspected our stock and made a list of any items we require to replace for the coming season.'

'Good. Well, we'll go through that now.' Miss Frobisher raised her lorgnette as Sarah put down the list in front of her. It might be 'Abigail', Sarah thought, seeing the haughty profile. She had thought about it in bed recently.

She chose her wardrobe carefully for London. It had to be smart but not ostentatious, and yet demonstrate that she came from a superior fashion house. And console Miss Frobisher a little in default of Nessie. Discreet French grey seemed the only choice. Miss Frobisher favoured black for herself, and frowned on brown. Minnie helped her with the details, padding slightly the jacket to make up for Sarah's lack of fullness in the bosom, 'You need the fullness up there to let the jacket sit right,' and raising the hemline at Sarah's request since Lanvin and Chanel were raising theirs.

She also, at Sarah's request, made for her a one-piece undergarment of pale satin trimmed with a deeper hue of ecru lace, discreetly boned, because Sarah hated corsets which dug into her slim frame. The blouses were specially made, and a pom-pom was specially dyed to match the French grey felt hat Sarah had chosen to complete the outfit.

'You will out-dazzle Aggie,' Minnie said, grimacing at her from the floor where she was kneeling. She was already complaining of arthritic knee joints.

'You mean the A stands for . . . ?' Sarah couldn't bring herself to repeat it. The name was too redolent of the shawlies who stood waiting for the trams under the Umbrella at Bridgeton Cross.

'Aye, everybody knows that. "Aggie, the Wee Bachle", we call her in here.'

'Oh, Minnie!' Sarah put her hand to her mouth to hide the smile. Wee Aggie. It was true that Miss Frobisher lacked height, and had a certain curvature in her calves, which was only glimpsed on the rare occasions when she sat down carelessly.

They travelled first class to London, Miss Frobisher saying that porters never paid any attention to you if you didn't. She slept most of the time, at least her head rested on the white linen seat-back. The lines of her face slipped, she looked tired and old, but she was her usual authoritative self when they had lunch and afterwards afternoon tea, giving Sarah with her refined manner a demonstration of how a lady behaved when travelling first class.

Sarah admired her. Nessie's name was never mentioned. The conversation was confined to instructions on how to behave at the shows of the various houses. 'Charles et Cie is recognised in London as small but exclusive,' she said. 'Remember you are a stand-in for my daughter until such times as she can join us.' This was to be the line taken. Sarah had only seen Nessie once, a gawky, bespectacled schoolgirl of sixteen, but ducklings could turn into swans. There must be something in the Swiss air which fostered romance. Maybe she should go there herself.

They installed themselves in Browns Hotel (the only place to stay), and immediately were sucked into a whirlwind of activity. Miss Frobisher in action was a fearsome sight. Some of the other buyers visibly quailed before her. 'Just copy me,' she said to Sarah, who thought it would be better to temper her own behaviour with slightly less acidity. But then she wasn't the owner of Charles et Cie. Nor the daughter of the owner. Just a stand-in, as she had been reminded.

On the only free afternoon they had, Miss Frobisher said she was going to retire to her room and have tea sent up, and Sarah, not forgetting Major de Vere's advice, paid a visit to the National Gallery.

It was vast. That was the first thing which struck her, and everybody seemed to know where they were going. She wandered aimlessly from room to room, surrounded by canvases, stopping when she saw other people stopping, being completely overwhelmed by the amount of exposed flesh, flying cupids, suffering Christs, infant Jesuses, weeping Marys, and finding no pleasure in them.

When she decided to go, defeated by the crowded walls, she came across a painting labelled 'Still Life', but the lemons portrayed looked far from still and as if they were about to roll out of the painting and on to the floor so that she felt like putting out a hand to catch them. It was a pity, she thought, that she hadn't Major de Vere with her to show her the one he had been talking about.

She lost her way and found herself in a room where the bare flesh had entirely disappeared, and there were only quieter pictures of the countryside. She stopped at one which showed a simple avenue of trees, still, calm, stiller, much stiller than the still life which had worried her. She could walk right into this one, much easier than the Highland landscapes which because of their vastness made her wish to be a bird so that she could fly over them.

The sky was vast but tranquil, the road beckoned her. She could almost feel the fresh air on her face, like the fresh air when she had sat on the wooden bench watching Major de Vere digging. Well, that dream of delight had gone . . .

That evening in bed she closed her eyes and again walked into the picture she had seen with a familiarity which pleased her. She didn't want to know where it was, nor where the road led to, she didn't want to know its end. It was like her life.

*   *   *

Miss Frobisher was pleased with her performance at the spring shows. 'You have a keen eye, Sarah,' she said in the privacy of her sanctum (the continued use of her assistant's first name was the only reminder of her confidences about Nessie). 'It's invaluable in the fashion world, a keen eye and attention to detail. And something I can only call *je ne sais quoi*, a flair, to *know* when something is right. It's a combination of experience and natural taste. When Nessie joins me in the future, I hope to develop in her those instincts which, being my daughter, I'm sure she will have.' Miss Frobisher was making the best of a bad job.

'She's young enough to learn if she hasn't done so already,' Sarah said judiciously.

'You have a good head.' Miss Frobisher was approving. 'What age are you?'

'Twenty-three.' It sounded ancient as she said it. Even Nessie was married at nineteen.

'I shall expect a run-down of the entire costs for the trip on my desk tomorrow morning,' Miss Frobisher said. 'I'm going home now. The expense has to be set against our final charges.'

'I'll see that you have it,' Sarah said, wondering if the grocers in St Enoch Square would be shut before she got there. And thinking also how tired and woebegone the poor soul had looked. And, later, being appalled, as she worked on the figures in the big account book, how much Mrs de Vere had paid for her simple black dinner dress.

Mary and John were glad to see her back. 'What was it like?' Mary asked.

'Full of shops like Glasgow. And parks. The buildings are beautiful on the river Thames, grander than on the Clyde, although Carlton Place takes a lot of beating. And the people talk louder and quicker than we do. Everything is quicker. And the taxis are quicker. And the women kiss.'

'For God's sake!' John said. 'Did you pay a visit to the gallery of the Houses of Parliament? Shout down and ask them why they don't stop profiteers from profiteering? Tell them that the boom's over? We're in for massive unemployment?'

'I've had enough of that talk,' Mary said. And to Sarah, 'He may be going on short time.'

'There's nothing fixed, Mary. I told you that. She worries,' he said.

'Aye, I nag when I'm tired. I'm off to bed. I'm glad you're back, Sarah.'

'Give her a kiss,' John said.

'Away you go, you daft loon. This isn't London.'

'Aye, she's no' her usual self.' He paused. 'Some folk are better at having children than others. You would have thought that Mary . . . she had a miscarriage when you were away.'

'Oh, poor soul! She needs a holiday.'

'Well, we're in luck. Your cousin, Andrew, in Fifeshire has invited us for a fortnight to their place. I'm that pleased. You can imagine how I feel when Mary . . . it makes me feel it's my fault.'

'It's nobody's fault, just bad luck. You have a lovely lad in Lachie. You'll have a wee girl one of these days, just wait.'

'You're an understanding lass, Sarah. I'll say that about you.' He looked boyish, embarrassed. 'But, when you love . . .' He stopped himself, shook his head.

Later, in bed, Sarah thought, well, here I am again on the outside of a marriage looking in. She would see how it felt being alone when they were in Fifeshire. It would be a trial fortnight for her. She hoped John was holding Mary in his arms just now. Marriage had its trials, and as he had said, when you loved, it sometimes increased them. But there were compensations. She felt lonely.

Chapter Thirteen

1922

'Well, it's no' for want o' tryin',' Mary said two years later. She looked at John with that look which unintentionally left Sarah out.

They were just back from Langside church where Sarah's new niece had been christened. 'Bella' was the name the parents had chosen, John's mother's name and a common enough one in Glasgow, but John, in a sudden flight of romantic fantasy, had astonished everybody by saying that in Italian it meant 'beautiful'.

She certainly was, a perfect baby girl, winsome, and totally unlike her brother, Lachie, who from his infancy had looked like a boy and sometimes a bruiser. Any aggressiveness, however, disappeared when he examined his new sister minutely, from her hands to her toes. He treated her with the same wonderment as John.

'Wee Bella,' he repeated incessantly. It was soon apparent that he would lay down his life for her.

Domestic life at Millbrae Road seemed at last to be on an even keel. There had been no further threat to John's job, but he was still immersed in meetings on behalf of the workforce of Dixon's. Mary, fully occupied with two children and now well and able to cope with them, said in a way John's absence gave her more time.

Sarah, relieved of her domestic duties, was able to devote most of her energy to Charles et Cie. It was apparent that Nessie's default had been a bitter blow to her mother however much she disguised it. More and more she relied on Sarah, and she was now privy to most of the business affairs of the firm as well as her salon and buying duties.

She was astonished when she found out how poorly the seamstresses were paid, and being a devotee of Robert Owen, thanks to John, brought the matter up with Miss Frobisher on one of their confabs, as tactfully as she could.

'I've found out that the seamstresses in the London houses are paid a lot more than ours, Miss Frobisher.'

'Well, that's London!' Her employer looked astonished at her comment. 'They aren't likely to go and work there!'

'You never know. The young ones might. And they're better informed now. There's a lot of talk about fair wages for workers. Even if they don't read the papers themselves they'll hear the men talking, sons, husbands. Workers know their rights now, and if they don't get them, they're likely to strike.'

'I think that's a bit fanciful, Miss Lane,' Miss Frobisher said, delicately showing Sarah that she had stepped too far.

'I doubt it.' It was high time her employer moved out of the ambience of Court Dressmaker which surrounded her and took a look at what was going on today. 'My brother-in-law is a shop steward at Dixon's, and he says it's like a boiling vat, the discontent, and that one of these days it will boil over and then . . .'

Miss Frobisher held up her hand. Her voice was icy. 'I hope you're not comparing the workers at Dixon's with my girls in the work-room. They're as different as chalk from cheese . . .' A year or two ago Sarah would not have dared to reply.

'They may be different, Miss Frobisher, but Jenny Carr's boy friend works there, and she'll hear him talking, and there's Minnie McConachie, for instance, one of our best workers, whose fiancé died after he was invalided home at the end of the war and who has to keep her old mother on her wages . . .'

'That may be, but I hope you aren't stirring up discontent amongst them, Miss Lane. As you know, I don't encourage too much fraternisation between Front and Back.'

'I assure you I've never discussed anything of that nature.

99

My loyalty has always been to you.' She met her employer's eyes. They had been indignant. Now they softened.

'I accept your word on that, Sarah, and I have to admit that I couldn't have managed without you these last few years. I trust your judgement. Perhaps you will bring the wages book to me tomorrow and we'll go over it together.'

'Thank you, Miss Frobisher.' But there was to be a sting in the tail.

'Of course I don't want you to be too sure that your position will last. I haven't given up hope that Nessie will see the mistake she has made and join me in the firm. As I've told you, it was her father's dearest wish.' Miss Frobisher raised her chin. 'As long as we understand each other.' Sarah withdrew, vanquished, as far as her employer was concerned. But there was still the wages book tomorrow . . .

Minnie said to her in the work-room later on, 'They're saying Nessie isn't married at all. It's just auld Aggie's way of saving her face. Somebody our Mrs Donaldson knows worked as a cleaner to the parents of a school friend of Nessie's when they were at Hutcheson's together, and they still keep in touch. Aggie's praying for the day when Nessie comes back with her tail between her legs.'

'Cleaners have a fertile imagination,' Sarah said, straight-faced, but when her eyes met Minnie's, her mouth turned down in a smile. 'Miss Laird of Milngavie would like this coat lengthened, Minnie.'

'I don't blame her with her ankles.' Minnie took it from her, her eyes wicked. Her hands were showing signs of arth-ritis as well as her knees, Sarah thought, seeing the swollen knuckles.

That summer, quite by chance, she met Ruth Crosbie when she was giving Bella an airing in her pram while Mary and John took Lachie to visit John's parents in Riddrie. 'We don't want him to feel left out in the cold because of his wee sister,' Mary had said, and Sarah had agreed to be the baby's nurse for the afternoon.

'Well, Sarah,' Ruth greeted her, 'don't tell me you've gone

all domesticated.' Sarah stopped. She had been making for the duck pond with a paper bag of stale bread, a time-honoured custom on Sunday afternoons.

'No, it's my good deed for Sunday, to let Mary and John visit his parents.'

'I haven't seen you in the library recently.' Ruth's tone was slightly accusing.

'No, I seem to be too busy for reading. I've been promoted and there's a lot of extra work, going to London to buy and so on. I've had to become interested in the business side as well.' She saw Ruth's resentful expression.

'Too high up for your friends? I've missed you and our talks.'

'I thought you were busy with your cousin? You told me she was staying with you.'

'So she was, but she took umbrage. The pettiness of some people! I was quite glad to see her go.'

'Maybe you like your place to yourself.'

'I do, for a time, and then I get lonely. Sundays especially . . .' Sarah looked at her in surprise. Ruth was the last person she would imagine as feeling lonely. 'You never came to visit me although you said you would.'

'Mary's been having a bad time for the last year or so.' She wouldn't go into details. Ruth didn't strike her as the kind of person who would be sympathetic about women's frailties. 'But things are going all right now. This little creature is evidence of it.' She smiled down at the sleeping Bella. Ruth gave the child a cursory glance.

'What about next weekend? I'll cook you some nice food, French, and we'll read and play music, and go out in the dark and walk . . . maybe you would like it so much that you would decide to move in with me. You know I told you before you were always welcome.'

It sounded appealing, to be away from domestic clutter, the pail of nappies underneath the kitchen sink, Lachie's bois-terousness, and when John came home feeling in the way. Sarah made up her mind. 'I'll come next weekend. Thanks. It would be a change.' She saw Ruth Crosbie's face glow, her eyes became full and soft. She was quite a good-looking girl when she got rid of her forbidding expression.

'We'll call it a trial run.' She laughed.

'If you like.' Bella stirred, whimpered. 'Would you like to walk along with me? They always settle if you push them.'

'No, thanks. I'm going the opposite way. See you on Saturday, then. Come in time for dinner. Seven o'clock?' Her whole appearance had changed, her cheeks were bright with colour, her hair looked thick and strong, her smile full. 'Cheerio!'

Sarah pushed on alone, tolerably pleased with the idea. Here was her opportunity if she wanted to leave John and Mary on their own with their children. She had always believed she did. Funny Ruth had shown no interest in Bella, she thought, looking down at the cupid-bowed mouth, the tiny dimpled chin.

The Saturday evening Sarah spent with Ruth was as she had described it. The casserole was rich and satisfying, she had some kind of joss sticks burning on the sideboard which, mingling with the smell of herbs seemed exotic and strange. There was cider to drink, a beverage unknown to Sarah, and afterwards with their coffee they had a strange drink in a tiny glass which Ruth called crème de cacao, and which went straight to Sarah's head, the fumes mingling with the rich smells already in the room. It was a far cry from the kitchen at Millbrae Road.

They went for the promised walk when they had had coffee, and Ruth, laughing, linked arms. 'I'll take care of you,' she said. Sarah giggled, ashamed that she had staggered.

There was something pleasing in walking in the dark. The mundane grocers' and newsagents' shops were different, their windows shrouded and mysterious, the avenues off the main road badly lit with only an occasional gas lamp. Some of the ground-floor flats still had their curtains undrawn.

'Do you ever look into lit windows and imagine what people are talking about?' Ruth asked her.

'I'm rarely out in a residential area like this', Sarah said. 'Usually it's only nearby shop fronts, chippies, Tallys.' That sounded common, she thought, but never mind. 'Yes, I think

I would make up stories about them, but I would never dare to walk out on my own.'

'I don't mind that. I'm intensely curious. Sometimes I loiter behind the hedge, just for a minute, hoping to see something really intimate.'

That was a strange word to use. 'I don't know about intimate. I like to see the children jumping about. You don't hear them behind glass!' She laughed. 'Lachie can be really rowdy. A proper little boy.'

'Children don't interest me. It's the relationship between people that makes me . . . conjecture.'

'You mean between husband and wife?'

'Not necessarily.'

'I suppose that's true, but it's generally couples.'

'Playing mummies and daddies, nagging at each other, or shouting at their children. I don't see the point of that kind of relationship.'

'Mary and John aren't like that. They're a devoted couple.'

'Doesn't that automatically make you feel *de trop*?'

'Sometimes . . .' She would rather not have remembered that feeling. She looked at Ruth, whose eyes seemed to glow in the dark.

'You're a sensitive girl. I knew that the first time you came into the library. You were looking for something, but you didn't know what it was.'

'Isn't everybody?' Sarah said, thinking that was a clever thing to say, suitable to the type of conversation they were having. 'What are *you* looking for, Ruth?'

'Me?' Ruth paused. 'To find my heart's desire . . . in someone.'

'You mean, get married?'

She laughed. 'It isn't the only thing in life. You mustn't have such plebeian views.'

Sarah didn't think she had those. 'You wouldn't like children sometime?'

'No, they leave me cold.' Sarah didn't reply. She had thought everyone felt a tenderness towards children, whether or not they owned them.

'Have I offended you?' Ruth was laughing at her. 'You mustn't feel that you have to think like everyone else, want the same as everybody else. You must analyse your own feelings, go deep down into yourself. Be honest. Ask yourself . . .'

'I only want to be happy, and not harm anyone else.'

'Oh, you are too easily satisfied! You aren't nearly demanding enough! I'll have to show you how much more there is . . . I've had enough walking.' She spoke abruptly. 'We'll go back now.'

When they were in the sitting room again Ruth played French records, Debussy, she said they were, and poured some wine for her. It was rosy, in large glasses. 'Smell it,' she said. 'Smell is important. Bring all the senses into every experience.' This time Sarah remained cold sober, and just a little tired and nostalgic for the flat in Millbrae Road. You're a baby, she told herself. Ruth read to her from *Sons and Lovers*.

'I remember getting it out of the library a long time ago,' Sarah said, feeling it was all too much, the intensity.

'Did you like it?'

'No, I returned it. I found it . . . upsetting.' She had blushed when she read some parts of it.

'Life is upsetting, ugly. Look at Glasgow with its ugly people, ugly thoughts. The only way to be happy is to make a life for yourself, or better still, with someone who feels the same as you do, make it unique, precious, contained in a kind of capsule, just the two of you. In short, learn to *live* . . .'

Sarah laughed uneasily. 'I've been doing that for a long time,' she said, finding the laugh turning into a grimace. Like the smile on drunk women when they sat in tramcars, swaying, a happy, simple smile.

'You've been *existing* only, earning your living, but not being aware of life. You have to learn to liberate your mind. And your body. I think you were beginning to learn that. I remember your expression when you first came into the library.'

'Pathetic?' She didn't like this picture of herself.

'No. Don't make fun of yourself, or of me. You were seeking, you wanted to find the key to a richer, fuller life than the one you were leading. And you'll never find it if you continue to live with your sister and brother-in-law where your individuality is stifled. Don't tell me you haven't wished you weren't living in such an intimate fashion with them.'

Sarah could never tell this girl, anyone, of the times she had lain in the next room and heard the muffled noises of Mary and John making love.

'Actually,' she said with a trace of her employer's icy tones, 'the flat, or half of it, belongs to me. I have every right to be there. John is the interloper. He once said that to me.'

'How do you like it here with me?' Ruth asked, changing tack.

'It's very nice . . .' Sarah began.

'Oh, for God's sake stop using that word "nice"! You'll have to read a lot more before you learn that there is only one specific meaning for "nice". Oh, Sarah,' she broke off, her face perturbed, 'I've offended you. I'm sorry . . .'

'Don't be. I'm not easily offended. I'm a person in my own right.' She listened to herself. It must be the rosy wine. 'I have a responsible job. So I feel fine! Not offended.' She laughed. 'I feel quite nice, in fact.' Ruth didn't reply for a second or two.

'You have great charm, Sarah.'

She hardly heard her. 'You see, I have to remind myself . . .' Maybe she had gone too far.

'And great potential.' Ruth wasn't listening to her. 'Don't throw it away. Do you go out with men a lot? They must be aware of your charm.'

'Oh, yes, quite a lot.' She was reckless now. 'But "charm" isn't the kind of word they would use. "Awfy nice", more likely.'

'You're a caution.' They both laughed, and Sarah felt at ease, liking this girl who had strange ideas, and even stranger ways of speaking.

Ruth filled a bath for her, and when she had finished bathing and was in her dressing gown she could hardly keep her eyes open. 'I think if you don't mind, Ruth,' she said, 'I'll go to bed. How about you?'

'Me too. I had a sponge down while you were in the bathroom. Do you mind sharing a room? The spare room's chilly when the east wind's blowing.'

'No, that's all right.' She had thought she would be given a room of her own.

But it was large, with two single beds and heavily curtained windows, cosy because of the gas fire which made a funny, plopping noise from time to time.

'I don't think we need that when we're in bed,' she said, when Ruth tried to adjust it.

'All right. It's safer off.' She took off her dressing gown and Sarah noticed her firm strong legs. Ruth's nightdress barely came to her calves. In comparison, in her own long one she felt puny, fragile almost. Mary always said, 'You're small-boned, Sarah, compared with me, one of Pharaoh's lean kine.' She hopped into bed quickly and tucked her nightdress round her bare feet, a childhood custom.

'It's a nice comfy bed,' she said, and because she felt shy sleeping in the same room with someone she thought of at that moment as a comparative stranger, she yawned exaggeratedly, and continued, 'I'm really tired. I don't know about you.'

'I'm the same. I won't have to be rocked to sleep. Goodnight.'

'Goodnight.'

'You aren't afraid of the dark?' Ruth had got out of bed and turned off the gas chandelier. It faded gently, the room going from dusk to darkness because of the heavy curtains.

'Goodness, no!'

As her eyes got used to the darkness she began to distinguish the dark bulk of the furniture in spite of the heavy curtains. This is a strange situation, she thought, snuggling down into her pillow. The thought of a living person lying a few feet away from her was disturbing. She listened. Ruth's breathing seemed regular.

She wanted to think some more, to imagine what it would be like if she lived all the time with Ruth, slept in this room or better still in the smaller room Ruth had mentioned. How they would arrange the shopping and the finances, and how much rent she would be expected to pay. Nothing like that had been mentioned yet.

But Mary and John would appreciate having the extra room to themselves with a growing family. And the lack of restraint which another person in the flat imposed. She remembered John once saying that on winter mornings when he had to leave early he used to light the kitchen fire and dress in front of it.

And every Sunday, unless they were going to Riddrie, she would pay them a visit and have tea in that bright kitchen with the glowing fire and see Lachie and her lovely little niece, Bella. She was satisfied. It sounded like a good arrangement.

Sarah sat bolt upright, it seemed before she had been properly asleep, as if some noise had disturbed her. How long had she been asleep? She had taken off her wrist watch, and she lifted it and peered at the dial. Five o'clock in the morning already! It was confirmed by the grey light in the bedroom. She could make out the dim shapes of the furniture, and for a second she was confused, imagining she was still in her own room at Millbrae Road.

But, as she looked around, eyes narrowed, she knew it was unfamiliar, the heavy wardrobe with a mirror on the centre cupboard, and on the other side of the room she could make out a large dressing table . . . the furniture seemed immense compared with her own.

She heard the noise of a truck or something on wheels, maybe a milk float, or a barrow being trundled along. There was the faint rattle of the milk cans. In the semi-darkness she heard Ruth's voice and she jumped, startled.

'Aren't you sleeping, Sarah?' She turned and saw Ruth facing her in the other bed, her head propped up on her elbow.

'I was,' she said, making her voice falsely bright. 'I slept right away but something must have wakened me, something in the road.'

'Or maybe me. I was up. I do that if I can't sleep, get up

and look out of the window. I like to see the road quiet, no passers-by.'

'I never do that.' She lay down. 'You aren't rising yet, are you?' She was wide awake, very much aware of Ruth's presence. She would never sleep now. And her heart was beating rapidly. She put her hand over her chest to steady her breathing. She knew Ruth was getting up, heard the soft footfall of bare feet, then was aware that she had come in beside her.

'This is what I used to do with my cousin,' Ruth said, lying down. 'We would lie and talk, plan our lives, share secrets . . .'

'Did you?' Sarah felt acutely uncomfortable at the girl's proximity. It was the strangeness of another body so close to her. Never since she had slept with Mary as a little girl had she known anyone in her bed. In any romantic thoughts she'd had of men, Gus Carmichael or Major de Vere, she had never got as far as imagining them with her in bed. She lay still, feigning sleep, tense.

'Are you afraid of me, Sarah?' Ruth asked. Her face was close to Sarah's. Sarah felt her breath on her cheek, and with it a heavy female smell which filled her nostrils. Sweat came into her armpits with fear and she turned away.

'Afraid? I don't know . . . no, I'm not afraid, just . . . well, I'm sleepy . . .'

'I'll help you to sleep.' She felt Ruth's body pressing close against her back, her arm coming round her waist.

'You're . . . smothering me, Ruth,' she said, moving away to the edge of the bed.

'You're a shy little thing. You mustn't be shy. No one will know. Let me show you . . .' Her hand moved over Sarah's stomach.

The heat of the blush which flooded her cheeks seemed to sear her. She half-rolled out of the bed and stood for a second on the cold linoleum, not believing anything . . .

'What are you doing, you silly little girl?' She knew that Ruth was lying on her back, looking up at her.

'I'm dying . . . to go to the lavatory . . .'

'Don't be long, then. I'll miss you . . .'

She half-ran to the lavatory, a dark hell of a place in the middle of the square hall, felt for the chain and flushed the cistern, then stumbled into the small bathroom next door where in her shyness last night she had undressed. She threw on her clothes, half-buttoning, half-fastening. Her face was still scarlet, she could feel its heat, but now it was with rage. 'Virginia Woolf,' she thought, and in the old parlance of her mother, 'I'll give her Virginia Woolf!'

'Hurry up!' Ruth called. Her voice rang beguilingly.

Sarah slipped into the hall, her handbag was in the bedroom, she remembered, but her coat was here, hanging where she had left it last night. She threw it on, and fumbling at the outside door, felt the key in the lock. Ruth had said earlier that she always left it there. It turned easily, and she went out and shut the door behind her, not particularly quietly, because of her relief. Without stopping she went running along the long stone corridor of the close with its brick-coloured cement walls and out into the chilly early morning air.

She never stopped her half-running, loping, speed until she rounded the corner at Millbrae Road. There was a milk float at the close, and as she ran upstairs the milk boy was hanging the cans by their long handle on the doorknobs. He looked round at her in surprise. I must look a sight, she thought. She hadn't stopped to comb her hair, her coat was unbuttoned. He gave her a sly smile.

'I'll take that,' she said tersely, feeling her face fixed in some kind of grimace.

'Did ye have a good . . . ?' he started, but the grimace must have frightened him. 'Aw right, missus,' he said, and handing over the can, bounded down the stone stairs.

She hadn't her key. She realised it as she put her hands in her pockets. It was safely tucked inside her handbag in Ruth Crosbie's bedroom. Under her bed for fear of burglars.

She stood irresolute, and then fear flooded her. Supposing Ruth had run after her and was at this minute rounding the corner of Millbrae Road . . . she lifted her hand and gave a loud decisive knock with the brass knocker, a replica of

Culzean Castle, which Mary had bought in Largs and which she lovingly polished every morning. 'Doing the brasses' was one of her more enjoyable tasks.

John opened it almost immediately. She saw he had his heavy overcoat on over his underwear, long drawers and a semmit. 'In the name of God, Sarah!' he exclaimed, standing aside. 'What's the matter?' She pushed in past him.

'I'll tell you when I'm in,' she flung over her shoulder. He was following her closely into the kitchen and she turned to face him. 'I'm sorry to frighten you, John. I forgot my key. It was in my bag and I . . .' She felt she was babbling incoherently.

'You didn't frighten me, lass. I was just laying the fire for Mary before I got my clothes on . . .' He pointed to the sticks lying inside the fender, the rolled-up newspaper. 'But I thought you were staying with . . .'

'I was. Oh, John . . .' she wailed, unable to stop the sound and fell against him. His coat was open. She felt his hard body through the drawers, and in the midst of her misery a strong sexual thrust went through her, the first she had ever felt. She drew away from him and covered her face, dissembling to hide the feeling, its aftermath of a steady pulsing in her groin. 'I don't know how to tell you. All I know is I had to get away . . .' She drew in her breath, praying the shameful throbbing would die down, leave her in peace.

'Take your time.' He took her gently in his arms again. 'Cry away. You don't have to tell me. Here, here . . .' She was sobbing loudly, with fear, with shame, with a torrent of feeling. 'Don't bother with it the now. Tell Mary . . .'

'Tell Mary what?' Mary's sharp voice came from the doorway. 'I'm here. What's the matter?'

'It's this lass.' John turned to her, still holding Sarah. 'Here, you can deal with it better than me.' He released her.

'And whatever it is you'd be better to have some clothes on!' He laughed at her, and at the same moment the pulsing died in Sarah's groin and she knew it had been one-sided, would always be one-sided. He belonged to Mary.

'I'm making a fool of myself, Mary,' she said. Her tears

had dried. She drew her hands down her face. 'I left Ruth's house in a hurry because she came in to bed beside me and . . . I didn't like it.'

'Came into bed beside you!' Mary's eyebrows were up amongst her hair. 'Well, that's a new yin.' She turned to John who despite her advice was kneeling at the fire, deftly criss-crossing the sticks over the paper, arranging small pieces of coal on top. He was an adept firemaker. He set a light to it, the flames licked cheerfully round the pyramid, and he stood up.

'There,' he said. 'You get the kettle on and the frying pan out and I'll go and make myself decent.' He gave Sarah's shoulder a pat as he passed her. 'You're back wi' your ain folk,' he said.

When he came back they were both at the table drinking tea. The bacon was sizzling. Mary liked to let the fat run out before she fried the eggs. 'We're not going to talk any more about Sarah's weekend for the time being,' she informed him. 'She's had enough of it.'

'Aye, more than enough,' Sarah said. She and Mary had hardly exchanged a word, but the understanding had been there, a wish to 'let things settle'. She met John's eyes. They were smiling at her, a teasing smile.

'Well, we're always learning,' he said, sitting down at the table.

'She could do without a lesson like that,' his wife said. 'Do you remember, though, there used to be a woman who loitered about the Central Station wearing a collar and tie? And a man's haircut?'

'Did she give you the glad eye?' he said, helping himself to two teaspoonfuls of sugar.

'What a conversation to be having at half-past six in the morning!' Mary said. And then they were laughing, the three of them.

Chapter Fourteen

In the routine tasks of the household that morning, helping Mary with the children who were soon stirring, Sarah began, strangely enough, to feel sorry for Ruth. She knew she would never go to the library again, and that was a pity because it was the handiest one for her, and she had been getting on well with her reading. Her reason was embarrassment. Perhaps when she became really mature she would change her mind.

Mary and John had taken the right attitude, she thought, in that they hadn't taken any attitude, simply because they had believed they would never run across anyone like Ruth Crosbie (except the woman in the Central Station, of course, who, in a way, now clicked into place).

Their attitude of amused bafflement was better than the one she had taken, a mixture of fright and horror. Theirs simply said this is something which has never occurred in our frame of reference, and it was a pity Sarah had inadvertently become involved in it.

She also began to wonder if the extreme physical reaction she had experienced in John's arms had been aroused first of all by Ruth's advances. She knew now that it was against her own tendency ever to think of a woman in that way – all her romantic dreaming had been concerned with men – but she should be grateful to Ruth for showing this to her, and also that sexual feelings were not just confined to one sex.

She also realised that John had not instigated her arousal, nor even been aware of it. He had been sorry for her in her predicament, her laughable predicament, she thought now, sorry if she had been hurt. He had taken her in his arms the way he would have done with Lachie or Bella.

Sarah went to work on Monday morning feeling different,

as if she had attended a weekend course in self-knowledge. She was glad, however, when Miss Frobisher said she would like her to go to Helensburgh to see Mrs de Vere. 'There's a letter on my desk from her this morning, and she's thinking along the lines of a winter coat. She specifies you as being the only one who understands what she wants. Try and talk her into having it fur-trimmed, Sarah. I've just been offered some nice skins Mr Samuel had left over from his coats.' Mr Samuel was her favourite furrier in Sauchiehall Street.

'Certainly, Miss Frobisher.' Her employer would reap a handsome profit from that, she knew. And yet sable would suit Mrs de Vere. She saw the coat in her mind's eye, draped fur collar, lean line with inset panels to disguise her customer's girth. It would be nice, she thought (the word Ruth Crosbie didn't like), to take the train to Helensburgh, and she might walk along the shore road to Mrs de Vere's house. She needed 'a good blow' to get rid of the lingering smell of joss sticks and casserole in her nose.

Mrs de Vere received her in the drawing room. The nursery was a thing of the past, and she seemed genuinely glad to see her.

'Well, Miss Lane,' she greeted her, 'you have roses in your cheeks today. You are generally pale.'

'I walked along by the shore, Mrs de Vere,' Sarah told her. 'I spent a weekend with a friend and I was indoors most of the time.' How quickly any experience was taken into oneself, she thought, subtly changed, presented in a different guise.

'I imagine you must have many smart Glasgow friends,' Mrs de Vere said. 'Your fashionable appearance has given me quite an impetus. One of the last things Ronald said to me before he left was, "Don't let yourself go, Mother."'

'You have a distinctive style, Mrs de Vere. Everyone has.' But before moving into the sable trimmings she asked, teacup in hand, 'How is your son?' How nice this is, she thought, tea at the window of this gracious room looking on to the broad reaches of the loch, nearer, the expanse of lawn with a summer-house in one corner still overhung by roses. Like a picture in a calendar. Maybe she would rent a little house here herself looking on to the water and she could have a garden . . . All the time she was smiling and listening to Mrs de Vere, whom she had grown to like so much.

'Oh, he's thoroughly settled down now with his men on Salisbury Plain. Absorbed. That's Ronald. He loves his men. I don't think he could love a single person. It's the corporate body which interests him.' Strangely enough, Sarah knew what she meant.

'My brother-in-law is the same. It's the corporate body, the welfare of the men in Dixon's. And his wife and children, of course.' Not me.

'I used to think he would marry. Someone like you, actu- ally, Miss Lane, elegant, who would grace his dinner table. But of the same class.' She said this without any idea of giving offence. Sarah nodded, knowing her class. 'But I doubt if he will. If he has any allegiance, it is to the idea of family. He will always come back to where I am, and when I go, well, I suppose he will live for the army completely. His father was the same, but his allegiance was to the navy. They're a breed apart. Women are an adjunct only. Not really needed.'

'Your husband needed you.' Sarah took a sip of her China tea. She might even begin to like it.

Mrs de Vere paused. 'That's true. I suppose there have to be variations, otherwise the breed would die out.' She smiled at Sarah as if they had solved a conundrum. 'Now, shall we look at the designs you brought with you, Miss Lane? I should like this coat for my visit to Salisbury.'

'Of course. And I have brought some trimmings for you to see. Sable. I can see you in sable.' It would give the right impression in Salisbury, she thought. They had a pleasant hour browsing in magazines at the teatable which the house- keeper had cleared when summoned. Sarah thought she sniffed when she looked down at the rich display of fur.

When Sarah was leaving, Mrs de Vere asked suddenly, 'You're a dear girl. I suppose you have a life apart from Miss Frobisher?'

'Oh, yes. I share a home with my sister and brother-in-law,

and their children, as I told you. It's difficult for a single girl to live on her own in Glasgow.'

'But someone as beautiful as you will soon find someone who will want to give you a home. What a pity one has to marry, as one thinks, for independence, and then find it's bondage, really. I know I got trapped. Be careful.'

'I'll try,' she said. Mrs de Vere had some odd ideas. Perhaps it was because of having gone to Girton.

Chapter Fifteen

1923

She has a sweet face, Sarah thought, on her way to work. She had gone up on the top deck of the tram because she thought the April freshness of the air would penetrate there, and she was sitting at the open window on the back scanning the photograph of Lady Elizabeth Bowes-Lyon leaving for her wedding to the Duke of York.

They had discussed the wedding dress in the work-room many times. Minnie McConachie thought she would play safe because of her mother-in-law, the queen, and Sarah had agreed, as a recognised exemplar of fashion. This morning she was wearing a new Chanel suit, still in the pale grey favoured by Miss Frobisher, but short-skirted, loose, comfortable, with a silk blouse of the palest mauve.

Mary, looking her up and down, Bella on her knee, had said, 'Well, don't go up on the top wi' that skirt. The conductor will lose his eyesight!' But she had. If she was still shy, it didn't extend to her liking for wearing *le dernier cri*, as Miss Frobisher put it. It was a pity she was wearing a hat which covered her newly bobbed hair. She folded the newspaper neatly when she saw the tramcar swinging along towards Charing Cross, and ran downstairs, feeling free and unencumbered in the shorter skirt, and lower-heeled shoes.

Later that morning Miss Frobisher was closeted with a man from Bowie's, the Glasgow jewellers, silversmiths and purveyors of fancy articles, who sent a representative twice a year only, with a certain degree of ceremony. Mr Turnbull had recently been promoted to call on their best customers, since old Mr Bowie had retired. She had told Sarah she liked the new man. He was deferential, but not too deferential, he recognised her worth, and he brought only examples of the finest items for her inspection.

The first visit was for display and inspection only, the second one when, having made up her mind, she selected an article which she felt reflected the ambience and the quality of Charles et Cie. Replicas of her choice were distributed to her most valued clients in time for Christmas.

Personal jewellery was frowned upon as being too intimate; this year her choice had fallen on a shagreen-covered address book with gold corners and clasp, and which bore the imprint, in gold embossed lettering, of Charles et Cie. She emerged from her sanctum, well-pleased with her choice, Mr Turnbull in tow, a tall, chestnut-haired youngish man who filled his well-cut suit, and who gave the impression, with his briefcase and bowler hat in hand, of discretion and quality.

'Miss Lane?' She summoned Sarah who was seated at the mahogany desk in the centre of the salon, her pale grey suit matching the pale grey carpet, a picture of elegance with her smooth-haired small head, her long white fingers, her pale pink lips matching her pale pink nails.

'Yes, Miss Frobisher?' She stood up.

'I have to keep an appointment at five o'clock. Would you complete the order with Mr Turnbull for me?' And to Mr Turnbull: 'Miss Lane is aware of my choice. You may safely give the details to her, date of delivery in particular.' She glanced hurriedly at her watch. 'Take the matter in hand, Miss Lane. I'll see you tomorrow. Goodbye, Mr Turnbull.' She extended a regal hand, then swept out of the salon, her silver fox trailing over one shoulder, her plump legs immaculately silk-clad, what one could glimpse of them (not for her the Chanel skirt, Sarah thought), above her high-heeled shoes.

Sarah smiled at Mr Turnbull as she sat down again. She recognised him, of course. He had been accompanying old Mr Bowie for the last few years, ostensibly being shown the ropes, but expertly and discreetly conducting the whole operation. With the retiral of Mr Bowie, a bustling stout gentleman with a gold chain across his expansive waistcoat, he seemed to have gained an importance of his own. He had filled out a little, his hair, sleekly Brylcreemed, was still a rich chestnut which gleamed under the soft salon lighting. She thought he might be around thirty-five.

'Please sit down, Mr Turnbull,' she said, offering him a seat beside her desk. 'Have you your invoices?'

'Yes, certainly.' He snapped open his briefcase and handed over a sheaf of papers to her. 'All present and correct, I think. How do *you* like the address books, Miss Lane?'

'Very much. They look expensive.' She glanced at the papers. 'They *are* expensive.'

'Nothing but the best for Miss Frobisher.' He smiled at her.

More than they're worth, she thought, as she entered the figures in the accounts book open on her desk. She had seen similar address books in a shop in the Argyll Arcade priced at far less, but Miss Frobisher equated cost with quality. 'That's it,' she said, straightening her back and smiling at Mr Turnbull. 'A good day's work.' She wondered if he would take that as a criticism and said the first thing which came into her head. 'I expect you'll be glad to get home now.'

'Yes,' he said, shutting his briefcase and standing up, 'my mother keeps a check on me.' She saw the twinkle in his eyes. Surely he would be married at his age? 'Is there anyone waiting for *you*?'

'I live with my sister and her husband. I keep saying I'll get a place of my own, but . . .' She stopped herself confiding further.

'It seems you and I are in the same boat.' So he had been serious.

Sarah's young assistant was standing at her elbow. She turned. 'What is it, Annie?'

'It's after five, Miss Lane. Do you want me to close the door?'

'No, thanks, I'll do it on my way out. Tell the others to finish up at the back.'

'Right-oh! Miss Lane.' Miss Frobisher frowned on such expressions. Sarah let it pass since Mr Turnbull was still there.

'Can I escort you?' he asked when the girl had gone. 'We might even be going the same way.'

'I live on the south side.'

'I'm out west. Partickhill. Tell you what,' he smiled, and she thought of him suddenly as a person, not as the substitute for old Mr Bowie. He looked nice, boyish, and the skin round his blue eyes wrinkled at the corners when he smiled. He looked what Mary would call 'quite the gent', but she thought he might be different underneath his professional veneer, even 'quite a card'. That was one of John's expressions. 'Tell you what,' Mr Turnbull said again, 'we might even have a coffee, or a drink, if you're not in a tearing rush.'

'I think I could spare half an hour,' she said, smiling at him, he had that effect on her. 'Will you wait till I get my handbag and gloves?'

They walked down the hill to Charing Cross – it was only a hundred yards – and when Sarah stopped at the tram stop Mr Turnbull said, 'Tell you what,' (for the third time), looking even more boyish, 'there's a nice little howff I sometimes frequent in Berkeley Street. Have you time to go there for a coffee?'

'Well . . .' She thought it looked more sophisticated to hesitate.

'Boyfriend waiting?'

She smiled non-committally. It was too ridiculous to say, 'Mary will have the tea ready,' knowing in any case Mary would be delighted. And she must remember that Mr Turnbull knew her as Miss Frobisher's chief assistant, a person in her own right. 'Well,' she said, copying Mr Turnbull's playful manner, 'I don't mind if I do.'

'That's the stuff,' he said, looking pleased. 'Live dangerously.' He put his hand under her elbow and guided her across the street.

The café was divided into booths, each with a rose-shaded lamp. There were several couples occupying them already, the atmosphere was subdued, only spoiled by a faint smell of fat. Sarah noticed a couple who were tucking into mammoth plates of fish and chips, the tomato sauce bottle between them.

'The best fish in town here,' Mr Turnbull told her, 'if you're hungry and can't wait. Can I tempt you?'

'Oh, no, thank you.'

'Then you must have a drink. What will it be? Gin and It?'

'That would be nice.' She was not unused to cocktails. On her buying expeditions to London with Miss Frobisher, her employer had warned her against accepting more than one. 'These firms just want to fill you up so that you'll order more of their clothes than you want.' Her ready-made selection at Charles et Cie was kept only to appease customers who might be in a hurry. 'Good clothes are like an oil painting,' she had said to Sarah, 'they take time.'

Mr Turnbull called the waiter who leant over him in a conspiratorial manner, then sped away to return with Sarah's cocktail and a fair-sized glass of whisky. 'My tipple after a busy day,' he said to Sarah, smiling. She liked his manner. He made her feel at ease, unlike Gus Carmichael. 'This place does for popping into if you're in a hurry.' He looked around as he sipped appreciatively at his whisky. 'Yours all right?'

'Nice,' Sarah said, wishing there was a better word. She had never felt right saying 'lovely', although it was a favourite word of the London buyers.

'So you keep thinking you'll get a place of your own?' he asked, his eyes full of interest.

'Yes, but somehow I don't. You know how it is.'

'You feel you're needed?'

Sarah liked immediately his way of looking at her problem. 'In a way. John is out at meetings a lot – he's a shop steward, and there are the children. Lachie and Bella . . .'

'I can see you like them.' His eyes were on her, still full of interest.

'And you said you lived with your mother?' As near as dammit, anyhow, she thought.

'Yes, I haven't met the right girl yet.' His eyes were still smiling. She was enveloped in their warmth. 'Of course I

travel a lot, so my mother is far from being dependent on me
... but, still, what man doesn't like to be spoiled when he
comes home?'

'That's true.' Either the gin or the conversation was giving
her this feeling of rightness. 'I'm in the same boat in a way,'
she confided. 'Mary does everything for me. I've never liked
housework. But I can help with the children. They're wee
darlings.' Mr Turnbull had turned away as if he had lost
interest. No wonder, with all this domestic chit-chat. He
turned back again.

'Do you think you could call me Barney?' She was surprised.

'I think I could.' She smiled at him. 'I'm Sarah.'

'Nice name, Sarah.'

'Miss Frobisher likes formality at Charles et Cie. I quite
like to hear my own name.'

'She's a dragon, isn't she? You can't pull any fast ones over
on her, not that I'd want to, of course. Only the best is good
enough for our Miss Frobisher. But then I can see that by
her staff.' His eyes held hers, flattering her. She liked the look
of him, his air of cleanliness, good grooming, immaculate
dressing. She liked his roguish manner. She smiled, lips closed.
She was wise enough not to be drawn into criticism of Miss
Frobisher. 'So what do you do with your spare time? Don't
tell me you're at home with your sister and her husband every
night?'

'That would be telling.' The remark was foreign to her
nature. She had heard Annie using it when she was recounting
her escapades to the other girls in the work-room.

'"That would be telling," she says.' He seemed to like this
verbal sparring. 'Will you have another gin and It, Sarah?'

'Oh, no, thank you.' He raised his eyebrows at her, at
the same time lifting his hand to the waiter, who scurried
over.

'Another of the same, Jimmy.' He indicated his own glass,
and to Sarah, 'You're sure?' She nodded. Two pairs of eyes
were on her.

'Yes, quite sure.' The waiter seemed to be involved also.

'Quite sure,' she said again. He scurried away. She thought there had been the merest toss of his head. 'Do you travel a lot on business, Barney?' she asked.

'Oh, yes, London, of course, the big English cities, Birmingham likes our stuff, occasionally abroad. We're quite upsides with Edinburgh, Bowie's. And I'm angling for an American trip, believe it or not. Where's *your* favourite holiday place, Sarah?'

'Not so far afield, although I love London. I go buying with Miss Frobisher. The galleries there . . .'

'The Bond Street Arcades?'

'No, pictures.' She shook her head. 'I'm hoping one day I'll understand them.' She saw his blank look. 'I like the Clyde Coast too. Helensburgh. And Largs. It's the water . . . I'm afraid I'm lazy about going further afield.'

'You need someone to show you. Thanks, Jimmy.' The waiter put down another glass of whisky in front of Barney. He raised it to Sarah. 'Here's to jaunting about the world, and here's to our friendship. It's a long time since I felt such a rapport.' He sipped his whisky. 'I hope you don't mind me saying that.' He looked roguish. 'Of course, I've noticed you before, but you always looked rather aloof.'

'Did I? Well, Miss Frobisher doesn't encourage . . . chit-chat.'

'I believe that. I'm glad the opportunity occurred to meet like this. When I saw you sitting at that desk when I came out . . . so stylish. I always notice style.' He nodded decisively. 'I'm looking forward to many more opportunities.' He had been sipping his whisky as he spoke, and now he held up his glass. It was almost empty. 'See the effect you have on me? I'm quite nervous.'

'I can't believe that!' She laughed. She had never felt so much at ease with anyone. And calling him by his first name right away without feeling shy about it. Mary would be bound to like him too. She liked suitors to be well-dressed, gentlemanly, which was strange, since John didn't come under that category. He dressed badly since clothes meant nothing to him. Dixon's and the men there were his life, then Mary and the children in that order. Since the episode with Ruth Crosbie she had tried to sort out hers.

She would stop trying to change it. Marriage, of course, would be the most welcome change, but until that happened she would be part of John's and Mary's family and consider herself fortunate. There was the added advantage of the children, whom she loved dearly. John, she knew since that morning when she had been in his arms, thought of her only as Mary's sister. The fierce feeling which had swept through her was a need which she knew would never be satisfied by him, nor would she want to come between them. But it had felt natural. Even yet . . .

Since then she had put most of her energies into her work at Charles et Cie. She had been complimented by other buyers in London, also the wholesalers. She had an 'eye', they said. Her liking for clothes and her good taste in them was because of that 'eye', a talent for design, and line. She could never have worn or chosen any garment which offended her, could never understand women who wore colours which screamed at each other. She knew she was appreciated by Miss Frobisher, and that she might have offered her a partnership had it not been for her employer's belief that Nessie would return to the fold.

Instead of going to the library, she had bought books. She didn't wish to see Ruth Crosbie again. She learned to use them, to be able to find and read about any subject she was interested in, from art to social issues. She thought she had, in her own words, 'straightened herself out'. John was still and always would be her yardstick when it came to problems of the day with his wisdom and his moral integrity. What, she thought now, listening to Barney Turnbull, would John think of him?

He was being quite jolly, telling her about Bowie's and about the staff there, and how Mr Bowie had encouraged him. ' "The manner is all important," he often said to me.' He had finished his whisky now. 'He thought I had what it took, a "presence". He coached me, took me out to the best restaurants, introduced me to our clients. It wasn't that the other lads in Bowie's weren't as good as me,' she liked his deprecating air, 'some of them would have been a damn sight better, excuse the French, but it was the manner, and the height. Have you noticed how many Glasgow chaps are undersized? Wee Glasgow runts, to put it plainly. But wee smarters. Look at them in the war. They did all the fighting while I sat at a desk because I had it up here.' He tapped his forehead. 'Mr Bowie wangled an exemption for me . . . here am I talking too much about myself! It's this whisky. You're sure you won't go on somewhere else with me and have a decent meal?'

'No, really,' she said, smiling, 'Mary will have mine ready. And she would wonder . . .'

'Some other time, eh?' He nodded, understanding. He had the same situation with his mother. 'Good living,' he said. 'It's the quality of life that matters, good living, travelling, good food. And with a good companion.' A shadow seemed to pass over his face and then he was saying earnestly, 'I hope you're going to become that to me, Sarah.' He put out his hand and took hers. She noticed the gold accessories, a heavy signet ring, a braceleted watch, the gold pin set with a diamond in his tie. They gleamed, as did his chestnut hair.

Was he moving rather fast, she wondered, and should he be quite so sure about her, so soon? But he was sincere enough, and his eyes were moist. She liked him, she really did. He was not in the same class as Major de Vere, of course, but as his mother had pointed out, neither was she. Barney seemed just right. And how nice it would be to have him call for her in the evening! Mary would be pleased. She released her hand to look at her watch.

'Goodness!' she exclaimed, although she was not surprised. 'We've been here for over an hour! I must go.' She gathered her gloves and handbag together. Trams got fewer when the rush had passed. 'It's been really quite nice, Barney.' She smiled, feeling her shyness showing through a little because of the way his eyes were holding hers.

'It's been great for me. Are you *sure* you can't let me give you supper?'

'No, really. Mary will be waiting.' It was the first time that she had resented Mary.

'Well, she's the last person I want to offend.' He laughed gaily. 'I must keep in with Mary.' He got to his feet. 'My motor's in the garage for servicing since I was doing local calls. Courtesy of Bowie's. Supplied by the firm.' He was frank, which she liked. 'I'll get a cab for you.' He called to the waiter who was standing against the wall near their table. 'Check, Jimmy. And a taxi for madam.'

'Right away, Mr Turnbull.' They seemed to know each other.

'There's no need, Barney,' Sarah protested when they were in the street. She felt she was using his name a lot, yet was surprised how easy it was.

'I like getting my own way. Besides, I'd never send a pretty girl like you home in the dark.' A brisk wind blew up from the Clyde as they stood at the kerb and she shivered slightly. 'Here's one. Jimmy's been quick off the mark.' When the cab drew up beside them he had a quick word with the driver, then opened the door and handed her in. He wasn't coming with her. She had seen money exchanged. He said, holding the door open as she sat down, 'I told him it was the South Side. I'll leave you to give him your address.'

'It's Millbrae Road.' She wouldn't look surprised. 'Thanks,' she said. 'And thanks for the drink.'

'We'll have many more.' He smiled and shut the door, then spoke to her through the open window. 'Can I get in touch with you at your sister's?'

'We haven't a telephone.'

'Not to worry. There's Charles et Cie. You'll hear from me very soon, Sarah.' His eyes met hers, holding them, then he stepped back and the cab drove away. She saw him standing on the kerb, looking dapper, his briefcase in his hand. He raised his bowler, and she waved back.

Well, Sarah thought, leaning back, that was a surprise. Everything had happened so fast, as if she had stepped through an open door into a different world. He seemed so confident, so sure about her. Was she so sure about him? She pictured him, a bit like Jack Buchanan, she thought, although he was dark, but the same boyish air. She liked him, oh, yes, she liked him . . . she drew in her breath as she looked out at the streetlights, the people. All the big shops had shut now, but she could see the shadowy figures of the wax models in the windows, eternally posturing. Some draped in wraps like Greek togas. People queuing already for the cinemas. She craned to see what was on. Mary Pickford in *Broken Blossom*. She ought to go with Minnie. And they'd talked of *Miracles of the Jungle*. Or perhaps Barney would ask her to go with him. She liked him, oh, yes, she liked him.

Chapter Sixteen

'My, you're home early tonight,' Mary said.

It was a lovely evening in late April, even in the city streets Sarah had thought she could smell spring in the air. She remembered the pleasure of walking along the shore road at Helensburgh as she hurried along Millbrae Road. At least there were trees here, with their light green foliage, and there were children playing in the road with their girds and cleeks, racing down the middle of it as she had done when she was a girl. She had often beaten the boys because of her lightness of foot.

'I'm going out for a run in a motor,' she told Mary. 'It's that Barney Turnbull I told you about.'

'Oh, aye.' Mary's mouth pursed in a pleased smile. 'Lachie!' she shouted at her son who was climbing on to the wooden side of the kitchen sink. 'I'll swing for that one,' she said. 'Come down out of there! You'll break your neck.' Sarah laughed and went to rescue her nephew.

'He's just a boy. Watch, son.' She lifted him up and, her arm round him to keep him safe, pointed out of the window. 'See, there's a blackbird. It's looking for food to feed its babies.'

'I could catch it, so I could. Will we go down, Aunty Sarah?'

'No, that would be cruel. And I'm going out. I'm in a hurry.' She lifted him down and fumbled in her purse. 'There's a sixpence for you. You keep it safe till tomorrow and we'll go to the shops. What will you get?'

'Sherbet dabs! To dip in a paper poke!' She laughed at him because she was happy.

'Right. And we might have enough left for some dolly mixtures.'

'I only like the jelly ones.'

Mary said, looking at her, 'Somebody's happy the night. Do you fancy this Barney Turnbull?'

'He's nice and polite. Yes, I like him. I think you would too, Mary.'

'Well, you know he's welcome here any time.'

'I don't want to give him any ideas, but maybe I'll bring him to meet you and John the next time . . . if there is a next time.'

'Be sure and give us plenty of warning so that I can get that man to get in early. I'm a Dixon's widow.'

'I'll try. Well, I'll be late if I don't hurry. I want to get out before the sun goes.'

In her bedroom she quickly changed into a light dress and coat to match in pale blue – it was a relief to have a change from grey – both garments with the short skirts which she liked wearing now. She wouldn't tell Mary about the wolf whistles she got when she was waiting for the tram. Especially if the wind blew up Sauchiehall Street. She loved the feeling of freedom the new clothes gave. Did it reflect the slackening of morals since the beginning of the Twenties, she wondered, as she pulled on the Milanese stockings which had to be extra long, but could be bought in one of the Buchanan Street warehouses where she was well-known.

She brushed her bobbed hair vigorously, deciding that since she would be in a motor she could dispense with a hat. It shone smooth and fair, full of life. What a relief not to have to bother with hairpins. She fastened it in a mother-of-pearl clasp to keep it out of her eyes.

She had chosen to meet Barney at the Langside Monument near their flat. He was there, and when he saw her turn the corner of Millbrae Road he got out of the motor car and came towards her, smiling.

'Sarah! This is great! I took a chance telephoning you at your work.' He was leading her back to the motor car, settling her in, going round the other side to slip in beside her. 'It was short notice but I had been in London and just got back.'

'I happened to be free,' she said, smiling too. He looked even more handsome than she had remembered. His light grey suit and striped tie gave him an appearance of youthful smartness, like someone stepping out of the Automobile Club in Blythswood Square.

'You're even prettier than I remembered.' He turned to her. 'It's seeing you without a hat. Your hair's lovely. Shining, like gold sovereigns.'

'Thanks.' She couldn't stop smiling. 'It's much easier to manage. Men have no idea what it's like to wash long hair. And the soot in the Glasgow air soon makes it dirty again.'

'You're like me,' he said, starting the engine, 'particular about appearance. You have to be in our jobs.'

'I think I would have been, no matter where I worked. Mary says I'm pernickety.'

'That's what my mother says about me.' He laughed delightedly. 'Clean shirt every day. Of course, I take them to the laundry. I couldn't have her doing them.'

'No, you couldn't.' Again there was this feeling of ease with him. She had noticed the blue whiteness of his shirt when he came forward to meet her. And his hand on the doorknob of the car had been clean, the nails well-tended. John's were often dirty when he came in. The first thing he did was to go to the kitchen sink and give them a good wash. Strong hands. Capable. 'Where are we going, Barney?' she asked him as they sped through the South Side.

'I thought we might go past Carmunnock and on to the moors above East Kilbride. It would give us a good little run. And after that we'll drive into town and have a meal. There isn't a decent place out here.'

'You don't have to bother. Mary will keep me something in the oven.'

'I wouldn't hear of it! When I take out a girl I like to do it properly. The best or nothing.'

'Well . . .' she began, 'you don't have to . . .' She felt cosseted, special. Only the best would do for her, he thought. Mary would be delighted if she recounted the conversation.

They talked for a long time when he parked at the side of the road where they had a good view over the Clyde Valley. It was dusk already, and below them the lights of the city were magical, a starry valley with the main roads marked by lamps like small moons.

'I think I can make out Bridgeton Cross,' she said. And, pointing, 'That dark bit. The Umbrella. Have you ever stood under it?'

'Oh, yes. When it's raining.' They laughed together. She noticed his teeth, small and white, shining with cleanliness. He took such care of himself, she thought. That's what I like.

'It's a strange feeling up here,' she said, they were sitting close together, 'of being outside a teeming city looking down on it. I read a book by a man called Theodore Dreiser and he described the same sensation, outside looking in. I can imagine the people scurrying about like ants, lines of them, scurrying, wheeling in and out, busy, busy . . .' He was silent, as if he was thinking about what she had said, puzzling about it.

'You're a fanciful little thing.' He turned to her. 'My thoughts were on where we were going for supper. Maybe Danny Brown's would be best at this time. Do you know it?'

'Oh, yes.' She had hoped for somewhere exotic, unknown to her. 'It's a regular howff with some of the buyers I know.'

'They always give you a nice meal. I know the waiters.'

'You seem to know all the waiters,' she said, laughing.

'It's part of my job. I get an expense account. Mr Bowie prefers the fireside now. He says he's had his day of dining out customers.'

'Have we time for a walk?' she asked. 'I like walking on grass. Do you know what my dream is?'

'No?'

'To have a house with a garden some day.' She blushed suddenly. She was annoyed that her shyness could still catch her out. Once, in bed, she had tried to analyse why she blushed on certain occasions and had come to the conclusion that she saw innuendo in her own remarks where there was none intended, or where it escaped the listener. 'Preferably on the coast,' she continued. She willed the blush to fade.

'You're a sweet girl,' he said, 'I don't know what it is. Maybe it's the difference between your sophisticated appearance and your ... softness.' He means vulnerability, she thought.

'Soft?' she laughed. 'I don't like the sound of that.'

'I'm sorry. It's meant to be a compliment.' He said in a lower tone, 'Your hands are soft, for instance.' He had taken them in his. 'The skin is soft, the nails are smooth, my hands slide over them.' He raised her hands and kissed them, softly. She felt happy, that was all.

'Sarah?'

'Yes?'

'Would you think it forward of me if I asked you for a kiss?'

'Not if you asked me nicely,' she said. Annie's clichés came in handy.

'Please, please, Sarah?' She felt his breath on her mouth. 'Is that nice enough?' She was aware of his smell, musky and yet fresh, clean, not overtly masculine or hearty, but there was also an admixture of cigars, which was manly.

'All right,' she said.

His kiss brushed her mouth, and then his arms came round her and he held her close. The last time she had been in a man's arms had been those of John, and remembering, she also remembered that overwhelming thrust of desire which had shot through her. This was different, a sweetness, a protective feeling, as if it was her arms which were round Barney.

He kissed her again, and one of his hands came round to stroke her face, gently. 'If I had looked for a thousand years I couldn't have found anyone as sweet as you, Sarah,' he said. 'Holding you like this is bliss.'

She didn't answer. Should there have been more? Each man must be different, she thought. John had meant that strong arousal of her senses, a rebuttal of Ruth Crosbie and what she had offered. Gus Carmichael had been brash, had made her feel cheap. This feeling was gentle, tender, deeper, more lasting. She drew herself away.

'It's quite dark now,' she said. Mere pinpricks of light in the dark valley. She touched her bobbed hair. It was still smooth.

'Yes, quite dark.' His voice was trembling. 'I think we should go back before I forget myself.' He sat up, ran his hands over his hair and started the engine. She was content. 'Did you like me, Sarah?' he said as he drove.

'Yes,' she said, 'I like you.'

'Could it be more?'

'It might . . .'

'The luck,' he said softly, 'if I had looked for a thousand years . . . I've never felt like this before . . .' She put her hand over one of his.

The meal they had in Danny Brown's was halibut. It was chosen by Barney, vetted by the waiter. And the vegetables. And the ices. They drank white wine which he chose without consulting her but she sipped and said it was nice. Because she was happy.

When he let her out at her close at Millbrae Road they had made an arrangement to meet at the weekend. She didn't know coyness. She said she would like that, yes, Saturday and Sunday would be all right. Maybe they would drive down to the coast, and she agreed again, provided it wasn't Ayrshire, she stipulated.

'Another man?' he asked.

'Long ago.' She could scarcely remember Gus Carmichael's name.

She was so happy with this new tender feeling that she went straight to her bedroom and immediately to bed in order to savour it. She couldn't have borne any teasing from Mary and John. This was different.

Chapter Seventeen

Ever since the morning when she had run from Ruth Crosbie's house, Sarah had felt embarrassed to be alone with John. Had he read something in her eyes, she had wondered, a reflection of her sudden intense feeling when he had held her? If so, he had never mentioned the incident. 'John's deep,' Mary had said of him more than once. She accepted him as he was.

But now that she was meeting Barney two or three times each week and coming home later, she sometimes found John working at his books and pamphlets in the kitchen. Mary was an early bedder. She had always been, even before the advent of the children. She wasn't a reader. When her body was tired out with the practicalities of the day, cooking, cleaning, washing, minding children, she craved her bed.

That evening Sarah and Barney had sat talking in the palm court of the Picture House. He had been wistful. 'It's a shame you have to go home at all, girlie.' This had become his favourite endearment. Sarah had felt a similar reluctance.

'I don't want to have a bad reputation with the neighbours, creeping in at all hours,' and, tentatively, 'Maybe it won't be long before we're . . . together.' She had stretched her hand across the table to him. His blue eyes were sad. She loved him wholly, completely, a tender, but not completely satisfying love. Or did she mean 'satisfied'?

He felt the same, she knew, once in his motor car, his hand on her breast, she had heard his quick intake of breath. She had wanted to say to him, 'Don't let's wait', but had thought that they would regret it, or he would. He was such a gentleman.

'She's coming round to the idea,' he said, she knew he meant his mother, 'I know it's going to be hard for her. You see,' he smiled at her, 'I told her we were going to become engaged.'

'Not so as you'd notice.' He liked her to be playful, preferred her to hide any excess of feeling.

'Maybe you'll notice this.' He put his hand in his breast pocket and drew out of it a small blue velvet box. 'Open it and see,' he said, handing it to her. She took it, her heart beating rapidly.

It was a solitaire diamond ring set in a circlet of sapphires, the colour of his eyes, she thought. Hers were grey. And being his choice it was huge, brilliant, she felt the people at other tables were blinded by its brilliance.

'It's . . . beautiful,' Sarah said. She was almost speechless with happiness.

'Let me put it on.' He took her left hand and placed it on the third finger, seemed to look at it, raised her hand and kissed the ring. 'Are you happy?'

'Yes, happy.' She wouldn't spoil it by saying she would have preferred the darkness of his motor car where he could have put his arms round her, perhaps become passionate . . . engaged couples were allowed a certain licence.

'It suits you, girlie,' he said. He looked at her proudly, as if the ring had given her the finishing touch.

In the motor car she had thrown her arms about him in abandon. 'I feel a different girl,' she had said. 'I know it won't be long now.'

'Now, now, girlie.' He had stroked her face, then covered it with soft little kisses. 'No, it won't be long . . .'

'I'm engaged, John,' Sarah announced, sitting down opposite him at the kitchen table. She took off her glove and showed him the ring. Its rays seemed to flash round the kitchen disparagingly, highlighting the pail under the sink with the washing cloth draped over the rim.

'Mary'll be pleased,' he said, lifting his head from his papers. His eyes were tired.

'I like that.' She laughed at him. 'How about me?'

'As long as you're happy.'

'Oh, I'm happy! Barney's everything I ever wanted, so good-looking, so successful, so loving . . . yes, I'm happy.'

'Good.' His eyes were on her, direct. 'Have you fixed the date?'

'Not yet. It's his mother. She's the stumbling block, you know, the only son, and she doesn't keep well.'

'Oh, yes,' he said, 'I know.' He still held her gaze. 'Have you met her?'

'Not yet. I think she resents me. But maybe now that I'm his fiancée . . .'

'Anybody who saw you would be glad to have you as a daughter-in-law.'

'You're only saying that because you want rid of me.' It was the playful manner she assumed with Barney, which he liked. The remark rang falsely in the quiet kitchen. It was a mistake. She felt a rare heat in her cheeks.

'In some ways, yes,' he agreed. She heard the loud tick of the kitchen clock. John always left silences like this, she thought, so different from Barney who liked light chatter. She had imagined him on the stage, the gay young man-about-town, top hat and tails. She waited, heard now against the tick the rapid beat of her heart. She swallowed, moved nervously in her chair. 'Get off to bed, Sarah.' He spoke at last. 'You'll be tired with all that excitement.'

'Yes, I am a bit.' She got up. 'Goodnight, John.'

'Goodnight.' His head was bowed over his papers again.

But he was right, she thought, as she prepared for bed. The situation was untenable. A good word, that. She remembered a snide remark of Ruth Crosbie's when she had been speaking of John's standing at Dixon's. 'I bet they think he's lucky to have two women,' and seeing her horrified face, 'just a joke, Sarah. You're so young!'

But now that she had Barney, she knew it was foolish to imagine that John had been unaware of the effect he'd had on her that morning. There was nothing immature about him. But because of his maturity he would have banished it from his mind long ago, even if he had felt the same. It was of little or no consequence, part of life. What mattered in *his* was his work and his wife and family. He would never jeopardise that.

Besides, John would never be right for her. She could not bear to be a mere compartment in a man's life. With Barney she could share his work since it was like her own. He would consult her about it, as she would about hers, they both had that 'eye' so necessary in what they did. And she could never have felt tender towards John as she did towards Barney, he would have been demanding, too masculine for her. She needed someone to need her.

She went to sleep feeling she had persuaded herself. Barney's mother would soon agree to her son leaving her, she and Barney would set up a home together, choose the furniture together, the décor. He would get some things wholesale from Bowie's, and she had an entrée into some of the big drapery and furniture warehouses. Minnie would help her to plan her wedding gown, and she would be able to supervise its making. It was right, so right . . .

Chapter Eighteen

That Saturday after she had done out her room, her usual practice, she said to Mary and John at lunchtime, 'Would you believe it, I found a book which Ruth Crosbie gave me to read ages ago. About Mary Queen of Scots. I had completely forgotten it.'

John looked up from his paper. Saturday was a rare day with him, devoted to the family. 'I wonder if that was more than chance?' he said.

'What do you mean?'

'A dig from fate?' His mouth quirked. 'You've pretty well buried her or anything in connection with her, haven't you?'

'That's him again! Deep!' Mary was feeding Bella who was in a high chair beside her. 'You wee rascal! Did you see what she did? Spat out her good pudding!' Sarah laughed at the little girl banging her spoon and chortling with glee. Her fair hair made an aureole of gold round her face in the sunlight streaming through the kitchen window.

'She's like that Bubbles picture! Isn't she? Look at her, delighted with herself!'

'Don't laugh at her. It just encourages her. Here, Bella,' she proffered another spoonful, 'brown sugar, yummy yum.'

'You'll spoil her teeth,' John said, but his look was fond.

'All the same, John's right.' Mary wasn't as green as she was cabbage-looking, as she was wont to say about herself, 'you've never mentioned Ruth Crosbie's name since you ran away that morning. My, you were in a state!'

'I've grown up since then,' Sarah said. 'It just took me by surprise. Maybe I made a fuss about nothing.'

'You could take a walk round and show her your fine new ring.' Mary looked up slyly. 'And return her book.'

'Did you read it?' John asked. 'Sometimes I feel we should

know more about Mary Queen of Scots since we're living practically on top of where the battle took place.'

'And there are names to commemorate it all around us. How about Terreagles Avenue? And Darnley Street?'

'And Bothwell Terrace?' His eyes were bright.

'Would you like to read it before I take it back?'

'No, thanks. I haven't the time, worse luck. There's a rally tomorrow on the Green. The ILPs are getting their dander up and I've been asked to speak.'

'Are *you* going, Mary?' Sarah asked her.

'No, thanks. I can't watch John. I would be too embarrassed. You get over-critical when you're tied to a man. You'll know that now with Mr Turnbull.'

' "Barney" for goodness' sake!' And because lately she had detected disapproval in Mary's attitude towards him, 'So far I haven't found anything to be critical about. He seems perfect to me.'

'That wilny last, eh, John?'

'It might with Sarah. In a way she reminds me of Mary Queen of Scots.'

'Do you mind?' She pretended indignation. 'I haven't had half a dozen men . . . and I haven't chosen someone like Lord Darnley.'

'Nor Bothwell?'

'Nor Bothwell. *You're* more like him, isn't he, Mary?'

'My John's like nobody else but himself.' Sarah caught John's eye. The quirk was there again.

'Thanks for the compliment. In that case I'll no' throw you out.' He was in a rare light mood, Sarah noticed, thinking how different he was from that brash young lad who had shadowed Mary. Now he was a man, wiry, quick, strong-featured. He had an air about him. She was a lucky woman.

'I don't know what you two are goin' on about.' Mary was lifting Bella from her high chair. 'But I'm going to get this one ready. Are we or are we not going to Riddrie, John?'

'Oh, aye. I'll go and pick up Lachie and we'll be off.' Lachie went to a Saturday morning play group connected with the church which Mary said was the only peace she got.

When they had set off Sarah got herself ready with her usual care, parcelled the book and set off for Minard Road. She was full of trepidation at the thought of seeing Ruth Crosbie, but as she walked, the feel of her solitaire ring under the fine doeskin of her glove gave her a measure of confidence.

She stopped at the Langside Monument for a second, thinking of her earlier conversation with Mary and John about the ill-fated queen. She hadn't been altogether innocent, of course, the Scots always romanticised, liked legends. The Bad Queen and the Good Queen. Was Elizabeth jealous of Mary's success with men? Was Elizabeth frigid, unable to attract them? Who knew the real story? The real and shocking thing was that the English queen had had her cousin beheaded publicly. What a fate, she thought, walking on, but glancing at the old parish church behind it. Now, that would be a nice place to be married in. She could appreciate its Gothic beauty.

She walked down Langside Avenue, busy with people making for Shawlands Cross, and when she reached Pollokshaws Road was tempted to turn left and go there herself. In spite of the mellowness of the autumn sun, the copper-gold of the beech trees in the park on her right, her usual pleasure in being out of doors was absent. She was annoyed at herself because of the tremor in her hands, at the vague feeling of apprehension. Why should she worry about Ruth Crosbie now? She was in the past. To return the book would shut the door on what had been an upsetting incident, nothing more. She had been over-sensitive, stupid.

She would apologise to Ruth now, secure in her new status as an engaged woman. The fault lay in herself. She was unused to advances from another girl, to demonstrations of affection, to sharing a bed, far less with a woman. Ruth had perhaps shared hers with her cousin, thought nothing of it. She reached Minard Road and began walking down it to Ruth's flat above a newsagents.

Sarah was cheerful again. She felt right in herself, a professional woman, engaged to a smart Glasgow businessman, going to call on an old friend. There was the smoky smell of autumn in the air which she loved. People in the suburbs would be building bonfires. She would like that. In summer the city could be dusty, humid, sometimes near the Clyde the smells of diesel oil from the boats, rotting fish, refuse of all kinds, were nauseating. Discarded boxes of rotten fruit were left for days before they were cleared up. The dirty petticoat of Glasgow, she had read somewhere.

But here, away from Dixon's and the other ironworks clustering round Polmadie, the air seemed fresh. Had Mary Queen of Scots thought the same on her hill at Langside, that soon the battle would be won, that Elizabeth would stop hounding her, and that she would be in Bothwell's arms again, so different from Henry with his weakness, his vacillation and his slyness. He had never been right for her in bed . . . even here, on the eve of battle, she could tremble at the thought of Bothwell's caresses.

She thought of bed often, of being in bed with Barney. He was right for her, not as rough and demanding as Bothwell, nor weak like Darnley, so right, she repeated the words as she reached the entry to Ruth's flat. Her thoughts had carried her almost to the door.

But as she went up the stairs slowly, it brought back to her that frightened dash she had made a year ago, how she had sped fleet-footed back along the way she had come through the early morning stillness, just as the queen must have fled from the battlefield. Now she realised that it would have been more sophisticated to have got in touch with Ruth long before this, to have turned up at the library as cool as cucumber, treated the whole thing as a joke. It was no good looking sophisticated if you didn't act in the same way.

The main door she remembered with its panel of old Glasgow glass with its Art Deco women and the trailing acanthus leaves. She had said to Barney that she would like to find a flat with stained glass in the door and windows, it appealed to her sense of style, but Barney had said he liked everything modern, especially the bathroom, gold taps and white furry bathmats. And white-painted furniture for the bedroom and the lounge, as he called it, lots of lamps with tassels, and lots of mirrors. Not many ornaments, but a china bowl with heaped china fruit looked good.

Sarah pictured herself shopping in the furniture showrooms near Charing Cross, choosing cool dark woods, eau-de-nil carpeting, silk curtains of the same colour, 'toning rather than contrast' she had tried to impress on Barney, but he had laughed and said she was an odd little girlie, a bit too subdued.

And he had been strangely silent when she had spoken about the wedding although she had said she preferred it quiet, no retinue of bridesmaids, nor those tiny trainbearers tripping over her train . . . she lifted the heavy brass knocker and let it fall, feeling the trembling again, and hoping that when she took off her gloves the solid brilliance of her ring would supply the confidence she lacked. A strange woman opened the door, a woman with a loud hard voice and black hard hair and dangling earrings. 'Yes?' she said, staring at Sarah with bullet eyes.

'Isn't Ruth at home?' In spite of the confidence that she had drummed up, Sarah's voice trembled. The woman was still staring at her. 'Maybe it's a bad time to call, Saturday afternoon? She's maybe shopping? Or even doing an extra shift at the library? I know they have these extra shifts . . .'

'Are you a friend of hers?' The woman interrupted.

'I . . . was.'

The woman nodded, her expression not so much softening as becoming less hard. 'Was.' She repeated the word as if sampling it for her approval. 'Come in,' she said abruptly and stood aside, holding the door wide, and then, pushing in front of Sarah in the dark hall said, 'This way,' and led her into a bright lounge, it could only be called a 'lounge' in all its splendour of garish flower pictures – who would have thought sunflowers could look so fierce – its small tables loaded with photographs in silver frames, its glowing gas fire intensified by a shining aluminium reflector. It was a far cry from Ruth's dark exotic interior. 'Have a seat,' the woman said. Sarah lowered herself into the arms of a plump velvet armchair, the seat buttoned down as if to restrain its exuberance. She loosened her Liberty scarf, peeled off the white doeskin gloves and let the ring in all its radiance escape.

'Thank you,' she said. And, looking up at the woman, 'Are you a friend of hers, Mrs . . . ?'

'Rowan,' the woman said. 'Like the trees. No, I'm not a friend. I never knew her. We got the offer of the flat from the factor at a cheap rent and we jumped at it. He couldn't let it. It was bigger than we wanted, but it was a chance for Tom and me. We couldn't turn it down.' She paused, and sat down abruptly on a hard chair as if it was her natural element, although the twin of Sarah's held out its inviting arms. 'And neither of us minded.'

'Minded?' Sarah was puzzled. 'It's a nice road, handy for the shops and the tram . . . ?'

'Minded that she had committed suicide.' She sat back to watch the effect on Sarah as if she was expecting to enjoy it. 'I could see you didny know,' she said with satisfaction.

'Committed suicide?' Sarah repeated the words. 'No, I didn't know. I hadn't been visiting . . .' She felt sick with the shock, closed her eyes for a second, then took out a handkerchief from her handbag and held it to her mouth to hide the tremor.

'They kept it out of the papers, the factor told me. With her working in a library near here they wouldny want people put off borrowing books, and that . . .'

'How was she . . . found?' Sarah took the handkerchief away from her mouth.

'Through the library, the factor telt us. She didny turn up for two days and they got the polis to break in. She was in the bath. She had cut her wrists, he said, and the water was dyed pink – that made it more gruesome, like, being dyed pink.'

'I . . . can't believe it.' Sarah was beginning to get a hold on herself. 'I'm sorry. I would have come if . . .'

'Well, you weren't to know, were you? Was she a close friend?' Her interest seemed almost clinical.

'No, not close.' Sarah swallowed. 'I met her in the library. That was all . . . I had a book . . .' She indicated the parcel on her lap.

The woman nodded. 'There was a letter, the factor telt us, but he didn't know where it went. The polis maybe kept it.' Thank God I never wrote, Sarah thought. 'As far as he knew there was nothing incrim . . .' she had another go, 'nothing incriminating in it. Like names and that. My guess was that she had been jilted by some man. It's always the same thing. If they only realised that there's none of them worth it.' An impatient look suddenly took over and she stood up. 'I'm meeting ma hubby in the Ca'Doro at four. We always have wur teas there on Saturday afternoon when he's finished his work. Brechin's, the butchers. Makes a break. Then the pictures afterwards.' She nodded. 'Sets you up.'

'I'm keeping you.' Sarah stood, hoping she wouldn't feel dizzy. Barney had said she shouldn't drink because with a head like hers anything could set her off.

She went slowly down the stairs after the woman had shown her out. 'Any roads, one yin's loss is another yin's gain,' she had said, with the first sign of pleasure she had shown. Sarah had thought of asking, 'But you didn't mind?' except that it was evident she didn't. She and her husband had got the flat and she had soon eradicated all signs of Ruth.

In the bathroom . . . Would there be a pink tideline where the dyed pink water had reached? For two days Ruth had lain in it. All pink . . . And had the policeman and a colleague to place themselves at either end and lift her, limp and lifeless . . . she felt so sick at the Pollokshaws entrance to the park that she had to turn in and walk to the boating pond where she sat for a long time. Boy-men, sailing boats. Their sons looking on sulkily . . . she wasn't to blame, was she?

Chapter Nineteen

1924

Sarah was in the work-room arranging for alterations to be made to a suit which Mrs de Vere had bought last year, and which she now found rather tight. Mrs de Vere spent a large part of her time either sitting in her limousine or sitting at committee meetings, but Sarah had said, tactfully, that it could be made more 'comfortable'.

'All it needs is to be released at the armholes and waist,' she had said. 'You grow into a Charles et Cie suit, that's the beauty of them. The basic cut is there, and perfection can be easily obtained. We all alter from time to time.'

'You don't look as if you do, Sarah,' the lady in question had said. 'You're as slim as a reed, and twice as tactful.' There were no flies on Mrs de Vere, Sarah thought, smiling. 'Look, my dear, why not bring it back to me next Saturday and stay overnight? I could do with some younger company. Ronald is still in Egypt with his men, playing at soldiers.'

'That would be very nice. I'd like that. Thank you,' Sarah had said.

She had been surprised but strangely pleased. She had always liked Mrs de Vere, and it was flattering to think that she seemed to feel the same. She, unlike Mrs de Vere, felt the need for *older* company, not someone like Miss Frobisher who was immersed in her own affairs, but a woman of the world, which she felt instinctively Mrs de Vere was. And someone who lived a totally different life from her, who had a different viewpoint. She might even be able to help her with her problem . . .

'Yes, I can easily have it ready,' Minnie said. Her expression was bright this morning. Usually she looked tired and wan, and her cheerfulness seemed forced. Sarah knew that the last thing Minnie wanted was to be labelled as a 'Greetin' Teenie'.

'You look chirpy,' Sarah said. 'Have you come into a fortune?'

'No such luck, but I've got some good news, that's why. There's a cousin of my mother's coming to Glasgow this month and she's volunteered to take over for a week and let me have a holiday.'

'That's great! She must be an understanding soul. Where does she come from?'

'Perth. Yes, she is. She nursed her own husband for years and she says she knows what it's like. But she says only for a week, she's no angel.'

'Well, she's got a good heart.'

'I was wondering if you would like to come with me, Sarah? We get on well together and maybe you would be glad to get away from your folks?' She looked hopefully at her.

Sarah's heart fell. She had waited all this year for Barney to suggest a holiday together, but every time she tentatively raised the subject there had been a cast-iron reason why it was impossible, his mother was poorly again, there was a leather show at Harrogate . . . she had tried to hide her hurt.

'I'd really like that, Minnie,' she said, 'but it's Barney. We've talked about getting away together, but every time we try to arrange it his mother is ill, or he has another show to attend. Something always stops him.'

'Like what exactly?' Minnie's eyes were on her.

'I've told you. Work, or his mother . . .'

'Nothing's impossible if you want it badly enough. Forget it, Sarah.' She shrugged. 'It was just an idea. I'll go up and see some of my cousins in Perth. Anything would be a break.'

'I'm really sorry, Minnie. I would like a trip to the Clyde coast, for instance. I could have gone with Mary and John and the kids, but . . . tell you what, I'll talk it out with Barney and let you know definitely after Sunday. He's meeting me off the train from Helensburgh. I've been asked by Mrs de Vere to stay overnight.'

'Well, maybe that's more in your line.' Minnie was carefully putting the suit into a cotton cover. Customers' property was treated with respect at Charles et Cie.

'I'll definitely let you know by Monday.'

'It's all right. Don't put yourself out . . .'

Annie came rushing in, breaking up the conversation. 'She's looking for you, Miss Lane.'

'Thank you. You mean Miss Frobisher?' Annie was proving difficult to train. 'Not "she". I won't forget,' she said to Minnie and hurried out of the work-room, feeling miserable, and for the first time also a slow anger against Barney. Minnie was right in what she had inferred. Barney was adept at making excuses. Everything could be shelved, even marriage. The anger was now directed towards herself. They were engaged, weren't they? Why were they unable to make plans for the future? Why didn't she insist?

'Oh, Miss Lane?' Miss Frobisher's voice rang out across the salon when she went in. She was obviously annoyed.

'Yes?' She hurried forward.

'Where have you been? There's a client in the fitting room. Lady Boyd!' she hissed, 'and she insists that only you can help her to make up her mind. I didn't expect to have to search the place for you.'

'I'm sorry. I was in the work-room seeing to Mrs de Vere's alterations.'

'"Miss *Lane*, please," she said when I offered my services.' Mrs de Vere's requirements couldn't hold a candle to those of Lady Boyd's.

'I know her little ways, Miss Frobisher.' Sarah was placating. 'Is it the private fitting room?'

'Of course.' The lady was still angry, either at the delay or the slight to herself.

But, later, when they had both bade Lady Boyd good afternoon and Sarah had entered the amount of her purchases in the day book, Miss Frobisher softened.

'Very satisfactory, Sarah. She only came in for an afternoon dress. Very satisfactory indeed.'

'I showed her some of our new acquisitions. She fell in

146

love with the blue Lanvin with the one-sided drape, and the nutria-trimmed coat. She's going to London soon.'

'I have to admit you're good with her. She can be . . .' Miss Frobisher never said anything which could be repeated.

'I expect it's because I make sure she chooses what suits her,' and rewarded by Miss Frobisher's approving look she said, casually, 'Have you any news of Nessie these days?'

'Yes, as a matter of fact I had a letter from her this morning.' Miss Frobisher pursed her lips in a pleased manner. 'She's thinking of coming home – just for a holiday, of course.'

'With her husband?'

'No. I'm beginning to think . . . of course if you marry someone of a different nationality . . .'

'Of course,' Sarah said, trying to fill in the gaps. 'But it must be . . . exciting.' Miss Frobisher looked at her.

'You don't go into marriage for the *excitement*. With my dear husband and myself it was . . . cloth.' Sarah prevented her eyes widening. 'There was no greater thrill than to feel a fine piece of cloth between your fingers. We both agreed on that.' For some reason Sarah thought of Barney's hand on her breast. Once he had kneaded her nipple between finger and thumb, and she had felt the same sensation as that time in the kitchen with John. She felt colour rise to her cheeks, but fortunately Miss Frobisher was speaking.

'It's this Saturday you go to see Mrs de Vere, isn't it?'

'Yes. She's asked me to stay overnight. I accepted. I didn't think you would object.'

'I think it is a great honour. She probably thinks of it as a kindness. Weekends must be dull for girls like you.' Sarah's eyes opened and closed. She swallowed.

'Probably,' she said. Miss Frobisher had lost the capacity to make her angry a long time ago. Besides, she had never told her of her engagement, nor worn her ring in the salon. The only person she had taken into her confidence had been Minnie, and she had asked her to keep it a secret. She would make up her mind before she went to Helensburgh whether she would wear it there or not.

She felt shy, and yet was looking forward to the visit. She

147

needed to get away from Glasgow, to look at her problem from a different light. She recognised in Mrs de Vere a woman of intellect. That was what a good education did for you, made you broad-minded, not prejudiced, as Mary could be. There must be a word to describe someone like Mrs de Vere. Sarah had let her reading slide since she had met Barney. That was a thing she might discuss with Mrs de Vere, and no doubt she would be able to advise her on her choice of books.

One thing, she assured herself, travelling back to Millbrae Road that evening, unlike her weekend spent with Ruth Crosbie, she was certain she would be given a room to herself.

Mrs de Vere put her immediately at ease when she was shown into the drawing room by the housekeeper of few words, as Sarah thought of her. 'How nice of you to spare the time to come and see me,' her hostess greeted her, holding out her hand. 'Come and sit down and have some tea.' And to the housekeeper, 'Will you see Miss Lane's things are put in the rose room, Mrs Mason, please.'

'I brought your suit,' Sarah said from the comfortable sofa where she had been installed. 'It's in the hall.'

'Please put it in my room.' Mrs de Vere spoke to the house-keeper who was still there. 'I'll see to it later. And while you're here,' she poured a cup of tea, 'would you pass that to Miss Lane, please? She must be in need of it.' Sarah accepted the tea from Mrs Mason, whose face was expressionless. 'And a piece of your delicious Dundee cake, Mrs Mason. There, that's fine. You can go, thank you.'

Sarah put down the cup, saucer and plate with the cake on an adjacent table and drew off her gloves. Her ring winked reassuringly at her. Mrs de Vere didn't miss its brilliance even from a few feet away.

'What a beautiful ring! A solitaire, I see. I didn't know you were engaged, Miss Lane. May I wish you every happiness.' There was an immediate doubt in Sarah's mind. Did etiquette dictate that gloves be kept on? But Mrs de Vere was smiling kindly at her.

'Thank you. I don't usually wear it at work, but I thought, since this was a visit . . .' How easy it was to talk here, to feel at ease. It must be the gracious room with its wide windows giving on to the loch and Mrs de Vere's geniality.

'A friendly visit. I'm surprised your fiancé spared you. I'm greatly honoured.'

'He's away a lot. Actually he's been in Birmingham for the best part of a week, but he'll meet me off the train tomorrow.'

'He's in business?'

'Yes, he's well up in Bowie's.' Well established, she realised, would have been better. 'Since Mr Bowie retired, Barney has more or less taken over from him, visiting important customers and suchlike.'

'Well, there will be nothing to stop you from being married soon? Do try Mrs Mason's Dundee cake or she'll be disappointed.' Sarah nibbled, thinking that it was stodgy compared with Mary's, who if she said it herself was a dab hand at Dundee cakes. And black bun at the New Year.

'There's his mother. He lives with her, and she doesn't keep very well.'

'Ah, a demanding mother. Don't I know them! Pay no attention to her. Tell your . . . ?'

'Barney.'

'Barney, to flee the nest. I'm all for sons not hanging around their mothers. Thank goodness Ronald has the army. He would have been quite happy pottering around here. His father was the same, only in his case it was the navy.' Sarah sipped her tea with lemon appreciatively. She had opted for it when Mrs de Vere had offered her that or milk. It was a new experience.

'I thought we might have a stroll in the garden after tea, then come in and dress for dinner. That would give you a chance to come to my room to see that the suit fits, although I'm sure it will.'

'I'd love to see your garden. Barney prefers city life, shops, streets, restaurants, but my dream of delight would be to have a cottage at the coast' – she didn't like to say, 'a house like this', – 'and grow things.'

'It's a sad fact that we often marry men with whom we have little in common. Such a pity the other thing gets in the way when we're young.' Sarah didn't dare ask Mrs de Vere what 'the other thing' was, but she wasn't born yesterday as Annie at Charles et Cie said often, usually when she was recounting her outings with the current boyfriend. 'More tea, Miss Lane?'

'No, thank you, I've had a sufficiency.' Somehow that was wrong. Sarah got up and walked to the window to hide her embarrassment. 'What a lovely view. And, oh, look, yachts! It must be a race. Isn't the water choppy? Short little waves and sparkly on the top. And the sky's the same colour, with no sparkle. Leaden. It looks like rain.'

'It often looks like rain here,' Mrs de Vere said. 'Or it rains. A sunny day has to be welcomed with open arms. Yes, there's a race every Saturday. My husband was very keen.'

'Wasn't your son?' Sarah turned to her.

'No, horses. Nothing but horses. He didn't like the vagaries of the weather, he said. We sold the yacht after my husband died.'

'What was it called?' Sarah went back to her seat, still feeling thoroughly at ease.

'*Marina*. Very apposite. I've often thought what a pretty name it would make for a girl. But I didn't have any.' She smiled at Sarah. 'I expect that's what you look forward to with your Barney, a home and babies.'

'I think every girl does.' She wouldn't talk about the problem. It would be *infra dig*, as Miss Frobisher sometimes said. Besides, Mrs de Vere had given her an answer without realising it when she said that women often married men with whom they had little in common because of the other thing. *That* was what was making her want to be married. Actually she and Barney didn't see eye to eye about furnishings, but although she knew that was trivial, it might be indicative of a deeper lack of harmony. But there was the other thing which got in the way, the urge . . . she even felt, sitting on Mrs de Vere's sofa, a faint pulsing 'down there' when she thought of 'the other thing'.

'Shall we have our stroll in the garden now?' Mrs de Vere suggested, and when Sarah said yes, she'd like that and the tea had been delicious, the only *apposite* word, she registered, Mrs de Vere rang the bell at the side of the fireplace. In a minute or two Mrs Mason appeared, still glum-faced.

'Would you please show Miss Lane to her room, Mrs Mason?' And to Sarah, 'I expect you'd like to freshen up?'

'Oh, yes, thank you. And I'll change my shoes.' Her elegant high heels would not do for a stroll in the garden.

Mrs Mason led the way in silence to the wide staircase. Sarah said from behind her, deploring the gathered skirt over the broad hips, she would have been better with a well-cut flare, 'It's a lovely house, Mrs Mason.'

'Aye, but it takes a lot o' cleaning.' They reached the landing, and, opening one of the doors off it, she waved a hand. 'That's yours. The rose room, they call it.'

'Thank you.' During her years in Charles et Cie Sarah had come across quite a few people like Mrs Mason who refused to be drawn. She had learned to leave it at that. She went in.

It was scarcely rose, she thought, only delicately tinged in the walls, and the curtains were striped pink-and-cream, which she preferred to patterned, with flat, shaped pelmets. The furniture was also to her liking, well-polished and old, not shiny walnut veneer which Barney told her was the latest thing in Bowie's.

She was even more impressed by the adjoining bathroom, her first experience of such a convenience, furnished with everything you could think of down to bath salts. She used the toilet and flushed it with a feeling of simple pleasure. This was right, so right.

'You don't object when I call you Sarah?' Mrs de Vere asked as they strolled between the herbaceous borders.

'I like it,' Sarah said. 'It's like being on holiday here. It's a lovely feeling. They say you never miss what you haven't got but that isn't true. This is my idea of bliss, this garden. Look at those lovely flowers, the blue ones. What are they called?'

'Delphiniums.'

'And those clusters of different-coloured ones?'

'Stocks. Yes, the colours are pretty, aren't they? And the perfume is stronger after the rain. And the nicotiana. In the evening . . . You *should* have a garden. You take so much pleasure in it. Insist on it when you get married.'

She shook her head. 'Barney's the city type. He likes streets, the noise of traffic, restaurants. The rush and bustle. I do too, but it's only temporary because I work there. This would be my choice.'

'But you must have plenty of interests in common. Do you enjoy travelling?'

'I haven't had much opportunity. Barney does. He's always somewhere or other, for two or three days at a time.' Was she grumbling? 'But it's lovely when he comes back.'

'You're right. Make the most of the time when you're together. Convention nowadays . . .' She gazed down the herbaceous border. 'Sometimes you have to catch time by the forelock.' Sarah looked at her. In the soft dusk she imagined she saw for a second a young girl's face. There was the strong clean line of Mrs de Vere's features against the darkening sky, the folds under the chin were invisible, and her hair was richly black and swept back from the pale high forehead, except for a single streak of grey.

When Mrs de Vere turned to her she noticed how beautiful her eyes were, a deep hazel, almost black, the eyebrows highly arched above them. 'I was a girl in Buckinghamshire when I met my husband,' she said. 'A dashing young naval officer. What times we had when he came home on leave! Oh, we were wild! One doesn't see such gaiety nowadays, especially in Scotland. Look at Mrs Mason, for instance. Dour, isn't that the word?'

'She's typical of a certain age,' Sarah said, 'but the salt of the earth. She'll never let you down.'

'True, but she'll never lift me up. Ah, well . . . Our house near Thame was large, the houses where parties were held were the same, there was more opportunity . . .' Sarah saw a faint smile on her face. For what? she wanted to ask.

The only time she and Barney could be together was in the

car, and there was always a need to be back at the flat at a 'respectable' time, so as not to disturb Mary and John. Or the neighbours. 'Do you have lovely gardens in Buckinghamshire?' she asked.

'Oh, yes. The climate is kinder. Walled gardens hot with the sun where the wisteria hung in great purple racemes when we went out to wander there after dinner. In the moonlight, I remember, so often. We had a gazebo at the foot of ours. You could be there for a long time without anyone knowing . . . or bothering.' Her eyes seemed to have a light behind them. 'What bliss! My parents were elderly. They gave us a lot of freedom . . .'

'Life in Glasgow is very circumspect for unmarried girls,' Sarah said, still with the image of that magical gazebo in her mind. 'People watch you.' People like Mrs Mason, she thought, upright, sanctimonious. 'How you behave. And if you live with your parents, or in my case with my sister and her husband, you have to observe the rules, although they've never been spelled out. It's the difference between being a nice girl and a loose one.'

'Oh, that ubiquitous word "nice"!' Mrs de Vere said. 'I don't know what the Scots would do without it. Well, my dear, have you ever considered having a flat of your own?'

'Oh, yes, I've considered it often, but then, since I met Barney I thought . . .' No, she wouldn't mention her problem. 'If I had a flat of my own, Mrs de Vere, I'm afraid it wouldn't be considered . . . well, nice!' They laughed together.

'I'm beginning to understand the mores of a provincial place like Helensburgh.' That was a good word, 'mores', Sarah thought, one she hadn't come across. You could guess easily what it meant. 'We had a flat in Mayfair for the Season. Often our mother didn't want to go up to town. She was busy in the garden, you see. "Why do they have it in the busy season?" she would say. Oh, my sister and I had some fine times she knew not of! Shall we walk on? I'd like you to see the rose garden before it gets dark and takes the colour out of them. There are some lovely rugosas, although I think this part of the Clyde coast can't be beaten for rhododendrons. They're very prolific.'

The evening was very pleasant. Sarah changed into a champagne-coloured dress with a fringed skirt – one which had been especially made for a client in Kilmacolm who couldn't stand herself in it when she tried it on. 'My hips look like Ailsa Craig,' she had said, which Sarah thought was an apt description.

She had looked doubtful when Mrs Robertson had shown her the page in the *Ladies Journal* with a similar gown, had said diplomatically that the style didn't suit everyone. She knew the rumour in the work-room was that Mr Robertson was a ladies' man, and Sarah had wondered if poor Mrs Robertson had wanted to charm him back. However, she thought, putting on her amber necklace – a present from Barney – before the cheval mirror in the rose room, what was one person's loss was another one's gain.

That was what Mrs Rowan had said about Ruth Crosbie's flat. Would that young girl who was now Mrs de Vere have taken Ruth Crosbie in her stride? Probably. Sarah flicked the fringes of the champagne dress to restore her confidence before she went downstairs.

Mrs de Vere, in stately black, presided at the candlelit table, set with silver and glass. Even Mrs Mason's straight mouth as she served dinner didn't spoil Sarah's feeling of pleasure. In any case the atmosphere was enlivened by her husband who poured the wine and was altogether more cheerful. 'A fine claret, this, if I may say so, madam.' He was very stately in his role of butler, like the one Sarah had seen in a film at the Picture House with Barney, only in that one, he had been carrying a picnic hamper followed by a footman with folding chairs. Gloria Swanson in trailing chiffon and wearing a huge straw hat had been walking ahead holding a parasol.

'We may have a run round the loch tomorrow, Mason,' Mrs de Vere informed him, 'then lunch at Shandon. That will give your wife a rest.' And a rest for you too, Sarah thought, looking at the man's attentive expression, and seeing the flicker of relief in his eyes.

'Very good, madam.'

'Then I thought we might let Miss Lane see Hill House before we run her to the station.'

'A nice little trip, madam.' The atmosphere was pleasant, everyone liked everyone else, the food was beautiful, the wine Sarah sipped was mellow, like a ripe peach, she thought, she liked Mrs de Vere so much, smiling warmly at her down the table as she raised her glass.

'To you, Sarah. May I wish you every happiness.'

'Thank you.' She raised hers. 'And may I reciprocate?' She smiled equally warmly at Mrs de Vere and at finding the right word.

'Have you heard of Charles Rennie Mackintosh?' Mrs de Vere asked her.

'I know he helped Miss Cranston with her tearooms.'

'Helped her indeed. I wonder if the good people of Glasgow realise what a treat is in store for them when they decide on the cup that cheers.'

'Mary, my sister, likes the Ca'Doro. My favourite is Fullers in Buchanan Street. I know some of the buyers in the shops there who frequent it.' It was as if her tongue had been oiled.

'You must inveigle them into the Willow tearoom some time, or your Barney.'

'Oh, no, that wouldn't suit him. He likes restaurants. The Rogano is *his* dream of delight.'

'Ah, yes, I begin to see your Barney, a *bon viveur*, not perhaps a man for the fireside. But to go back to Charles Rennie Mackintosh, he built Hill House near here for the Blackie family. You'll see how he has adapted Scottish Vernacular to a contemporary style. I'll be interested to have your reaction.'

'I'm no judge.'

'Don't denigrate yourself, Sarah. You have exquisite taste. Try some of Mrs Mason's cheese soufflé, her inspired cooking is a constant surprise to me and restores my faith in human nature.'

There was no doubt the cheese soufflé was as light as the yachts had looked on the short choppy waves earlier, perhaps she had been wrong about the Dundee cake. 'This wine with the soufflé...!' She looked at Mrs de Vere, smiling. 'Delicious,' she said again. It was such a useful word.

'Yes, it's a fine year, that.' Mrs de Vere examined her glass as if the date was written on the outside.

When it came to herself, there was so much she didn't know, Sarah thought, wine, architecture, gardens, life in general. Mrs de Vere's mind was packed full of knowledge, a lifetime of learning, of living. She was able to live alone and have all those thoughts passing through her mind ... what an interesting life that would be. She would never be lonely. Was that why, if you were like her, and after the excitement of the 'thing' had passed and you were alone, no husband, and virtually no son, you could be quite happy? Because there was still plenty in life and you must stay alive to live it?

Her own mind, if she were truthful, had only two things in it, Barney, and clothes. She must start filling it up. John could help her there, but she didn't want to monopolise his time, or keep him talking in the kitchen when Mary was in bed.

'Could you recommend a book to me, Mrs de Vere, one that you particularly liked?'

The older woman looked smilingly at Sarah, her fork raised like a forefinger. 'Is there anything to beat the pleasure of reading in bed, alone? I hope you indulge yourself there.'

'Yes, I do, not perhaps so much at the moment.' She didn't want to tell Mrs de Vere about Ruth Crosbie, nor indeed did she think she could ever tell anyone about Ruth Crosbie.

'I'll give you a particular favourite of mine before you go upstairs. Edith Wharton's *The Age of Innocence*. An American, rather like Henry James in many ways. I think you'd like it.' Sarah would rather have had one about the age of knowledge, but thanked Mrs de Vere and said she would be very grateful to have it.

'It will keep you entranced,' Mrs de Vere predicted.

It did. But it didn't make her sleepy. Until two o'clock she tossed and turned, her mind a welter of thoughts and impressions, tea at the fire with lemon, the view of the yachts beating into the wind, the garden with the stately delphiniums, the sun-baked wall in the Buckinghamshire garden draped with purple racemes, what a beautiful sound that made, purple racemes, the gazebo where Mrs de Vere sat with her friends for hours in the darkness, or one friend more likely, her flat in town where she went wild with her sister unknown to her parents. Were there no nosey neighbours in Mayfair, or were they all behaving the same?

She began to imagine living in her own flat. It wouldn't be in such a strange, glittering place as Mayfair, but a *nice* flat (sorry, Mrs de Vere), in Hillhead maybe, with a tiled close and a mahogany rail on the stone stairs, old Glasgow glass on her door, freedom to come and go, to read and think, lying back on her own sofa, having Barney to visit her, no need for him to hurry home.

'My own flat . . .' The words were on her lips when she finally slept.

Chapter Twenty

She went running to meet Barney when she saw his tall dapper figure standing at the platform exit. He raised his hat and bent forward to kiss her, but in her enthusiasm she threw her arms round his neck.

'Hold on, girlie,' he said. 'You nearly bowled me over!'

'Sorry!' she said, laughing and disengaging herself. How handsome he was! She saw two girls who had been sitting opposite her in the compartment glance appreciatively at him as they passed. But he was hers!

'Oh, Barney,' she said, 'I've had a lovely time with Mrs de Vere. She has a lovely house and garden!' They were walking through the station concourse towards Gordon Street.

'How about the Central for a bite?' he said, interrupting her and glancing towards the hotel entrance. 'I've had a lovely time too.' And indeed he looked well, she thought, better than he generally did. His skin was glowing, there was a softness about his eyes as he looked at her, a look of love. 'The service is good there. I'll go in and book a table at the Malmaison for eight and we'll have a stroll around until then.'

'That would be nice,' she said. 'I'll wait here.'

When he came out she linked her arm through his as they walked along Gordon Street. 'You look really well.' She had been struck by his appearance as he came out of the hotel, as if there was an aura around him.

'Do I?' His face had settled into its usual playful expression. 'I had a gruelling time in Birmingham but I landed a few good orders. Mr Bowie will be pleased. The Station Hotel there is very good too. No expense spared.' They stopped at the corner, waiting for a space in the passing traffic. The junction at Union Street and Gordon Street was always busy.

'I like Glasgow at this time of the evening,' he said. 'All this hurry and bustle. It excites me,' and when she stole a glance at him she thought he did look excited, his eyes, and there was a flicker at the side of his mouth.

'I told Mrs de Vere that,' she said, 'that you liked . . .'

'Come on!' He put a hand under her elbow and they hurriedly crossed the street. She saw people walking into the Ca'Doro and thought a seat at the window would have been nice, watching the crowds. He said, as they walked along Gordon Street, occasionally stopping to look in the shop windows, 'What did you tell Mrs de Vere?'

'How you liked city life. We walked in her lovely garden and I said this is what I really like, but Barney . . .' Buchanan Street was quieter and they crossed easily into Royal Exchange Square. 'The buildings here . . . !' She felt uplifted, as if Mrs de Vere had given her new eyes. 'Those rows of columns, I think they're called classical, and that . . . gracious tower with the clock . . . I wonder who the man is on horseback? I wish I knew more about things. I think inside is the Stirling Library . . .' She looked at Barney. He seemed slightly impatient.

'We'd better walk back,' he said. 'I wanted to have a look at Wylie & Lochhead, but I don't think there's time.'

'No,' she said, turning obediently. 'It's almost too nice to go inside.' She tried to match his long steps. 'That's what I liked about Helensburgh, the air was fresh on my face. It was good even although the sun didn't shine much. And we went to Shandon Hydro for lunch.'

'You had lunch at Shandon Hydro?' Barney exclaimed, looking, she imagined, slightly envious.

'Yes, we didn't eat much either of us, but we talked a lot. Isn't it odd how two women, from different walks of life and different ages, can strike up such a rapport?'

Barney was busy guiding her across the busy corner again, past the Central Station entrance and the row of taxis. He didn't speak. When they were going through the Hope Street entrance to the restaurant he said to her, 'Clothes.'

'Clothes?' Sarah surrendered her light coat to an attentive

waiter. Another one guided them to a table, drew out a chair for her and unfurled her napkin. An outsized menu was handed to each of them.

'Yes, clothes,' Barney repeated. 'She probably wanted you to knock a bit off the price for her.'

She was surprised at him. 'No, it was nothing like that. Except when she tried on her suit we didn't talk about clothes at all. We talked about . . . life.'

'Life?' He looked at her over his menu. 'What is there about life to talk about?' And without turning his head to the waiter who was standing behind him, 'Go away, George. We haven't made up our minds yet.'

'Certainly, sir, take your time.'

As usual Barney studied the menu carefully. Wine and food were important to him. At Shandon Hydro Mrs de Vere had said, 'Do you know what I would like, Sarah? An omelette.'

'That would suit me fine,' Sarah had said. 'I hate to feel full up.' Mrs de Vere had lifted her hand and the waiter appeared, just like that.

'Is the asparagus fresh, Thomas?'

'Yes, madam. I can vouch for it,' he had said.

'Do you like asparagus soup, Sarah?' And when she had said she did, Mrs de Vere had given the order, 'Soup and an omelette for two. Fresh hot rolls. And a half bottle of my usual red.' To Sarah, 'We don't want too much at lunchtime, just a glass with the omelette.' Sarah had nodded, agreeing. Barney was inclined to keep filling her glass along with his own.

Now it was Barney in command, she thought. Mrs de Vere had consulted her, Barney never did. 'I'd like fish,' she announced.

'Fish?' He looked at her, eyebrows raised. 'I was going to let you try their roast saddle of mutton. And they have a good claret to go with it.'

'You have that, then,' she said, 'I'll stick to fish.' He looked at her, drawing in his breath, and then his face relaxed in a smile. 'Well, my girlie must have just what she wants.' George was summoned, halibut was ordered for her – she would rather have had plaice but she had shot her bolt, the mutton for Barney. 'Just as you like it, sir,' George said, 'slightly underdone.' The halibut, Barney assured her, as if in recompense, would have a rich, creamy sauce. She thought wistfully of the omelette she had eaten with Mrs de Vere. But she was happy.

'I missed you, darling,' she said. She felt shy saying 'darling', but she didn't like 'dear' – all the shopgirls called you that – and 'sweetie' reminded her of an American ragtime song she had heard, all about a sweetie who was hard to please. Her glass of sauvignon blanc made her bold ... 'I miss you more and more every time you go away. Now that we're engaged I want to be with you all the time.'

'Me too.' He nodded, and, sadly, 'If it weren't for Mother ...'

'How is she?' She had to ask.

'Complaining about my being away. I always have to placate her, bring her something, the way I do for you.'

'You don't have to placate me.' There was a touch of Miss Lane of Charles et Cie in her voice.

'Of course not. It's a pleasure. Guess what I've brought you this time?' He was playful, charming, and she shook her head, smiling at him, her own boy. That was the first time she had thought of him like that. It was just right. But she didn't feel comfortable receiving presents. She wished she could enthuse, say, 'Ooh!', the way Annie did.

She preferred the little soapstone Buddha he had given her some time ago, a sample, he said. Who would want that? But she had. It fitted the palm of her hand. She kept it on her dressing table and often she lifted it, cupping it between her hands. She thought of it as a talisman.

This time it was a sugar sifter in a box, crystal with a silver screw top, it looked like something she had seen in Samuel's shop window. 'For your bottom drawer,' he said, and she said how lovely it was, and wasn't it beautifully engraved, and the silver, it dazzled your eyes.

'For strawberries and cream in summer,' she said. 'Mrs de Vere says they have a glut every year and that I must come back and share them.'

'Mrs de Vere, Mrs de Vere,' he mocked gently. There was a fleck of brown gravy at the corner of his mouth, but as if he saw her glance, he wiped it off with his napkin.

'I'm sorry,' she said. 'It's just such a change for me not being at the flat with Mary and John, and in such lovely surroundings. If you had seen the water, Barney, those little choppy waves, and the yachts kind of dancing over it . . .'

He tapped the menu he was studying. 'Supposing you concentrate on your sweet?' Mrs de Vere said 'pudding', which must be right, but she wouldn't correct him. And when they were spooning their chocolate parfait, he looked up and said, 'When we're in the car, I want to have a serious talk with you.'

'Do you?' she said, trying to hide her delight.

She refused coffee, hoping he would do the same, but he took his time over it, had a brandy and a large cigar which the waiter deferentially lit for him.

It was ten o'clock when they parked on the hill leading to Cathkin Brae, at the side of the entrance to a large house hidden in the trees.

'We haven't a great deal of time,' Sarah said. 'It will be after eleven at least when we get back.'

'Don't fuss, girlie,' he said, putting his arm round her. The rich smell of his cigar was in her nostrils. 'I've been thinking . . .'

'What have you been thinking?' she asked, stemming her eagerness. It was about getting married, of course. He had decided to do something about his mother. At a pinch, she would offer to have her. She might not be as difficult as he said, and if they had a fairly large house she could have her own room.

'City types like us . . . I've a proposition to make. After all, you're a big girl now . . .' Her heart fell, it felt sore, a sad soreness under her ribs.

'What is it, Barney?' she said, and then, 'No, kiss me first.' She raised her mouth. His head came down, his lips were moist, one hand on her breast was fondling it, starting up the pulse, making her quiver under his mouth. 'Love me, love

162

me.' She didn't know if he heard her. He raised his head, sighing.

'I'm daft about you, Sarah, your sweetness. If I looked for a hundred years . . .'

'I feel the same, my darling . . .' Her hand caressed the back of his head, she felt the smoothness of the brilliantined hair under it.

'I've told you about Mother, but not everything. Before I went to Birmingham, I told her I was thinking about getting married, and she went into some kind of faint . . .'

'But why? We could have her too if she feels that badly . . .' She pressed her body against his and she thought he groaned.

'It's a shame . . .' he muttered.

The pulsing was stronger now, she wanted, wanted . . . 'Why is she like that?' she said. 'Most mothers . . .'

'It's because she's ill. She can't bear to have me leave her,' his voice was flat, 'and I can't bear to be without you, Sarah. It's an . . .' 'Impasse,' she thought. There was a word for everything. 'Sarah,' he said, his voice was low. 'Why don't we get a flat, share it, until I persuade . . . ?'

She ignored the implication at first. 'Maybe if I went to see her . . . ?'

'No, that would finish it. But to begin with, a flat for us where we could meet comfortably instead of this hole-and-corner affair.'

'People would talk.'

'It's only because it's Glasgow. Provincial, narrow-minded, conventional . . .'

'Conventional mores,' Sarah said, thinking of Mrs de Vere. She pulled away from him, waited until she had steadied her voice. 'It's really Mary I'm worried about, you see. She's been like a mother to me since our own mother died. John's different. He doesn't care what people think, that is, individuals. It's society at large he's interested in. He's a law unto himself. Except that he would never go against Mary.'

'Are you sure?' Barney said.

'Yes, she's the mother of his children. Family life is sacrosanct to him.' She found the right words came to her more easily now, it was a question of practice, and reading.

'Are you sure he wouldn't be sorry on his own account? That he's always fancied you?'

'Barney!' She pulled back from him. 'I don't like that remark.' She heard her voice, shrill, splitting the darkness in the car.

'Sorry, girlie. Just a wee joke.' Watch your mouth, she wanted to say to him, like a woman in a pub, or 'Watch your gob', if it was a pub with sawdust on the floor. She was surprised at her swift anger, and tried to placate him.

'Mary's different from what she was. She's grown like my mother. When she was a young girl she was quite a tearaway. Of course she had an awful anxious time during the war. She's very stoical, but she worried herself sick about John. It's part of the scheme of things, isn't it, when you're married, to worry about your husband, and yet it's natural, marriage . . .' She realised as she was speaking that she was making a mistake talking about marriage. She felt him move restlessly beside her. She tried to be playful. 'Not that I'm hinting, of course . . .' She heard her false laugh and was ashamed.

'I'll come straight out with it, Sarah.' She could feel him tense beside her, his straightness. 'As I've said often before, Mother is the stumbling block. I feel just like you do that we ought to be together, and this is my suggestion . . .' He paused. Was he afraid to ask her outright to have his mother with them? 'I don't mind . . .' but it was lost. 'So,' his voice was firm, the firmness he used when he was assuring a customer that what he was selling to them was *absolutely genuine and of the best quality*, she had heard him with Miss Frobisher, 'supposing we find a place, a private place where we can be together . . . for the time being . . .'

'You mean, not tell her?'

'Yes, for the time being. I could stay with you as often as possible. After all, I do leave her alone when I have to go off on my trips. I employ a good woman to take care of her . . .'

'We could have a secret marriage,' she said. She hated the feeling inside her, of a supplicant. That was not the Miss Lane of Charles et Cie, respected by customers, sometimes by Annie, nor indeed was it the Sarah Lane who had spent an enjoyable stay with Mrs de Vere of Helensburgh, two women of the world with mutual interests.

But then, Mrs de Vere despised the conventional morality of the provincial town. Hadn't she said so? She'd had a wild time in London with her sister when they were young, and in the gazebo in the Buckinghamshire garden. She had probably thrown her cap over the windmill many times.

'Marriages are never secret,' Barney was saying, 'however hard you try. What I'm suggesting, Sarah, is an in-between stage, just till I get her used to the idea of someone taking her place. I know I'm partly to blame letting her rule the roost when I was younger. But when my father died we had only each other . . .'

'I can see that,' Sarah said, 'but it's unhealthy to cling to a son. Anyone would tell her that.' It was Mrs de Vere speaking.

'That's the theory, girlie, but think of a lonely frail woman. Put yourself in her place.' 'She could have got herself up and going.' Sarah could hear Mary's brisk voice in her ears. When their parents had died so suddenly it was Mary's stoicism which had supported them. She it was who had got them up and going. 'We've lost a good father and mother,' she had said, 'but the last thing they would have wanted would have been to see us unable to cope . . .'

'Mary would kill me,' she said.

'Look here.' He was strangely masterful, taking her in his arms. 'Who do you love? Me or Mary?'

'It's different.' The rich smell of the cigar he had smoked hung between them. 'Mary's like a mother to me . . .' Suddenly she felt herself melting into him. 'But you're my boy . . .' That's what he was when you got right down to it, her own dear boy. What was she quibbling about? They loved each other. Marriage was not possible just now. Why shouldn't she have a flat of her own where Barney could visit her occasionally? It was as simple as that.

'All I want,' he said, kissing her, soft sweet little kisses all over her face, 'is to share a cosy little nest with you where I could come as often as I could manage, say, two or three times each week, until such times . . .' his voice tailed off, 'and you in it so neat and pretty amongst our own things, nice china and glass – I can get it wholesale from Bowie's, good food and wine – I could bring a bottle when I came . . .' He noticed her silence, and drew her close so that their cheeks were together, the way dancers did the tango. 'I've worked it out and the way I see it is that I would be able to tell her fairly soon . . .'

'That we were getting married?' You never miss a chance, do you? She hated herself.

'That's exactly what I do mean.' He wrapped his arms closely round her, swaying slightly backwards and forwards as if it were they who were doing the tango. 'Just think of it, you and me in our wee home together . . .' Jack Buchanan, she thought. My boy sees himself as Jack Buchanan.

And she knew that for ever and ever he was her boy, her own dear boy, so playful, so captivating, so loving, ruled by his mother, certainly, but if they had a place together and she made it really comfortable and inviting, it would give him the courage to tell his mother that he wanted to get married and his mother would see the joy in his face and say, 'All right, son.'

'All right, Barney,' she said.

Chapter Twenty-one

When she went into the flat John was busy with papers although it was close to midnight. 'Hello, Sarah,' he greeted her. 'Mary's gone to bed.'

'Wasn't she at her sewing bee?' This was a recent ploy of Mary's. They had collared her at the church and induced her to join.

'Oh, aye. When she came in she said her eyes were tired, but if you ask me it's her tongue that's tired. When they women get together they're like a load of chattering monkeys.'

'Well,' she laughed, 'you don't talk a great lot, John.'

'That's true enough. I'm poor company at times. But since Ramsay MacDonald came in it's been nothing but strikes, railways, dockers, trams, shipyards, miners. It all affects Dixon's. Any increase in their wages, if they're lucky, is offset by the cost of living. You have to be a philosopher, or better still, a historian.'

'What's the rumour about MacDonald accepting a Daimler? Is it true?'

'Aye, it is. It's on the records. Power corrupts. And thirty thousand pounds' worth of shares in McVitie and Price's to run it. Running it on biscuits, eh?' He laughed. 'Who said I didn't talk enough?'

'Maybe it's not Mary's kind of talk.'

'I'll remember that.' He looked at her, smiling, his lean face seared by the deep lines on either side of his mouth. 'Where did you get to tonight?'

'We went to the Central Hotel. The Malmaison.'

'My, he does you proud, that Barney! What's it like? I've never been in it, nor likely to be at those prices!'

'You pay for service, and, I expect, the best meat in Scotland. Barney likes a good tuck-in.'

'And a dram to follow, I daresay.'

'That's it, John.' She went on, before her courage failed her, 'I'm thinking of getting a flat of my own.'

His eyes were direct. 'Is this Mr Turnbull's idea?'

She was stung. 'No, it's mine, mostly. You've got your family growing up. I love them dearly as you know, but I think I should go.'

'I see.' His eyes were still on her.

'Do you not like Barney?'

'He's affable enough. I just wonder . . . he's well-off, isn't he?'

'He lives well, yes.'

'You know people will talk.'

Sarah flushed. 'I don't care about them. It's Mary. She thinks she's been given a special dispensation to look after me. You know that.'

'I know that.' He looked at her squarely. 'You're fond of him?'

'More than fond. You should know how you feel about Mary. I want that for myself, what you've got.' She met his eyes. He knows what I'm thinking . . . that morning when I ran away from Ruth Crosbie's flat.

'I should go ahead,' he said. 'It's your life, Sarah. There's nothing to keep either of you . . .'

'There's his mother. She's being very difficult. That's what keeps him from marrying, you see.' It sounded feeble. For a moment she was Miss Lane of Charles et Cie, shrewd, evaluating . . .

'And he's thirty-five?'

'Maybe a bit of a mother's boy, but that's in his favour.'

'A soft heart? You should know.' His eyes seemed to see through into her skull.

'And you'll break the ice for me with Mary?'

'She's no' a dragon. She's got a loving heart, but, yes, I'll break the ice for you.'

'I'll miss you both, and our talks.'

'You're part of us, and there's always a place for you, well, it's your place as well. Tell him from me he's to take good care of you.' His eyes held hers.

'I'll tell him.' She wanted to weep, to weep with him. Why should she when she was so happy? 'I'm for off, then,' she said.

'Have a good sleep.' She saw him with clear eyes, the tired face, and loved him, a different love than she had for Barney, deeper . . .

'What's this I'm hearing from John?' Mary said to her the following evening when she had put the children to bed. Her face was stern. Sarah might have known. She didn't like the idea. 'He was telling me about your intentions.' Intentions, Sarah thought. At least she was accepting it.

'I'm glad he broke the ice.' She sat down at the kitchen table, inwardly shaking. 'Did they go to sleep all right tonight?' Sometimes the children went mad, chasing each other, shrieking, for half an hour or more. She called it 'letting them have their win' oot'.

'Aye, I told them I was havin' no nonsense.' She's got them tamed too, Sarah thought, meeting her sister's eyes. Here I go. She remembered how as a little girl Mary had taken her to the public swimming baths, and when she had stood teetering at the edge she had pushed her in.

'Mary,' she said, 'I've been feeling for some time now that I'm getting in yours and John's way. You've been very good to me including me in everything you do, holidays, your friends, but it's not right.'

'I promised our mother I'd look after you.' Mary was wary, lips pressed together.

'I know that, and you've been the soul of kindness, but Mother wouldn't think I'd still be on your hands now, a drag on you. Barney says . . .' That was a mistake.

'It's Barney Turnbull that's put you up to this.' For the first time she saw clearly the dislike of him in Mary's eyes. She didn't like him because he hadn't talked of marriage. She had never said it, but it was in her every tone, every gesture. 'All those expensive presents,' she had once said disparagingly. What she meant was that if he could afford them he could afford to get married.

'We're engaged, don't forget,' Sarah flared with an unusual burst of temper. 'I can surely do what I like at my age! I've got a responsible job, I'm paid well, you've never even taken half of what it needs to keep me . . . besides, I want to entertain my own friends, be independent.'

'Unmarried women don't set up on their own in Glasgow. You know that well enough. It doesn't look nice. People talk . . . And,' she looked aggrieved, 'you know I've never stopped you having your friends from the shop, Minnie, as often as she can come, or church people. I've gone out of my way for them . . .'

'But not Barney.'

'I did so invite him. But he's away a lot, and besides,' her face softened, 'well, I get anxious about you, your future. I'm frightened I'd say too much. John's warned me.'

'I know you mean it for the best, Mary, but I've made up my mind.' She got up. 'Barney's picking me up outside. I'll be late.'

'That's another thing. He never comes up for you, like . . .'

'Like what?' Like other people.

'Oh, forget it. It's my big mouth again. On you go. I'll have cooled down when you . . .'

'Mammy!' It was Lachie. 'I want a drink of water . . .' A well-known ploy. The two women's glances met. Sarah smiled and Mary shrugged, then her face twisted to hide a smile as she got up. 'Enjoy yourself,' she said, turning from the kitchen tap as Sarah rose and left the kitchen. Mary could only express love with John, she thought, shutting the outside door quietly behind her. She could hardly see the stone landing for her tears.

Chapter Twenty-two

1925

She thought it would have been easy to find a flat, but summer came and went, and after that there were trips to London with Miss Frobisher for the autumn shows. She was leaving more and more work to Sarah. Nessie was behind it, Sarah thought, but if that was so, her employer was keeping it to herself.

In winter the factors' offices shut at five o'clock, and there was only her lunch hour in which Sarah could call on them. Barney encouraged her in her search, but took no part in it. It seemed that having made the suggestion to share a flat he was leaving it to her to find one.

She had confided in Minnie, which she regretted. 'I'm looking for a flat to rent, Minnie. You'd think it would be easy.'

Minnie had looked up from her sewing machine, her eyebrows raised. 'How did Mary take it?'

'Well, you can guess. She doesn't approve, but she knows she can't stop me.'

'Is it because of Mr Turnbull?'

'I suppose so. I know John has told her to keep off the subject. But I'll be glad to get away. The atmosphere has changed. I imagine even wee Bella looks at me with reproachful eyes.' Her voice broke and she turned away. 'Well, I'd better get back to the salon.' Minnie's voice recalled her.

'I think you're making a mistake, Sarah.'

'Taking a flat? It's not so uncommon. I believe in London girls . . .'

'This isn't London. Besides, it's not the flat. It's the fact that you have a . . . friend. Mary knows people will talk, think the worst.'

All her frustration burst out. 'I like that, Minnie McConachie! Maybe you don't remember telling me that your biggest regret was not . . . giving into your man during the war!' She could have bitten out her tongue.

'That was entirely different!' Minnie's face was red. She slipped the hem of a tweed skirt from under the machine foot, and instead of snipping the sewing thread with scissors, bit through it with her teeth. Mrs Laing's, Sarah registered, one of their most fussy clients. 'It was wartime, he could have been killed any day, and in any case, he was prepared to marry me!'

'And who says Barney won't!'

Annie burst into the work-room followed more sedately by two of the other seamstresses. 'It's your turn for tea, Minnie. Hey, are you two having an argument?'

'You'd be better employed downstairs in the packing room,' Sarah said, her chin high, and to the two women who had quickly taken their places at their machines, 'We'll never get that girl trained!' They smiled, and under the busy whirr as they pedalled, Sarah left the work-room. She felt shaken, and went to the Ladies where she examined her face in the mirror, noticing the tick at the side of her mouth. To splash cold water on it in the hope of calming herself would ruin her makeup. She reapplied her lipstick, patted her hair and went out. If she could have patted her sore heart too, she thought, she would have felt better. Minnie was right.

In the *Evening Citizen* which she read in the tramcar going home, she noticed an article about the great Paris Exhibition of 1925 which was due in April. 'Clean lines, exotic colours,' she read. 'Art Deco is born.' She thought of Mrs de Vere, and her enthusiasm for Charles Rennie Mackintosh. '*Avant garde*,' she had said, 'even a touch of Art Deco.' Perhaps she could introduce a little of the new feeling in the flat when she found it, in cushions and lamps, cut out Barney's predilection for tassels and bows.

And as if her luck had turned, when she came to the Property Section and glanced down the columns, an advertisement in a square box caught her eye. 'Superior flat to rent in Grove

172

Street, two bedroomed, modern bathroom, one up. Immediate occupancy.' It's ours, she thought, somehow I know it's ours.

The factor told her there were several applications already when she called at his office at nine o'clock the next morning. She had decided to risk Miss Frobisher's displeasure for once. She would say the tramcar's trolley bar had broken and she'd had to wait until it was mended. It *had* happened to her once before. It was a white lie. In the end, by giving her business address which clearly impressed him, he handed over the keys if she promised to let him know that day. He couldn't leave his office as his assistant was off with flu.

She saw the flat at lunchtime, a quiet cul-de-sac off Albert Road, liked the bathroom, thought the rest would have to be redecorated before she could live in it, and raced back to the factor's office in Virginia Street. She signed the agreement, paid a month's rent in advance and was given the keys. She was weak with excitement and lack of food for the rest of the day.

Barney seemed surprised that she had succeeded, almost as if he had forgotten that he had proposed the idea.

'Aren't you going to congratulate me?' They were having coffee in the Ca'Doro. He couldn't spare any more time that day.

'You're a clever girlie,' he said, saluting her with his coffee cup. 'Decent ones are as scarce as gold. But it's going to take quite a time to furnish it.'

'Not if you leave it to me,' she said. 'You see, I told Mary quite a time ago and I'm anxious to leave. It's uncomfortable, I can't quite describe it.'

'You're a wee devil when you get started,' he said. She had never thought of herself like that.

'We'll have to talk about finance, Barney. What we can both put towards the furniture, and I'll pay the rent. The flat's in my name.'

'Oh, you shouldn't have done that!' But his eyes looked relieved. 'I'll write you a cheque right away. You go ahead and get it looking nice for us. And don't worry about money.'

His cheque book was already on the table. He bent over it, wrote, then handed a cheque to her, filled in and signed for one hundred pounds.

'Oh, Barney, that's far too much,' she said.

'There's plenty more where that came from, but it'll get you started.'

'Well, thanks very much.' She folded it, thinking that if anyone saw them they would think she was being paid for favours, which in a sense she was. 'And, Barney, would you mind if I don't buy at Bowie's?' She thought of their tassels and bows, their pleated frills. To her surprise he didn't protest and said she must please herself.

Sarah went to the shop she had admired so long, 'Interiors', near Charing Cross, and bought sparingly. She found the clean lines she was looking for, the material in stiff silk for curtains and cushions. The one hundred pounds was swallowed up in no time, and she bought the bed herself. There would be no three-piece suite yet. The antique chest would hold Barney's clothes, the capacious lobby presses in the flat would hold hers. When it was a *fait accompli* she would steel herself and tell Mary.

She dreaded it. Ever since she had told Mary she would be leaving, her sister had been quieter than usual, and she fancied, so had the children, as if she had warned them to be good. 'It's sad,' she told Barney, near to tears, 'I'll miss Lachie and Bella.' And my talks with John. She thought of the quiet kitchen, sitting across the table from him, listening, her eyes on his earnest face, the deep-set eyes with their direct gaze.

'It will be a lot quieter when we're on our own,' Barney said. 'You'll be glad to be rid of these squalling kids.'

'Oh, Barney,' she said reproachfully, but reminded herself he was unused to children. Will it be too quiet, she wondered. She knew she was bad at adapting, disliked change. She had worked in Charles et Cie now for eleven years, had always lived with Mary, and then Mary and John, when he moved in. Perhaps she needed to learn how to be more flexible.

'Have you told your mother?' she asked him.

174

'Oh, yes.' She wondered if it was her imagination that his eyes slid away from hers.

But when he took her in his arms and his hand, surer now, stroked her thigh under her skirt, and her pulses began to race, she knew it was all right. He was and always would be her own dear boy, married or not.

'I've got a flat, Mary,' she said the following morning. 'My things are all packed and I'll send Baxter, the carrier, round for the rest tomorrow, if that's convenient. I'll not be too far away, Grove Street. It's nearer for my work.'

'Well, I see the deed's done.' Mary's face was set. 'So you're leaving right away. No time wasted, eh?'

'It took ages.' Maybe Mary had thought she had dropped the idea. 'I didn't want to bother you with the details until I was fixed somewhere. The stairs I went up and down!' But Mary didn't smile.

'Oh, aye,' she said.

'I'll be back often, and you'll come and see me, and Lachie and Bella and John. It'll be quite fun for the wee ones, Aunty Sarah's house . . .' The look on Mary's face made her run dry. She should have said something about how much she loved her, and appreciated all she had done for her, cooking, cleaning, making her part of the family, she should have had something prepared because both of them were so bad at that kind of thing. 'Gosh!' she said, looking at her watch, 'is that the time? I'll be late if I don't get a move on!'

Mary walked stiffly to the door with her, but in the dark hall she stopped suddenly and took Sarah in her arms, nearly knocking her backwards with the force of her grasp. Sarah could feel the matronly bust pressed against her own thinness, the awkward love in the gesture, they who so rarely embraced.

'You look out for yourself, Sarah,' Mary said, as suddenly disengaging her. 'And remember, this is your home as well as ours. You can come back at any time. I'll no' say any more. Have you got your umbrella now?' She took it from the stand and gave it to her, then opened the door.

'Cheerio!' Sarah said, turning at the top of the stone stairs to look back at her sister. Mary lifted her hand. Only when she had reached the bottom of the stone stairs did she hear the door close.

The feeling of disappointment in herself was strong all the way to Charing Cross. Even to think of Barney gave her no relief, nor did it remove the feeling of shabbiness. You did that badly, she told herself.

Chapter Twenty-three

It was strange taking the tramcar to Grove Street instead of the more familiar route to Langside and Millbrae Road, but the strangeness was overwhelmed by the feeling of excitement. She would be opening the door to Barney this very evening.

Sarah even managed not to think of her sister's disapproval of the whole scheme. She would invite her for tea soon, and when Mary saw the flat, and how happy she was in it, she would accept the situation. 'It's her fondness of you which makes her anxious,' John had said to her one evening, but when she had surprised herself by saying, 'But you're fond of me and you're not anxious,' he had said, 'Working for the men cured me of taking things personally. Detachment's a great virtue.' There had been the familiar quirk at the side of his mouth, but he had turned his eyes quickly away from her as he spoke and dropped the subject.

But now, in the tram swaying down Albert Road, the constant feeling of joy intensified as she got up for her stop. 'Mind yersel',' the conductor said sourly as she jumped off too soon and went half-running towards Grove Street. Her mind was full of loving housewifely decisions to be made.

Should she buy some of those custard tarts from Currie's before they shut, and some morning rolls? A tart for his last cup of tea and a roll for his fried bacon and egg at breakfast? John liked it with the doughy inside removed to make a nest for the egg, and fried in the bacon fat. Yes, she thought, I'll go, but only if the shop isn't crowded. This pleasurable anxiety, not being able to bear the wasting of time before she got home to have a bath – it was necessary to get out of her shop-dress smelling of different women – added to the excitement. She would shake that gardenia talcum all over her body and silk it into her skin. Fortunately Currie's was on the point of shutting. She made her purchases.

Now, having set the table, changed and bathed, she heard Barney's key in the door. The happiness was unbearable as she ran into the dark hall and felt the harsh brush of his blue serge suit against her, the smell of the solidified brilliantine (the one Bamber's sold), felt the featherlike touch of his moustache against her mouth. Her heart ached with the unaccustomed joy of it. She had never had a man before.

She felt shy, girlish, as she waited for him in the lounge. 'Just freshen up first, girlie,' he had said. She heard the toilet flushing. Well, of course ... Did she look all right? She smoothed the mauve marocain of the dress down her hips, feeling there the stiff silk of the mauve and white striped sash-belt. The same silk outlined the neck and elbow-length sleeves. It had been expensive but worth it. The taffeta looked well against the marocain.

He came into the room with his quick stride, face flushed – he must have stopped at one of his howffs first and had a drink, the Grosvenor or the Corn Exchange – well-cut suit, double-breasted, from one of the best tailors in Buchanan Street, smoothly-polished brown leather shoes, hand-made, the brilliantined chestnut hair echoing the colour of the shoes. Everything had to be of the best for Barney, she thought with love, hand-made silk shirts and pyjamas, the finest linen for handkerchiefs, and shrewdly, that he just avoided being a dandy because of the width of his shoulders and his athletic build.

'Home to the love-nest!' he said, coming towards her and taking her in his arms as if he had rehearsed it. His breath smelled of whisky and good cigars, but his nearness, the brush of his pencil-line moustache (Ronald Colman they called that kind in the work-room), his masculinity, made her giddy for a moment.

'Don't call it that, Barney,' she said, releasing herself, laughing, 'it's my bachelor flat. Mary doesn't like it for one, I can tell you.'

'Well, I told you before, you're a big girl now.' He dismissed that, looking around appreciatively. 'You've done it up really well, nice pieces you've got there, but I think it would have been better if you'd had the curtains draped and swagged. More toney. I've a young friend ... had a drink with him tonight as a matter of fact ... who's an interior decorator. Just set him ... just set himself up in business.'

'No.' She shook her head. 'I don't want to change them. Nothing too opulent.' She had a fear of it looking like a brothel, she was nervous, trembling. It had been a difficult day. She had thought she had better tell them of her change of address in the shop. Miss Frobisher had raised an eyebrow.

'You've left your sister's house?'

'Yes, Miss Frobisher.'

'For your own place?'

'Yes. The children ...'

'Do you think that's wise, Sarah? After all, you're a single girl.'

'Oh, it's becoming quite the thing nowadays, Miss Frobisher.' She was airy. 'The head buyer at Copland's has a flat of her own and some of her friends too.'

Miss Frobisher looked doubtful. 'Well, that may be. I just hope you haven't embarked on anything unladylike. There's the reputation of Charles et Cie to think about as well as your own. You have to bear that in mind.'

'I haven't forgotten it.' She knew how valuable she was to the firm. No one else had the knowledge of the clients and their tastes. At first she had trusted her memory, but as she was promoted up the ladder over the years, she had invested in a solid red-covered ledger, alphabetically indexed, where she entered any wishes, foibles or peculiarities of the figures of their wealthy clients.

Lady Maladon might have been surprised to read the note against her name: 'Take off the size tag if it's ready-made. Swears blind she's two sizes smaller than she is.' And the Honourable Liza Bailey might not have liked her description: 'Short legs and long body ... never let an assistant show her anything high-waisted.'

'You've made a lovely job of the table, Sarah.' Barney was

talking to her. 'It's a treat for me. We've always eaten in hotel restaurants, the best of course!' He threw back his head. He was a hearty laugher.

'That's a lace cloth of my mother's. Mary insisted on me taking some linen. But there's nothing elaborate to eat, just a chicken and a fruit salad. I thought it would be enough.'

'Ample.' He looked slightly doubtful. 'And I've brought a bottle of bubbly.' He took her in his arms again, his blue eyes looking sincerely into her own. She could see the tracery of red veins in the whites. 'You won't regret this, Sarah. It'll give us the privacy we need. You've been such a cautious girlie. And I'll help you with the rent, of course.'

'I don't want that, I told you.' She spoke sharply.

Barney put his cheek against hers, stroking her back tenderly, long, smooth strokes down to the taffeta sash. 'Well, I can help in other ways. We're both mature people. We know what we're doing, and it's only temporary after all.'

'You mean until we're married?' She felt ashamed, saying that, as if she was bargaining her body against a promise, but it made her position seem tolerable to her. Besides, it was for Mary's sake too. She had noticed those sharp eyes.

'Kept woman.' The words had been going through her head all day as she had dealt with her usual patience and skill with the elegant clientèle of Charles et Cie. Not so elegant, she thought now, wrinkling her nose. When she had knelt down at Mrs Cowan's hem to pin it . . . 'Only you know the length I like, Miss Lane . . .' there had been a fishy vaginal smell in her nostrils. With her two-bathroomed house in Whitecraigs you would have thought she could have kept herself clean.

They went to bed before dinner because Sarah drank more champagne than she was used to and her inhibitions left her. She undressed, teetering unsteadily on one black patent court shoe and then the other (Barney had gone into the bathroom saying gaily, 'I won't look'), got into her oyster satin nightdress (wholesale from Daly's because she knew the head assistant in lingerie), and slipped under the silk sheets and the rose-patterned double quilt. She couldn't believe in her situation, nor in the double quilt so opulently puffy after the simple counterpane in Mary's bedroom. Nor could she quite believe in Barney, coming through the door in his pyjamas, switching out the light, and clambering in beside her. 'Got to watch the electricity bill, eh?' Jovial.

He was jovial all the way through (the oyster satin was slipped up, the pyjamas down), adroit, quick even, a matter of a few thumps, some heavy groaning and then a long sigh. It was over before it had begun, almost, and Sarah was left trembling and unsatisfied and wondering what she had done wrong. There should have been pain, blood (she had prepared for that), tenderness, transports of delight, flesh against flesh. Then he had jumped out of bed, gone to the bathroom, come back smelling of soap and talcum, and cradled her in his arms.

'That's what it's all about, girlie. I wasn't too rough, was I? My God, you were lovely.' And then, quickly, 'But it's not all sex. It's going to be grand having this place to come to after my business trips, knowing you'll be waiting for me . . .' His voice faltered. 'Are you all right, Sarah? Did I . . . satisfy you?'

She was trembling, filled with a great disappointment, a greater need. It had to be worth leaving her sister's house, making Miss Frobisher suspicious of her, it had to be worth more than that . . . she clung to him, not speaking, begging with her body, and after a time he tried again and this time it was better. She lay shuddering with happiness, lost in some kind of sensual dream, prolonging the shuddering to impress him, suddenly fell asleep. She was wakened by Barney tickling her ribs.

'Come on, girlie. This won't do at all. The cook's gone to sleep and I want my nosh.'

She turned to look at him. From the light of the street lamp she could just see his face in the unlit room. It looked dark, as if the blood was near the surface of the skin, blacker over the cheekbones, the light caught the blue of his eyes. His lids fell and he slightly turned away as if he couldn't bear her gaze. The movement made him look like a grown-up child except for the thin line of his moustache. She kissed him and got out of bed. She thought it was going to be worth it.

The time passed, a routine was established, Barney away, coming back, the joy lasted. Sarah was a real woman now, fulfilled. In the work-room Annie said, having more courage, or cheek, than the others, 'Miss Lane's got a boyfriend. Her eyes are shining all the time.'

'Get on with your work,' Minnie said, but her eyes went to Sarah as if to check Annie's observation.

Mary, urged by John, Sarah was sure, issued an invitation to them both for high tea, and she and Barney went, shining, well-groomed people, into the warmth of Mary's kitchen. Mary greeted Barney in her usual downright fashion.

'We don't have a dining room here like Sarah. We need all the rooms for bedrooms, except the parlour. I hope you don't mind eating in the kitchen.'

He was his usual affable self. 'Mind, Mrs Gibson? I like it! Many a cosy meal Mother and I have in ours. It's easier for her now that she's not so good.'

'What's wrong with her?' Mary asked. Downright.

'Old age, I'm afraid. It comes to all of us.' He sighed. 'I have a good woman coming in to see to her. I'm away a lot.'

'So I believe. Here's John,' her face softened, 'my better half.' The look of love which passed between them warmed Sarah's heart as it always did. Everything shared.

'We're no' strangers,' John said, shaking hands with Barney. 'Well, sit down and make yourself at home.' And to Mary, 'They're both fine. Bella's asleep and Lachie's on the point of it. I've read him a story.'

'I was going to let Barney see them,' Sarah smiled at John, 'but maybe we'd waken wee Bella.'

'That's the last thing we want to do.' Barney looked relieved, she thought. 'But believe me, I hear plenty about Lachie and Bella. Sarah's always singing their praises. I hear you're a busy man like me, John. You don't mind me calling you that? Sarah says Dixon's would be in revolt if it weren't for you.'

'That's a bit of exaggeration. Aye, I've to do a fair bit of travelling, but not with a bag of samples.' There was a twinkle in his eye.

'I don't exactly knock on doors.' Barney laughed heartily. 'Do you remember the old women who used to come round with their sheets full of all kinds of haberdashery and open them up on the landing?'

'Aye, there's a few left yet. No motor cars for them.' John nodded. 'And hard work carrying those huge bundles up and down stairs all day. Thank God we're beginning to stamp out slave labour at least.'

'Don't let this man get up on his hobby horse,' Mary said, 'or you'll be here all night. Draw in your chair.'

The evening wasn't a success in spite of Mary's excellent tea of fish pie and fruit salad. She harped on a bit about men who were tied to their mother's apron strings, and the virtues of having a family before it was too late. Her remarks were pointed, to say the least. It was obvious she didn't like Barney, and that John had no rapport with him. Their lives were lived on a different plane.

It was different with Minnie and Mary when Sarah asked them both to tea one Saturday afternoon in June. John was taking care of the children to let his wife out. The rapport had been there from the very beginning. They greeted each other like old friends.

'It's a pity all the same you didn't find someone else,' Mary observed, 'a good-looking lass like you.'

'No, when I lost my lad at the end of the war, that was the end of romance for me.' Minnie looked sad and yet justified.

'Aye, you're like me. But I was lucky. My John came back. Sad, sad days, though.'

'And there's ma mither.' Minnie looked around the room. 'Well, Sarah's fixed herself up here all right. A real little nest.' Sarah held her breath. Would she express her disapproval to Mary? 'We're all waiting with bated breath for the happy announcement.'

'Not as much as we are.' Mary nodded grimly, also avoiding Sarah's eye. No, she wouldn't ask them together again.

She welcomed Barney on his next visit still with the same joy, but subdued. She didn't think he noticed. She was always relieved when her period came, although he had told her he was 'taking care of things'. She listened attentively to his account of his recent visit to the theatre to see Noel Coward's latest play. 'We died laughing,' he said. He sometimes entertained his clients.

In bed she said gently, 'Not tonight, Barney.' She had always been shy about this, but he seemed relieved. 'It's just as nice to be friends,' he said.

'Do you think your mother liked me?' she said. 'Put your arm round me, Barney. That's nice.' They had gone to see her last Sunday, Sarah agreeing with Barney it would be better not to tell her that they were sharing a flat. She believed he was away from home a lot on business, he had said. Better to leave it at that.

'I'm sure she did. She doesn't see many people. Luckily that was one of her good days.'

Sarah had thought the old lady had looked far from frail. And she had also said when Barney was out of the room that it was 'high time that one was getting tied up'. It was all very puzzling. She wouldn't let her mind dwell on the subject. 'I had Mary and Minnie McConachie from work here last Saturday. I don't think I told you.' He didn't answer. 'You never come on Saturday.'

'That's devoted to Mother, you know that, Sarah. We both have our responsibilities.' He seemed to hesitate. 'Work's crowding in on me these days. As a matter of fact, two or three times every week is getting difficult.' It was like a stab in her heart.

'Oh, I've plenty to do, Barney.' The last thing she must do was complain. A married woman could, not her. 'Don't be a drag on your husband,' she had read in a magazine. But in any case she was a business woman, able to run a successful career and quite able to have her own social life. 'Don't apologise,' she said. 'I'm quite content in our flat as long as I know you love me, and that we will be married . . . eventually.' The pain in her heart was now like the one in the pit of her stomach, gnawing . . .

'You're a dear sweet girlie and I don't deserve you.' He turned to her and she put up her hand to caress his cheek. It was wet.

'You're my love, Barney, always will be. Have no doubts about that.' She took him in her arms.

Chapter Twenty-four

Life for Sarah was so busy that she ceased to worry about not being married. She now knew one or two saleswomen in the Sauchiehall Street stores who had discreet 'men friends' with whom they spent occasional weekends, but quite apart from that, Barney, she told herself, was 'different', tender and loving, and although he couldn't visit her so often because of his mother, their relationship had reached a stage of mutual tolerance and recognition of their respective occupations.

He thought she was the most elegant and clever young lady in Glasgow, she loved his gaiety and laughter, his taste for luxury. She adored him, his smart appearance and sophistication, and she gave up, if she had ever entertained it, the idea of going to see his mother on her own. It would destroy Barney's faith in her if he ever found out.

Miss Frobisher had gone to Switzerland to visit Nessie, looking perturbed but still dignified. Sarah's intuition told her there was something wrong, and that it was not a familial visit, but she was left in charge of Charles et Cie, and she enjoyed every minute of it. The work exercised all her powers of organisation, taste and tact, and they had never been busier. This was in part due to Mrs de Vere, who by speaking in glowing terms of her to her County friends, had advised them to go to Sarah for advice on their wardrobes.

Occasionally, during September, she had slight feelings of malaise, but dismissed them as being part of the strain she was working under. Another time, on one of her necessary trips to London, she was surprised that the hotel fare seemed to nauseate her. She needed a holiday, but it was impossible when Miss Frobisher was away. The gnawing in the pit of her tomach was back.

A month later, however, she received a letter from her

employer saying that she would meet her in London and they would do some buying together before they returned to Glasgow. She was sorry her temporary reign was over, but in a way it was a relief. Perhaps she and Barney could arrange to have a few days' holiday together.

The two women put up at Brown's Hotel as usual. Miss Frobisher looked even more drawn and tight-lipped, but brightened a little when Sarah told her of the increase in sales.

'You have done very well in my absence, Sarah,' she acknowledged. 'Of course they miss the *ambiance*, so to speak, but I'm sure you made a good deputy.'

'I did my best,' Sarah admitted. 'Don't hesitate to leave me if you want to visit Nessie again. I really enjoyed it.'

'I'm sure you did.' She seemed to peer at Sarah as if she didn't believe her. 'There isn't much chance I'll be going *there* again.' She drew her glance away, catching Sarah's surprised look, and raised an imperious hand. 'I'll leave it for the time being.'

'Of course.' Sarah knew her employer too well.

She had a commission from Mrs de Vere to look at suitable wedding outfits – her son, to her surprise, she said, was being married, and she had also promised to go to a show of modern paintings in the Hayward Gallery. 'Be my eyes for me,' she had requested. Sarah was alarmed, therefore, when trying to make sense of the jumble of colours, that she suddenly felt faint. She sat down on a seat against the wall, and after a time made herself look again at a painting opposite. To her relief, the jumble of brush strokes and dashes of paint assembled themselves into some kind of order and became what looked like the depiction of a stormy moor. She was relieved to feel her normal self, and on the strength of it bought an expensive catalogue for Mrs de Vere.

She would also tell Barney about the paintings, she decided, and see if she could persuade him to come with her next time she went to London. He liked what he called 'pretty scenes', or 'Frenchified ones', which generally meant very buxom women behind café bars, and whose embonpoint gave Sarah an immediate sense of inferiority. But, hadn't she noticed recently that her normally small bosom was becoming larger? She brushed the thought away. Instead she would think of her dear boy.

'You are far too good for me,' he had said when they had last been together, and she had been touched and said that she considered herself lucky to have met *him*, such a smart man-about-town, she had added, like Jack Buchanan. He had laughed, and springing to his feet had executed a neat little routine. He had beautiful feet, always in those expensive red-brown highly polished shoes. Then, to her surprise, he had suddenly knelt at her feet and put his head in her lap. When she had gently raised it his eyes had been wet.

'There's nothing to be sad about, silly,' she had said, taking his head between her hands, and he had looked at her sadly and said, 'Isn't there?' She had felt then the most exquisite mixture of sadness and happiness, and had known irrevocably that he was her own dear boy and always would be.

But it was no good. All the thinking about Barney didn't take her mind away from her problem. She went to Mrs de Vere's house at her request on a beautiful September day in an agony of mind. She *knew*. There was no avoiding it. She was pregnant. Because of a bout of early morning sickness she wasn't eating and was actually slimmer, and with worry the lines of her face were more sharply drawn. There were hollows under her cheekbones making her grey eyes seem larger than ever in the matt surface of her carefully made-up complexion. What, she wondered, would Mrs de Vere think of her? Would she be suspicious? Would she make any comment?

The sight of the loch, calm today, with a few motionless white sails breaking its blueness, the far-off misted hills, had a dreamlike quality, and yet a finality. Never again . . . Was this how all pregnant women felt, she wondered. She had heard the state gave to some a new beauty, but that was reserved for those who had a husband who could tell them so. They would never know the loneliness of her particular fear.

Barney didn't know, she felt sure. For the first month or so she hadn't believed it herself. She had convinced herself that the pressure of her way of life, running Charles et Cie, living in sin, if you wanted to call a spade a spade, had upset the normal workings of her body. And, although he was responsible, she couldn't say he had been pressing in his sexual attentions. That was the ironical part of it.

What he had said that first night so long ago had been true. It wasn't all sex. What he wanted was a love-nest to visit occasionally, softly lit, food cooked for him, she in negligées which he took pleasure in choosing as well as buying, shell-pink chiffon, mauve-dyed guipure lace, oyster slipper satin. For some reason that she didn't understand, he was not the marrying kind. He knew that. She remembered that evening when he had put his head in her lap, and when she had raised it his eyes had been wet.

He wanted the flat at Grove Street and her in it as a background to his life, a place to fill with the presents he brought from his many sorties to firms, fitted hide suitcases with silver boxes and bottles slotted inside for holding all manner of lotions and creams, crystal powder bowls, silver-backed brush, comb and mirror sets with sprays of enamelled flowers embossed on their backs, manicure sets in satin-lined crocodile leather cases. But her most treasured possession was the small soapstone Buddha, which she often held in the hollow of her hand for the comfort it seemed to give her. Apart from that one item, all of them made her feel more like a kept woman than his lovemaking did.

But it had at last to be accepted Barney would never marry her. And despite his less than passionate embraces, made up for by his loving tenderness, there was no doubt about it, she was pregnant at an age when most women nowadays were finished with child-bearing.

'You're seeing things at their best today,' the taxi driver said. 'You frae Glasgow?'

'Yes, I am,' she said.

'I wouldny like to live there, dirty, smelly place. See, when I get out in ma wee boat at night to do a bit of fishing, I wouldny change that for all the tea in China.'

'I'm sure you wouldn't,' she agreed, fixing her eyes on the scene before them so that she would remember it.

Mrs de Vere greeted her with affection. 'You do look as if you needed a holiday, Sarah, so delicate. Come in. Mrs Mason has the tea ready.'

It was like coming home, the teatable set in the wide window embracing the view of the loch, Mrs Mason bringing in the tray with the silver tea service, the Queen Anne teapot. (She had looked it up.)

'And how are you, Mrs Mason?' she asked. Her many sojourns in London hotels had given her almost as much *sang froid* as her hostess.

'I canny complain,' the woman said, as if she could quite easily, and giving Sarah a keen look. They said some people 'knew', especially people like Mrs Mason who had probably encountered pregnant unmarried women more often than Mrs de Vere.

'Did you see anything to suit me in London, Sarah?' Mrs de Vere asked. 'I saw you left some boxes in the hall.'

'Yes, I did. Something which I think will be just right for the wedding. You'll see what you think.'

'I always like your choice. I can hardly believe in this wedding, even yet. I always thought Ronald was a confirmed bachelor.' Sarah thought he had that look too. 'And an eminently suitable young lady, good family, rides to hounds. Sensible. Ronald says she won't mind at all being left at home when he does short tours abroad with his regiment. Her parents are delighted to move into the dower house and give them the family home. A few years older than Ronald, but that doesn't matter. What do you think?'

'As long as they love each other it doesn't matter at all. A happy marriage is the most important thing.' She found Mrs de Vere was looking at her keenly. She said quickly, 'I hope you'll like my choice for the wedding.'

Mrs de Vere took her glance away from Sarah and handed her her teacup. She breathed in the familiar fragrance. How could she ever have liked coarse Indian? 'What colour is it, may I ask?'

'Mauve. Two shades, really, mauve and lilac. There is a slotted lilac scarf at the neckline, and the two-tiered skirt repeats the theme. Very subtle. I thought the line was lovely, and I ventured to buy a hat in mauve with lilac trimming, large-brimmed.'

'It sounds just right, but with your taste . . . I may say Lady James is delighted with your choice for her. The bride's mother. Even more important than the son.'

'I'm glad. It gives me great pleasure when clients are pleased too.'

'You're an artist, Sarah, an artist. Try a cucumber sandwich.'

'Thank you.' She smiled. 'I went to the Hayward Gallery. I brought the catalogue for you.'

'How lovely! I'll have a good browse in bed. Oh, I do wish you could stay longer. Especially now.' Mrs de Vere looked wistful. Sarah nibbled her cucumber sandwich, waiting rather apprehensively. What did she mean? In this spacious room, with her friend – she had allowed herself to think that – she had almost forgotten her problem. She had even contemplated, but dismissed the thought instantly, of confiding in Mrs de Vere, asking her advice. How could she? It was *her* problem. She was the only one who could solve it. 'What do you mean, Mrs de Vere?' she ventured.

'It's rather a bombshell. Elizabeth and Ronald would like me to consider moving to the village where they will be living, in Somerset. There's actually a cottage for sale at the moment.' A sickening ache had started in Sarah's heart as she listened, screwing it slowly, viciously.

'Oh, yes?'

'I would be near her and her parents when Ronald was on his tour of duty. As I said, Elizabeth wouldn't always accompany him. Besides, she has hunt commitments.' It was worse now, like a vice, slowly going beyond endurance, causing a cold sweat to break out on her forehead. Oh, God, she thought, not again. Her friend, her dear friend, without Mary's and Minnie's prejudices, leaving . . . Mrs de Vere's face became a concerned blur. Sarah managed to put the Spode cup down carefully before she leant forward in her chair, her head swimming.

'Sarah! My dear child! Aren't you well?' She felt the kindly hand on her shoulder. Mrs de Vere must have risen and was bending over her.

'It's all right . . .' She managed to speak. 'I expect I'm over-tired.' By an effort of will she raised her head.

'You're far from well. Put your head forward again. I know what will help.' She was aware that Mrs de Vere went to the bell at the side of the fireplace, and in a minute or two there was the clatter of feet and the door opened.

'Is it more water, madam?' She heard Mrs Mason's rough voice, Clyde coast, she thought, harsher . . . the last person she wanted.

'No. Miss Lane is not feeling well. Bring her a small glass of brandy. I expect it's the heat.'

Sarah made a great effort and raised her head, pulling herself straight in her chair. With her slowly clearing eyes she saw, or thought she saw, the look of suspicion on the woman's face. 'I'm quite all right now.'

'On you go, Mrs Mason,' Mrs de Vere said. 'A small glass of brandy, quickly. Now, you'll come over to this couch, my dear, and put your feet up.' She was helping Sarah to rise as she spoke, guiding her towards the couch. 'My mother used to give me a tipple when I had tummy ache. Women's stuff. Did the trick.'

'I'm a terrible nuisance . . .' She lay back as she was instructed, and closed her eyes. If she could only tell her . . .

In half an hour she had fully recovered, she had a warm comfortable feeling in the pit of her stomach, and there were only the remains of the ache in her heart, but that was perma-nent. 'I'm really ashamed of myself.' She smiled at Mrs de Vere sitting across from her. 'I think you were right. It was probably the heat of the sun in the window.'

'You work too hard for other people, Sarah. You're worn out. You must take things more easily.'

'I'll try. Spring was busy with the fashion shows.' She said with false brightness, 'Let me show you your outfit before dinner.'

'Certainly not.' Mrs de Vere was firm. 'You'll rest here quietly for an hour and tell me about the Hayward, then you will go upstairs and have a leisurely bath. We'll have an early dinner and so to bed. You need looking after.'

Sarah leant back on the cushions. 'I'm being spoiled. Do you think you'll give up this house and go to Somerset?' The thought depressed her even further.

'Yes. My mind is more or less made up. I've always been a bit of an alien here, although I have done my best to take part in the affairs of the community. This place was my husband's choice because of the sailing, not mine. I'm well into my seventies, you know.'

'Are you? I shouldn't have thought it.' Which was true. There was still a vigorous quality about her. She would follow the hunt in her car – she had seen that in the *Tatler* – and have her daughter-in-law's parents as friends, and settle into a picture-book village with thatched roofs and be happy to be nearer her son. Mrs de Vere had moved and was sitting beside her on the couch. Impulsively Sarah put out her hand and touched hers. 'I'll miss you, Mrs de Vere,' she said.

'And I you.' She clasped Sarah's hand firmly in her own. 'I've always wanted a daughter. Just like you.' But you've got one now, Elizabeth, on a horse. Sarah could imagine her, dark-haired, dashing, shining riding boots, jumping, no, clearing, a fence. All *she* had was her problem. Mrs de Vere became brisk. 'Now, off upstairs with you, and we'll have an early meal. I'd like to send you back with some colour in your cheeks.'

Sarah smiled, rising. 'Miss Frobisher doesn't approve of colour in the cheeks of her sales ladies.'

'Oh, that woman has no soul! Nor sense of humour. Let's go up together.' She put her arm round Sarah as they climbed the stairs, and that at least was a comfort. But, in the end, you were on your own.

In the morning she felt well, calm, fatalistic, even. Dressed and in her right mind, which was a saying of Mary's. The wedding outfit was tried on with resounding success, a softer, more elegant Mrs de Vere emerged in front of the mirror, the large hat shaded her rather too pronounced features, the two-tiered skirt, accordion pleated, smoothed the broad hips and stout legs.

'You're a genius,' she told Sarah. 'The colour is perfect for me.' And, shyly for her, 'I don't think you know, but my name is Violet.'

'So the outfit is very appropriate?'

'You must have been inspired.' And, as she stood in her pink corsets, she assured Sarah, 'We shan't lose touch. I'll write and tell you all about the wedding, and my new cottage, and you must address me as Violet. I regard you as my friend.'

She embraced Sarah warmly at the door when the taxi arrived. 'You're the only thing I'll truly miss,' and, lowering her voice, 'certainly not . . .' The little backward movement of her head left no doubt in Sarah's mind who she meant. Sarah smiled and raised her eyebrows with a slight nod.

'Thank you for everything, Mrs de Vere.' She would have to practise saying 'Violet'.

Mrs de Vere looked straight at Sarah. 'And take my advice, my dear. Don't put off your marriage any longer.'

'I'll remember.' She managed to smile as she turned to go down the steps. The pain in her heart was back again, the slow, vicious, familiar pain.

'Back to smoky old Glasgow,' the taxi driver said smugly.

'Oh, I don't know,' she said with her chin up. 'There's more to do there than here.' He didn't talk for the rest of the journey.

Chapter Twenty-five

The days were drawing in, and when Sarah shopped in Albert Road she imagined there was a smell of Halloween in the air. The city bakeries had cakes decorated with sugared flying witches on broomsticks, the fruiterers had pyramids of rosy apples and green pails of tawny chrysanthemums at their doorways.

She had the habit, sometimes, when she was walking in and out of shops with her basket, of tracing in her mind the route to Millbrae Road, up Albert Road to Pollokshaws Road, round Queens Park Drive skirting the park, along Langside Road to the monument at Battlefield which always gave her a fleeting stab of sadness at the thought of that lonely queen, then turning into Millbrae Road towards the flat. The mental journey induced in her a feeling of nostalgia at this particular season.

There were the memories of the tin bath filled with water placed in front of the kitchen fire, the gales of laughter as they 'dooked' for apples, each with a fork held between their teeth. Once there had been a party, Annie Baxter and her husband and children, a fellow-worker of John's, Jim Roberts and his wife with theirs. The men had hollowed out turnips and placed the stump of a candle inside so that the light shone through holes for eyes and nose and an open mouth with fearful forked teeth, making the children scream with delight.

Mary had cooked a huge supper, and afterwards John had summoned everyone into the dark lobby where he blackened a few unlucky faces with soot from the side of the potato pot. What laughter there had been when the gas was turned on, the pointing fingers, the vows that John would pay dearly for his prank.

Late in October Sarah decided she would go early that

week to Millbrae Road. Which evening would depend on Barney's visit. She would take a basketful of Halloween fare, including a cake decorated with one of the fearsome witches, Chinese lanterns, since hollowing out a turnip was beyond her, and presents for the children. It would be the last time.

When she rang the bell she could hear Lachie's excited voice before John opened the door. 'Sarah!' he said, holding it wide. 'You're laden like a packhorse. Come away in!'

'A sudden notion. Hello, Lachie!' She put her arm round his shoulders as he danced at her side. 'I thought you'd be in bed by this time.'

'Mammy's out. Daddy's letting me stay up a wee while.'

'When the cat's away the mice will play,' she laughed as they went into the kitchen. She set her load on the table. 'And where's your wee sister?'

'She's in her bed. Have you brought something for me, Aunty Sarah?'

'Lachie!' His father reproved him. 'None o' that!'

'Don't worry. I have as a matter of fact, Lachie. A surprise present because it's nice to get one not at birthdays or Christmas.' She rummaged in her basket and produced a wrapped box which she handed to him. 'Ask Daddy if you can open it.'

'Well, if you're a good boy and thank your aunty nicely,' John said.

Lachie had torn off the paper and opened the box as his father was speaking. 'Oh, great! A tramcar! And you can turn the wee handle at the front for where it's going. Oh, great, isn't it, Daddy?' He held up the gaily painted toy to show him.

'What did I say about thanks?' John demanded.

'Oh, yes. Thanks very much, Aunty Sarah. Everybody at school will be jealous. Oh, great!'

'Bella will get hers when she wakes up in the morning.'

'If you ask me it will be before that,' John said. 'Look!' He pointed towards the door. The little girl stood there in her nightgown, rubbing her eyes and flushed with sleep. 'You waked me up, Lachie,' she accused, 'with your shouting.' She looked at Sarah, blinking. 'Where's ma mammy? You're no' ma mammy.'

'You know your aunty, Bella,' Sarah said, holding out her arms. 'Come up on my knee.' The little girl trotted over to her and was lifted up. 'Look at these wee bare feet.' She pulled the nightgown over them as she held the warm little body in her arms. 'Where is Mary, John?' She looked at him over Bella's head.

'At Annie Baxter's. Every now and again it comes over her like a drug that she's got to go and see Annie Baxter. She fights against it but only Annie Baxter will do. So off she goes. Fortunately the drug wears off when she is satiated and she comes back.' His mouth was turned down in a smile as he looked at Sarah, who was laughing at him. 'She'll kill me if she finds this one up.'

'Just for a minute till she sees what's in her parcel. It's on the top of the basket. That's it. You open it, John.' He did and handed over to his daughter a baby doll in a box, secured at neck, arms and legs by elastic thread.

'My tramcar's better,' Lachie said with masculine disdain. Bella, sitting up, ignored her brother.

'I want it out.' She looked at her father imperiously.

John saluted. 'Right away. Scissors. Kitchen drawer.' He rummaged amongst the various objects and found them, took the box from Bella and freed the doll from its elastic binding. She snatched it back and cuddled it against her chest.

'It's *my* baby doll. I'm going to call it Bessie. Wee Bessie.' She rocked it in her arms. 'Coorie doon, wee Bessie,' she crooned.

Sarah looked at John. Lachie had climbed on his knee clutching his tramcar, and was leaning against him, half-asleep.

'We'll let them stay for a while, eh?' she said, and he nodded, smiling, over Lachie's head.

'Just for a wee while.' She felt deeply at peace with the firelight flickering on them and the children quiet except for Bella's sleepy crooning.

'What's going on at Dixon's these days?' she asked.

'A constant fight for a minimum wage.' He spoke quietly. 'It doesn't suit Ramsay MacDonald at all.'

Sarah nodded, too contented to ask why. This was so different from her evenings with Barney. 'A Cottar's Saturday Night scene,' she wanted to say to John to make him smile. He was following his own train of thought.

'You fight for better conditions, a minimum wage and such-like, but it is the inevitability of the decline in heavy industry which you can't ignore. It's a weight on my mind all the time. I'm not daft. I know I'm fighting for a dying cause. We've not managed to get the new light industries here because we hung on to the old ones for so long. The north will die and the south will rise because they've been smarter than us. That's the real dichotomy between the north and the south. They can see further than us, quicker . . .' She kept quiet, sensing that he only wanted to talk. After a time she spoke.

'What can you do about it, John?' The little girl was heavy against her. She had stopped crooning. Soon they would have to put the children to bed and she would go home. She would have liked to sit here like this with the fire warm on her face and causing rays of light in front of her eyes when she half-closed them. She didn't want the evening to end.

'Damn all,' he said. 'I'm like that wee fellow who put his finger in the dyke. All I can do is warn people. Educate them. Keir Hardie saw that education was the key. I tell you, Sarah,' his face was suddenly drawn, 'we're rushing towards disaster.'

'I never saw you so pessimistic.'

'Me, pessimistic?' His sudden swift smile banished the sternness. 'I don't know the meaning of that word. I'm just a realist. I'll go on trying to do my best for the men. They're the salt of the earth. I'll sink or swim with them.'

'Well, you'll have a clear conscience.' Their eyes met, and she thought, there is a rare understanding between us. She drew her eyes away, whispered, 'Do you think we could get these two to bed before Mary comes back from Annie's? She'll blame it on me. She thinks I'm too soft.'

He laughed. 'Aye, you're right. She'll blame it on you. You

have a rare way with weans, Sarah. Are you no' thinking of getting married yet?'

She met his gaze. 'I'm thinking of it all the time. It's Barney who finds it difficult because of his mother.' The words rang falsely in her ears. She thought of a remark Minnie McConachie had made to her after her visit to Grove Street.

Perhaps in a subconscious desire to win Minnie's approval she had said, 'Barney took me to visit his mother the other day.'

'Oh, aye?' Minnie looked up from her machine. The old friendliness was absent. 'How did you find her?'

'Well, old, certainly. But not as frail as I would have thought. Barney said it was one of her good days.'

'Oh, aye,' Minnie said again.

'Of course she can't go out of her house alone to get her messages or that kind of thing.'

'Is that so?' Minnie said. 'It's no' what I hear.'

'What do you mean, Minnie?' She felt her hands begin to tremble, clenched them at her sides, then tried to relax by unclenching them again. Why was she so apprehensive?

'Well, our neighbour has a friend who knows her. Lives in a street off Byres Road.' So did Barney's mother.

'Does she?' She tried to divert Minnie. 'Barney has made their flat really nice. Comfortable. Well, it has to be. She's in it all the time.'

'Our neighbour's friend meets her for coffee in the tearoom above Boots in Byres Road. Quite often. So she says.' Minnie held Sarah's eyes.

'Oh, no.' Sarah shook her head. 'She must have made a mistake. Anyhow, it's only a friend of your neighbour's. You've often told me she's an awful gossip.'

'Aye, she talks a lot.' Minnie looked slightly taken aback for a moment. 'But there would be no point in saying that, would there? I mean . . .'

'Not unless you were talking to your neighbour about Barney and me,' Sarah thought but didn't say it. She had never had a quarrel with anyone in Charles et Cie since she came. She wasn't going to break that reputation. She raised her chin, said lightly, 'It's a great place for gossip, Glasgow. Tittle tattle. Well, it passes the time. And I must really get on, Minnie, or we'll be accused of the same thing.' She had gone out of the work-room with a straight back. The trembling was back . . .

'You should go and see his mother on your own, Sarah,' John was saying. 'You could win anybody's heart. She couldn't object to you as a daughter-in-law.' Perhaps it wasn't his mother to blame. She tried to smile.

'Are you getting worried about my reputation as well?'

John shook his head. 'Not a bit of it. I leave that to Mary. You could be a scarlet woman for all I care. You're just Sarah to me. Always will be.'

She felt her eyes fill and stood up with the sleeping child in her arms. 'I'll put this wee one down. Are you coming with Lachie?'

'Aye, on you go.' He was on his feet. 'My, what a weight this one is! Too big for carries.'

In the dark bedroom they tucked in their charges. She felt suddenly that she was wrongly taking Mary's place.

'Not a murmur from Bella,' she said.

'Same here.'

In the dark doorway he put his hand on her shoulder, stopping her. 'Think of what I said, Sarah.' He spoke softly. 'I don't want to see you hurt.' She stood for a moment, feeling his nearness, aware of the quietness of the house, the sleeping children.

'I'll maybe do what you said.' She spoke softly. She knew she never would.

In the too-bright kitchen where the taps gleamed and the brasses glinted on the mantelpiece she fussed with her basket. 'These are a few things for Halloween. I'll leave them here.'

'You shouldn't be so generous, Sarah, but thanks. But are you not waiting to see Mary? She'll be in any time.'

'No, I don't like being too late out.' She wanted to say to him, 'I know I'm making a mess of my life. Mary's right. You probably feel the same.' She smiled brightly at him. 'Tell Mary I was asking for her.'

'I'll tell her. You're sure you won't wait?' He looked concerned.

'I'm sure.'

'We've had a rare time, eh?' he said to her at the door.

'Aye, a rare time.' They stood, their eyes meeting and holding for a long second, then she smiled, said, 'Goodnight', and ran down the stone stairs. When she reached the close the wall tiles lining it seemed to run together in a blurred mélange of colour.

Chapter Twenty-six

Sarah was in an agony of indecision the last night Barney spent with her before he went on an extended trip to the United States. When he had told her on an earlier visit that he was going, she had felt at first numbness. After her disappointment at the thought of losing Mrs de Vere, this had seemed the final blow. Both had been in a way her hostages to fortune.

She couldn't confide in Minnie McConachie, nor indeed anyone at Charles et Cie, and the thought of Mary knowing she was pregnant was impossible. She couldn't let her down, knowing how highly she had always thought of her younger sister, how she had placed her on a pedestal, a superior being. It had always embarrassed her, but she had tried to live up to Mary's estimation of her.

John would have been different. He would not have been shocked. She imagined him looking at her with those steady eyes of his, seeing her heartache and misery, and saying, 'Well, it's not the end of the world. We'll help you.' Always 'we'.

She listened distractedly while Barney talked about his trip, the voyage on the *Aquitania* (his young friend, the interior decorator, was going on business too as it happened), the exciting places they would visit there, New York, Philadelphia, Chicago, then all the way across America by train to the West Coast and California where Barney had lots of contacts.

He was an agent for woollens which were made in Paisley, and the Americans went daft about Scottish wool, the way they went daft about Scottish whisky . . . he always took some bottles of Johnny Walker with him for gifts to his customers.

After dinner they rolled up the carpet and danced the Charleston to a new ragtime record he had brought with him, their hands on each other's shoulders. She was wearing, since it was their last night, a green chiffon dress with a handkerchief-pointed hemline edged with beads, and the points swirled about her silk-stockinged legs.

Glancing down, she thought how pretty it looked. If Barney thought the same he didn't say, but then he was concentrating, his smooth brilliantined head cocked sideways. '*Tata*, te *ta* ta . . . We'll have a *blue*. . . a *new* . . .' His shoes were shining nuttily brown, the pointed toes were decorated with a punched design, high-arched, a lovely foot for a man, she thought again. 'Nifty footwork, eh?' It was as if he knew what she was thinking.

'Gigolo!' She smiled at him provocatively, but she felt heavy and lumpen like a cow blundering through a gate to be milked. 'How long will you be away, Barney?' She couldn't keep it back.

'Not a moment longer than I can help, girlie, but the amount of travelling I have to do is frightening!' His cheeks were shining like Halloween apples, shining with pleasure at the thought. 'It could take three months.'

'Three months,' she echoed. What state would she be in at the end of three months? She would have to leave her job, make arrangements . . . her agony was so great that she had to bite her lip to prevent herself from telling him.

' "With your wee head upon my knee . . ." ' he sang gaily.

'I can't dance any more, Barney. It makes me feel sick jigging up and down.' Perhaps she could shake it away.

'That's your beef olives, girlie. I must say they were great. Just like mother used to make.' He hardly ever mentioned his mother now. 'You've become a fine wee cook since you got your own place.'

'Thanks for those few kind words.' She flicked her chiffon points flirtatiously, wanting to weep. She didn't think anything of the sort. She didn't like cooking at all, and the fiddling business of tying thread round strips of stuffed steak had always struck her as ridiculous and time-consuming. It was a popular dish of Mary's when she was having company, more unusual than cold ham and salad, or salmon soufflé made with a tin of John West's and three eggs. Mary! In three months, if she were still in Glasgow, she wouldn't need to tell Mary. She would notice! She had eyes like that woman in 'A Window in Thrums'.

In bed that night it was the best there had ever been. Desperation made her abandoned, Barney didn't laugh as much as usual, and he worked away manfully to satisfy her need with the regularity of one of the pistons on a Clyde steamer.

Like a deluge of cold water the thought came to her that far from being overly enthusiastic he had never enjoyed this part of their relationship, that it was a necessary adjunct only, his rent. She was the culprit, holding him close when he wanted to rush away to the bathroom. She now saw it had been his attempt to prevent a baby. All along they had both been too shy to discuss contraception, although she had heard hushed talk once in the work-room about 'French letters'. How could she mention anything like that to him, and that she had heard Boots stayed open late for the sale of them?

But tonight was a special effort on his part to be passionate because of her, the last effort required of him before he went away . . . with the interior decorator. She examined that with the calmness born of despair. Barney said they were 'good chums'. 'Oh, Sarah, you'll be the death of me,' she heard him say in her ear, and then mutter, or did she imagine it, 'so messy.'

In any case, he was out of bed quickly and off on his usual visit to the bathroom where he would run the tap noisily and then anoint himself liberally with talcum powder. It didn't matter now. There was only the smell of sex to kill. At that moment, knowing she was pregnant by him, her love changed but didn't die. How could it, she asked herself. He had been her only lover. He would always be her Barney, her own dear boy, the one man she had ever loved, who had brought gaiety and romance into her life, who had taught her the meaning of sexual passion, or had she taught herself?

She would always feel tenderness for him, even when the passion had gone. Everyone had different ideas of what they wanted out of life. Barney had only needed comfort and tenderness from her. Perhaps his problems were even deeper than hers.

She was in torment for nearly a week after he had gone, lying awake night after night. She couldn't go to see her doctor, who was also Mary's, but what was the point when she knew she was pregnant. She had helped Mary through *her* pregnancies. She had learnt from her the signs, the tight breasts, the feeling of nausea in the early stages, but above all, the conviction. She *knew*.

She would have to leave Charles et Cie. That was the first thing. Should she tell Miss Frobisher she was getting married? No, that would be a mistake. There were ways and means of finding out if it were the truth. Nevertheless, she would have to leave before she or the other girls suspected. At the moment, the salon dress, grey box-pleated marocain with a low waist and white organdie collar and cuffs, was ideal concealment, but that wouldn't last much longer. And what if her ankles became swollen? Mary's had.

Around the fourth month of her pregnancy on a gloomy November day she knocked on Miss Frobisher's door and at a command entered the private sanctum hung and upholstered in grey velvet. Nothing but the best would do for the refined clientèle she entertained. She liked to put it that way. Coffee with silver, sugar and cream was always served in the morning, and in the afternoon China tea was offered in Rockingham cups flanked by a bonbon dish of petits-fours.

'How nice, Sarah.' Miss Frobisher welcomed her graciously. 'It's not often I have a visit from you at this time in the morning. I was just looking through my correspondence.' Her attenuated vowels were as exquisitely refined as her egg-shell teacups. 'What can I do for you?'

'Well, it's like this, Miss Frobisher.' The half-formulated ideas swirled in her head. 'I've thought of branching out on my own lately.' She added lightly, 'Perhaps my little experience while you were in Switzerland gave me the taste for it.' Miss Frobisher's expression didn't change. 'I'm not getting any younger,' she smiled, getting no answering smile, 'and you've taught me so much. Of course, I wouldn't set up anywhere near you, indeed I thought of Largs. We used to go there for our holidays.' She stopped speaking, surprised that her hazy thoughts had been expressed in a fairly lucid manner.

It wasn't altogether fiction. Before Barney had appeared on the scene she had thought of starting her own salon sometime in the future. She had missed her chance in marriage, she had decided. She was on the shelf now. Why that should be, she hadn't been able to understand. She thought she had a nice enough nature, was nice enough looking, but perhaps there was something off-putting about her. Mary had once said that because she was so well-dressed young men were fearful they couldn't live up to it, or keep her in the style to which she was accustomed. She thought it was more than that, a kind of vulnerability underneath her quiet manner which made them uneasy. Barney's advent at that time had been just right, not too young, well-dressed, and with enough money to indulge himself in luxuries.

Largs presented itself at this minute as somewhere she could hide. It was true they had gone there on holidays when they were children, and later. The Ayrshire coast had always been a favourite of their mother's, and it had nostalgic memories for her. Helensburgh, with an understanding Mrs de Vere near at hand, had been a possibility until she had told Sarah her son was being married and that she was moving near him. If only Ronald had fallen in love with *her*. But, as his mother had pointed out, Sarah wasn't of the same class.

She looked at Miss Frobisher. 'You've always been kind to me, paid me well after my training . . .' Miss Frobisher brushed that imperiously aside with a wave of her heavily beringed, swollen-jointed hand. She then put the hand on her high bosom, pearl-grey (to match the curtains).

'The doctor said I had to watch my heart . . .' She looked pathetic, difficult for her, then brisked up. 'You were good material, Sarah . . .' she laughed, crack-belled, 'and you know I'm a good judge of material. An investment of my time and money.' She sobered immediately, perhaps disappointed at Sarah's lack of response. 'But that's by the way. To leave Charles et Cie, after the training we've given you . . . well,

I'm more disappointed than I can say. I never thought you would pay me back like this for all my kindness . . . no, it was you who said it . . . and desert me like this.'

'I didn't want to . . .'

'I never deceived you. You can't say otherwise. You knew right from the start that you could never step into my shoes because of Nessie. I had promised her father on his death-bed she would succeed me.' This was a well-worn phrase which the ladies of the salon had heard many times in case they got above themselves. Mr Freitzel, a Jewish tailor, had opened Charles et Cie twenty years ago and had founded its reputation on his good cutting. His wife had always been the front man.

Sarah couldn't resist it. 'But Nessie got married!'

Miss Frobisher sat up straight. 'That,' she said, 'is a thing of the past.' (If it ever existed, Sarah thought.) 'My visit to Switzerland, although I didn't say at the time, was to help her with her . . . divorce. She will be home quite soon now. A costly visit, but worth it in the long run.' She raised her eyes to the ceiling as if seeking Mr Freitzel's approbation. 'She will forget all about the unpleasantness when she comes home to help me.' What unpleasantness, Sarah briefly wondered, but in the end it didn't matter that Miss Frobisher hadn't confided in her. Family came first with the Jews. She had always known Miss Frobisher was a selfish, secretive woman.

'I have to look to the future, Miss Frobisher. Especially now.' That could be taken two ways. 'I think you will understand that.'

Miss Frobisher ignored this. 'You made a great mistake in setting up in a flat of your own, Sarah.' She touched her thick black bun of hair, looked down her Jewish nose. 'I wrote to Nessie at the time and said so. Nice girls don't do that sort of thing in Glasgow. If you were hoping to catch a husband, let me tell you that's the wrong way to go about it. Anyone would have told you what kind of man you'd catch.' And why didn't you warn your daughter about the wife-beater, or the womaniser, or whoever it was she got entangled with? A flame of anger swept through Sarah. She stopped herself speaking, because Miss Frobisher was right. Barney would never marry her, nor would he be a father to the baby, although it was his. It wasn't his style.

'I'm giving in my notice, *Mrs Freitzel*.' That was the only piece of insolence she allowed herself. 'Miss Frobisher' had been her employer's elegant cover-up for those wealthy but racist Glasgow matrons who wouldn't have given their custom to a Jewess.

But there was still Mary to contend with. After a week of bitter weeping she set off to visit her sister like a knight on a crusade, fully accoutred. Clever makeup, a loose coat and a cleverly cut dress was her armour. She wore the crocodile shoes Barney had given her as a going-away present, and carried a crocodile bag to match. Her rolled umbrella was of copper-coloured silk, her hat French felt turned up at the front by a diamond pin.

Mary's eyebrows lifted when she opened the door. 'Well, well, Queen Mary, no less.'

'Working garb. I've got news for you, Mary.'

'Come in. You haven't been too quick in coming to tell me if you have. I thought you'd got lost. Come away and let's hear it.' In the dark hall she stopped Sarah, putting her hand on her arm, her voice softer. 'Will you be getting married, Sarah? Is that it?'

'No, not yet. Barney's had to go on an extended trip to America. Maybe when he comes back. No, that's not the news.'

Mary pushed open the front-room door, her face showing her disappointment. 'I'm sorry about that. Come and sit down anyhow. Have you had your tea?'

'Yes, I took it before I came.'

'John's working late tonight and wee Bella's asleep.'

'Where's Lachie?' It would have helped.

'Mrs MacIntyre's taken him home with her Jackie from school, so we can have a good long chat. It's more comfortable here than the kitchen with the three-piece. Slip off your coat. My, what a gorgeous hat!'

'No, I can't stay long, I'm sorry. I've got a lot to do. The thing is, Mary,' she tried to steady her mouth, 'I'm going to set up a business in Largs.'

'Largs! Set up a business!' Mary turned to her. 'What would you do that for, in the name of Heaven? I thought you said you might be getting married?'

'Well, that wouldn't matter, would it? Barney's away a lot, and I've always hankered after a business of my own. It would keep me busy.'

'There are other things that keep women busy.' Mary's voice was sharp. 'Whereabouts in Largs, if I'm permitted to enquire?'

'I forgot to ask . . .' She tried to laugh. 'Barney's fixed it all up for me. You know he does a lot of trade with his cardigans and suchlike around the Clyde Coast, and it's somebody he knows who's giving up . . . an elderly lady.' It was bound to be. Where those lies came from she didn't know. They came pouring out of her mouth, tasting like vomit.

'Well, I don't know.' Mary looked at her, looked away. 'You fair give me the shocks these days, Sarah, clearing out one day, buying a business the next. But it's your life.' Her eyes came back to search Sarah's face, hoping to read the answers there. 'I tell you what. Jennie MacGilvray would look after the house and the weans for a week. You know, the wee hunchback.' She, at least, in Mary's eyes, had a tangible reason for not being married. 'She's as clean as a new pin and right fond o' weans. I'll come down with you and help you settle in.'

'No, no, there's no need for that. Don't bother Jennie.' Sarah was terrified. 'There's an assistant there, and the old lady will stay on with me till I get the hang of it. She might be offended if I brought you.'

'I don't see what would offend her in that.'

'You know what old folks are like.'

'And a house goes with it?'

'Yes, above the shop.' She spoke wildly. Nothing mattered now.

'I can see I'm not wanted.' Mary sniffed. 'I'm sure I don't

know . . . you've never been much good about a house . . . are you sure you don't want me to come?'

'Yes, I'm sure. I'm grateful all the same. You know that.' She saw the flicker of relief in her sister's eyes. She had never left her family for more than a few hours, saying you knew weans and what they got up to and she might come back to find the house burned down. 'It's just that I'd like to have a go at doing it for myself. It'll keep me busy while Barney's away. Later on, in the spring next year, maybe at Easter, you can all come and spend your holidays with me. Lachie would love it, getting down on the shore . . .' She was generous because next year meant nothing to her at this moment. The present was fearful enough.

'But this is just November!' Mary shook her head. 'I can't understand you these days at all. That man's done something to you. You would have been far better to have stayed an old maid in this house. We were happy enough, weren't we?'

'*You* were happy enough.' A shuddering sigh escaped her. 'You were married to a good husband, the salt of the earth.' There was a silence. Both women stared at the gleaming fire-brick elements of the gas fire Mary had lit. She thought it was dangerous but consoled herself with the fact that the room was generally only used on Sundays. Mary moved in her seat, put out her hand and touched Sarah's.

'That was a selfish remark. I'm not well-known for my tact.' Sarah shook her head, turning away. Oh, to tell her, to let her big sister take all the worry on her shoulders, to say, 'Come back and I'll see to everything . . .' She heard Mary's voice, falsely bright, 'And what did Madame Tutti-Frutti have to say when she heard?' She had never given into saying 'Miss Frobisher', because as she had once pointed out, she wasn't one of her clien*teel*.

Chapter Twenty-seven

Sin, as they said, had to be paid for, Sarah reflected, as she spent the next few weeks dismantling the flat at Grove Street, the love-nest . . . She had to be out this month, the factor had told her. It was a highly desirable flat. She would go to Largs when she had finished and find somewhere to live. It had to be Largs. That was what she had told Mary.

She wept to begin with as she packed her belongings with her usual care – Charles et Cie had taught her that. The green chiffon she had worn when they danced the Charleston the night before he left had a bitter-sweet memory. The bulkier things would go into boxes and be sent to that furniture repository (what a grand-sounding name that was) at Carleton Place on the Broomielaw.

She hoped it wouldn't be too damp near the river, but it would never do to get rid of everything in case he came back. She thought of the black water lapping at the stone walls of the repository, the floating orange skins, sometimes worse things that the girls in Charles et Cie had whispered about . . . sailors don't care.

She would leave a note with Mary telling her where the boxes were, and if the worst came to the worst, they could all go to her, John and the children. What would John do with expensive toiletries? (Barney always bought everything in threes from Bamber's.)

She tucked at the bottom of her suitcase some half-finished jars Barney had left, brilliantine, face lotion, talcum powder. She would be able to smell them sometimes and think of him, of dancing with him in those neat nutty-brown shoes you could see your face in, of coming back from the bathroom in his Paisley silk dressing gown with the broad black satin trimming, of taking it off and jumping in beside her like a loveable puppy . . . it was comfort he had wanted, only comfort . . . and an accommodation address.

And because she couldn't bear not to take them with her, the scent bottle with its silver stopper which had been his first gift, and the soapstone Buddha to keep by her for comfort. And if she was no longer . . . here, Mary could have the lot, and then Bella. She was a lovely wee girl with John's steady goodness. She could have told John more easily about the baby than Mary. That was funny when you thought about it. He was near to being like . . . Jesus Christ.

She sat back on her knees feeling her face redden at the sacrilege. And then the pain in her back made the blood recede. Bending over and trying to fasten the locks, you could tell there was something there, inside her, resting uncomfortably beneath her ribs as if it hadn't found a good place yet. She was silly to take the green chiffon. Her waist was thickening already. She would never be able to wear it again.

When she eventually got to bed, her last night in the love-nest, she thought, her mouth screwing painfully at that, she was dry-eyed and loaded with sleep. But with the sleep came nightmares. That woman at Elderslie Cross whom she had heard about . . .

She went into the dirty close chalk-marked by the children and patch-stained by urine – it was a fine place where the drunks going home could relieve themselves, climbed the dark stone stairway smelling of cats, stopped to rest on the first landing and looked through the grime-streaked window on to the back court. No grass there, unlike Mary's, where everybody tried to keep it nice.

On up, more slowly now, passing a woman with a plaid shawl round her head who gave her a sly glance and said, 'Is it Mrs McCafferty you're lookin' fur?' Not answering. And the woman herself, opening the door, dirty fingernails against the jamb, grey cardigan pulled across her bulging front with a safety pin, saying, 'Come in, hen, and hae ye brought the dough?'

The kitchen darkened by the half-drawn blind. 'We can get water frae the jawbox.' The dirty sheet spread on the table, the ash spilling between the bars of the grate, the cat sitting on the warm ash, swaying slightly as it dozed and stared into the hot coals . . .

Sarah woke in terror at the moment when the woman was bending over her holding something which looked like a long steel knitting needle, and sat up shivering.

Where did she get those images? She had never been near Mrs McCafferty, only overheard whispers in shops as she stood waiting to be served. Piecing them together. The house-wives with their string bags would never have told *her* anything. She was too well-dressed, too immaculate in her well-cut suits and real lizard court shoes, compared with their fur-trimmed slippers, their floral pinnies, and their cameo brooches, or more often, safety pins, holding their blouses tightly shut as if to preserve their chastity.

If only things had been different. If she could have been honest, said to Miss Frobisher, 'I'm having a baby, but I've got about five months to go yet. I'm feeling fine but although I'm not married I'm expecting the father back in good time. I know I couldn't be in the salon . . . Lady Grizel for one would be black affronted . . . but I've always liked the work-room. I could help there. I know the ladies' fads and fancies.'

She was going off her head with worry. Imagine such a thing! But how good it would have been to have the company, maybe have a wee bit of interest and kindness from the girls instead of disgust, and the afternoon cup together with the Fry's chocolate cream bar. Minnie would have come round. Going back to this flat which she had made so nice, with her own bed with the rose-coloured quilt for softness, waiting for Barney.

Maybe even slipping round at nights to Mary's with her knitting bag. She would have confessed to Mary, who would have been generous and said, 'Never mind. I've got some good pattern books left over from Lachie and Bella. "Bairnswear", they're called.' Sarah remembered them. They had nice pic-tures of laughing babies wearing matinee jackets with satin ribbon slotted through . . . she would have to stop this crying. It did nobody any good.

Chapter Twenty-eight

Largs was bleaker than she had ever seen it, even on wet days in summer. It had a general, all-over greyness with its pebbly shore and the stone houses with their prim Calvinistic fronts looking as if any decoration would be sinful. A lot of Glasgow's brightness came from the reflections of the lights in the wet streets, and the general air of vitality, a scurrying, joyful kind of vitality peculiar to northern cities, a cocking a snook at the climate.

The man in the corner newsagents at Brisbane Street sent her to Mrs MacIntyre who 'took in ladies', and apparently one look at Sarah satisfied the landlady that she came into that category. The tweed coat and skirt were impeccable, the helmet-shaped hat of good quality fur felt had a nice grosgrain ribbon to it. The upturned brim revealed a sweet face, a little pale but ladylike for all that. And as Mrs MacIntyre's sharp glance seemed to be saying, 'If that isn't a real crocodile handbag and a silk brolly, well, I'm a Dutchman.'

The room she showed Sarah was clean with a preponderance of white, white Madras cotton bedspread, white net curtains, and a white pleated paper fan in the grate. The light was white, sea-white. Sarah summoned her courage. 'I'd need a fire,' she said, shivering inside Forsyth's best Otterburn tailor-made, 'I'm a coldrife creature.'

'Oh, I'd see to that,' Mrs MacIntyre said. 'Jimmy, that's my husband, would either bring up a pail of coal every morning or we could find you a wee radiator. But there's fine heavy curtains and no draughts. They're good stone houses, these, none of your single-brick gimcrack things like these up above the town built by the council.'

'How much is it?' Sarah asked. I could go further and fare

worse, she thought, echoing unconsciously one of her sister's sayings.

'Two pounds a week, three good meals a day, and Jimmy would carry them up for you. We close the dining room in the winter. He's on a war pension, ma hubby, got his kneecap shot off in the Somme, but he's gae skeigh on his legs all the same.'

'Has he never worked since then?' Sarah enquired sympathetically, but also to deflect the woman's steady gaze on her.

'Him? He works all the time, especially in the Season. I couldny do without him at the Fair especially, better than three women, but, of course, we're quiet the now.' The piercing gaze was there again. 'You'll be down for a wee holiday, then, Mrs Lane?' The gaze darted momentarily to the simple gold wedding ring. Sarah had bought it in Argyle Street before she left, standing in front of Samuel's glittering display before she plucked up enough courage to go in. 'Or have you no' been too weel?' She put on a look of concern.

Sarah had prepared her story. It was no good saying, as she had contemplated, that she had a bad chest and was there for her health. Any Largs landlady knew full well that her town was recommended for its bracing qualities rather than its mildness. Nor that she was a lady of leisure. That would only have two connotations: one, that she might have a 'follower', or worse, 'followers'; or, two, that she was soft in the head. A lady who was comfortably off and of good character would choose Torquay or Bournemouth where it was well-known they had palm trees, soft winds, afternoon orchestras and Botanical Gardens to stroll in.

She took a deep breath. 'No, I'm quite well, thank you, but I'm a widow, and for a time back I've been thinking of setting up in business on my own. I used to come to Largs when I was a wee girl. I always liked it.'

'Oh, I see.' Mrs MacIntyre rested her arms on her shelf-like chest. 'Whit kind o' business?' Her stance said, 'convince me'.

'Fancy cakes and pastries, that kind of thing. High-class, of course.' In her feverish planning of ways and means to conceal her condition she had hit on the bizarre idea that any occupation where she wore an apron, preferably voluminous, would suit her best. She had reflected wryly that Miss Frobisher would have fainted on the spot at the mention of the obscene word 'apron'. The girls were given a yearly allowance to cover the expense of their well-cut 'afternoon dresses' for the salon. The only apron Sarah was in the habit of wearing was of the 'tea' variety, a scrap of flowered silk, frill-edged, to protect her skirt when she was washing up.

'Do you do a lot of baking yourself?' She motioned to a chair with her hand. 'Sit down, Mrs Lane.' Her eyes had gone smaller, calculating. She didn't look the type, this one, for baking. She was too refined. Her hands were too well-cared for.

'Thanks.' Sarah sat down, wished immediately she hadn't. It might make the woman suspicious. 'No, but I know the ins and outs of it. My father had a similar business in Glasgow on a large scale. My sister and I were on the retail side.' She had a vision of Mary's outraged expression if she could hear this pack of lies. Their father had been a master joiner all his days, a self-effacing man who couldn't have stood behind a counter and served the public if they had trebled his salary.

'We've got a real good baker and confectioner here already,' Mrs MacIntyre said. 'Craig's. They've got the monopoly here. It would serve them right if they got some competition.'

'Oh, I wouldn't want to take any of their trade away,' Sarah said earnestly. 'But I could maybe learn a thing or two from them. Perhaps get taken on for a time . . .' Her fancy was running away again with her.

'You mean, serve behind their coonter!' Mrs MacIntyre looked horrified, her eyes raking the fur felt, the Otterburn tweed, the crocodile handbag.

'It wouldn't be as an ordinary shopgirl. It would be as a kind of trainee. My father always said you had to learn a business from the bottom up.' Sarah wished she hadn't let her tongue run away with her quite as much. She had no intention of applying for a job in Craig's, lowly or otherwise. Mrs MacIntyre was bound to have a spy in the camp.

But her prospective landlady had subsided. 'A canna tell a lie,' she said, 'they make awfy good aipple tairts.'

Sarah moved in with the MacIntyres and took care not to do anything in a hurry. She had to give the appearance of a widow who was comfortably off and was looking around for a suitable investment. The money she had drawn from her savings bank account would last easily for six months. After that, it wouldn't matter.

Mr MacIntyre, Jimmy, as grey as the town itself, grey-haired, grey-faced, grey hand-knitted gensy, brought her the *Largs and Millport Weekly News* with her breakfast. 'There you are now, Mrs Lane. You have a good prowl through that. But take your time. If you want my opinion, there are plenty of sharks in Largs.' Sometimes, looking at the grey sea, and how the long waves curved and rolled towards the shore, Sarah wondered if they lurked there too. She had periods of light-headedness when the future, she decided, was not to be borne. Her depression and despair would be so great that she was tempted to give up the struggle there and then, but a face had to be put on things, at least for a few months. Barney might write. He was bound to write. And then she would pluck up her courage and tell him . . .

The effort of preparing herself to go out each morning exhausted her so much that it would be eleven o'clock before she went down the Turkey-red carpeted staircase with its brass stair-rods. 'Is that you away for your constitutional, Mrs Lane?' Mrs MacIntyre would say, coming from the kitchen to stand in the doorway. It was necessary to smile, to pass the time of day, to appear normal.

She would set out for a brisk walk round the town, or at least that was how she described it to Mrs MacIntyre, but more often than not she would take the bus along the coast in the Fairlie direction, then get off and walk slowly back, sometimes going into a café for a cup of tea if she could find one open. The island across the water, the Great Cumbrae, seemed to cast a cold, whale-shaped shadow on her as she walked, like the cold shadow which lay constantly on her heart.

What was she going to do? Barney would come back from America and find the flat empty. Mary would be worrying long before that and wondering why she hadn't kept in touch. She had written her a short note giving her her new address and asking her to pass it on to the Post Office. She was very busy with the shop, but she would write soon.

Sometimes on those wintry forenoons her agony was so great that she felt like someone deranged. She would stop and stare unseeingly in shop windows, or walk by the deserted shore, on wet days her only companions being the big, aggressive grey gulls. She would contemplate crossing the pebbles and walking into the sea to end it all, but she would restrain herself, as from a forbidden pleasure. That had to be reserved for later, when no further concealment was possible, when she had reached the end of the road, *when there was no letter.*

At other times she would reproach herself for having run away. That had been stupid. She would forget her pride and write to Barney tonight and tell him of the coming baby. He would come winging back from America and ask her to marry him right away. *But she didn't have his address. He had said he would be moving on all the time. . .* And then a modicum of sense would return to her and she would decide to go back to Glasgow and confess to Mary, throw herself on her mercy. Oh, the bliss of that, she would think, to be back in her own city amongst her own folks, away from this alien town in which she moved like a ghost.

Each day she made herself wait. Barney might come of his own accord. He would search her out and tell her how wrong he had been not to propose long ago. 'Silly boy,' she would say. The smell of the brilliantine and his rich cigars would be in her nostrils for a moment instead of the sea-wrack.

It was on one of those dreary excursions that she came across what might be the answer to one of her problems, a shop to let in the middle of Fairlie, diagonally across from the small Post Office. She stood under the notice board pretending to examine the windows with the casual interest of a passer-by. In the left-hand one there was a notice which said 'Teas', surrounded by a small but fresh display of cakes and scones on three-tiered stands. In the right-hand window there was a meagre collection of knitted goods, tea cosies, gloves and ladies' sensible underwear, combinations and long knitted vests with set-in sleeves. The shop was what Mary would have called a 'Jenny Awthings'.

Sarah looked up at the notice board again. 'Apply to J. & A. MacPherson, 3a Main Street, Largs.' She decided it would be more discreet to obtain information from them than to go into the shop for a cup of tea and perhaps be faced with more questions than answers. There would be plenty of Mrs MacIntyres.

She walked quickly back to the town, turning over the advantages in her mind. It was only ten minutes' walk from the centre of Largs, so for the time being she could keep her lodgings, although there might be a flat above which would be even better. Since teas were served with home-made produce, there would be an excuse for that voluminous apron she had set her heart on. And a crowning advantage, she remembered that in the drapery window there had been a few pairs of stout salmon-pink stays. She had decided she must soon buy a pair. Tight lacing and loose clothes would conceal her condition almost to the end. Or nearly to the end. That was as far as she could bring herself to visualise.

She was shown into Mr John MacPherson's room by a young girl with cheerful buck teeth. 'Is it Mr John or Mr Andrew you want?' she had asked, and Sarah had assured her it didn't matter. 'Come away through, then. Mr John's no' busy. You look fair chilpit. The Largs winds are very searching although they say we're on the Gulf Stream.'

Mr John, white-haired, red-faced, also smiling, was sitting toasting himself in front of a blazing fire. There was a smell of hot blue serge in the room. He invited Sarah to sit down and take off her coat, but she declined, loosening it at the neck only, although the room was like an oven. The young girl went away.

'I'm interested in the shop to rent in Fairlie village,' she told the solicitor. 'Could you give me some particulars, if you don't mind?'

'Well, that's easy enough, Miss . . . ?'

'Mrs Lane.'

'Ah, yes.' She had taken off her gloves. 'To tell you the truth you're the first enquiry we've had. Not the best time of the year for business. Would you take a cup of tea? I could get Isa to make you one. You look . . . cold.'

'No, thanks.' She knew of her paleness. Stays *and* rouge. She made a mental note. 'You're very kind, but it's too near my lunch.'

'I'll get to the point, then. The owner is a Miss Lindsay, an elderly lady, and she's been trying to get it off her hands for some time. You see, I'm being quite frank with you, Mrs Lane. It's not a bad wee business if she had built it up, but she's getting on and she's let it run down. She's an old maid and hasn't any relatives nearby. She's now willing to let it for a year in the hope that it might then be purchased by the rentor.'

'I wouldn't have to buy it then?' There was no future.

'No, no, nothing like that, but naturally it would be an admirable arrangement. The turnover is not great, but I think it would cover costs, and, of course, trade improves once we're past the worst of the year. Folks like to take a walk out from Largs, have a stroll round Fairlie, go up to the Fairy Glen, it's a real nice wee place, Fairlie, in the summer.' She was hardly listening to Mr MacPherson. It would see her to the end of the road, unless Barney turned up. Barney . . . his voice seemed to echo in her ear. '*You've become a fine wee cook since you got your own place . . .*'

'Is there a flat with it?'

'No, regrettably, that's been let to a retired couple. They come and go from Glasgow.' She would have to stay where she was with the MacIntyres. It didn't matter. She had some time yet before the end of the road.

'Did the owner do the baking, Mr MacPherson?' she asked.

'I'm afraid that's not in my line.' Her line was showing

couture dresses to rich spoiled ladies, fingering silk and satin, not floury dough.

'No, not for some time, I believe. She'd get someone nearby, I daresay. There's always some widow woman willing to earn a shilling or two. And if you didn't want to continue with that side of things, well,' his eyes twinkled, 'I'm sure you'll have plenty of ideas. The rent's moderate. Two guineas per week, paid monthly.'

'I'll take it,' Sarah said. It fitted in exactly with the lies she had told Mary, almost as if God approved of them.

He nodded, pleased, and held out his hand. It was warm, cushiony and slightly damp. 'I'm sure you won't regret it, and we'll be glad to have you in our little community. We're nice enough when you get to know us, and the Fairlie folk will soon take an interest in you when you move in.' Pray God not too much, she thought. 'Now, then.' He look a typewritten foolscap page from his desk drawer, glanced at it, slid it towards her. 'Here we are. If you'd just sign the contract at the bottom, please.' He said pleasantly, as she bent over it, pen in hand, 'If it's not too inquisitive, though I'm afraid we're famed for it here, what brings you to Largs?' 'Sarah Lane', she wrote, using the wooden-backed blotter beside her. At least it was her own signature. She sat up straight, sliding the contract towards him.

'Since my husband died,' she had told so many lies that it was becoming easy, 'I've wanted a little business of my own, preferably on the Clyde coast. Glasgow holds many sad memories for me. Before my marriage I was in an exclusive shop there, and well, time gets heavy on your hands.'

He nodded. 'Well, you strike me as the type who could work up Miss Lindsay's into a good going concern.' Mr Mac-Pherson ran his eye over the document. 'Yes, that's quite in order. Who knows,' he went on, looking up and smiling at her, 'in a year's time you might even decide to buy?'

'Who knows?' Sarah said, getting up. She had risen too hurriedly. A dreadful coldness struck her despite the heat of the room. Her brow was wet, and the solicitor's red face seemed to be dissolving like a jelly in front of her.

'Are you all right, Mrs Lane?' His voice was anxious and far away. He half-rose from his chair.

She made a great effort, her eyes cleared, she even managed to smile. 'Perfectly. It's just coming in out of the cold, and your room's so nice and warm.' His face was in focus now. He looked reassured.

'I'll say goodbye for the present, then.' He held out his hand.

Who knows, in a year's time, you might even decide to buy. . . The solicitor's words echoed in her head as she hurried back to Mrs MacIntyre's. The landlady liked to serve lunch on the stroke of one. 'Who knows?' *She* knew. Mr Mac-Pherson with the red face and the twinkling eyes would be the centre of his cronies long before a year. She could see him in the lounge bar of that hotel on the corner of Main Street, dark mahogany and brass, a glass of whisky in his hand. 'You could have knocked me down with a feather when I read it in the paper. Such a nice young woman, not that type at all, you would have thought. A sad business, poor soul.' Would he say 'poor soul'? She thought so. She hoped so. He had seemed a kind sort of man. But there was still hope, she told herself, rounding the corner of Brisbane Street and shivering against the wind, still hope . . .

When she got back to her room there was a letter waiting for her with an American stamp on it. She tore it open, her heart fluttering against her ribs, colour rushing to her cheeks. 'Oh, Barney, my boy, my boy, I misjudged you . . .' She was half-crooning to herself as she started to read it. For a moment the words danced before her eyes, and then they settled into his regular sloping handwriting.

Dearest girl, I know you're going to get a shock when you read this letter, but if you feel bad it's nothing to how I feel writing it. I was too much of a coward to tell you to your face. I thought this would be the kindest way to do it, and believe me, Sarah, when you read this, you'll think, I know you'll think, that you're well rid of me.

I'm going to stay with Iain in America for a time, maybe not come back to Scotland at all. We'll see. He says folks here don't think the same of two men living together. They're easier-going.

I know I was always light-hearted with you, at least I hope you thought that, but for a long time I've been worried nearly out of my mind. I spoke to the doctor but he could give me no help, said I should find a good girl and settle down with her.

Well, I couldn't have found a better girl than you, Sarah, always so gentle and loving, ready to do anything I asked, even leaving your sister's house and setting up on your own. It seemed to work for a time, didn't it? I hope I made you happy, because I did try . . . remember those good dinners we had together . . . you were a great wee cook . . . and that night we danced the Charleston? You were wearing a lime-green chiffon dress with floating points and those shiny silk stockings I'd bought you – they were Milanese, the best – and I thought any other man would go mad with desire. It was then I knew it was no use. I'll never forget that night, the happiness in that flat you'd made so cosy for us, and the sadness. I pray to God you'll never know the sadness I felt.

Sarah, how can I say this without hurting you? It's me and Iain. That's why I could never marry you, though I know that was what you wanted, what every girl wants. You're so loveable, so trusting. Mary didn't like me, because she saw deeper than you. Or maybe you didn't want to see . . .

But it's me and Iain, always will be, at least I hope it always will be because he's ten years younger than me. But I don't think of that. I'm happy with him the way I can never be happy with any girl. That's the cruellest thing I've ever had to say, and to say it to you, who were so good to me, breaks my heart.

I hope you'll come to realise it would never have worked, and that you're well rid of me. But try not to think of me with too much bitterness. Think of the happy times and try to forgive me. You had one part of my love and as much as I could give. I hope you'll find someone some day who can give you everything.

Barney.

Chapter Twenty-nine

She couldn't remember going out of the house at Brisbane Street, or whether or not she had spoken to Mrs MacIntyre. There had been a rich smell of cabbage in the narrow hall as she went through it, and she knew they would be sitting down to their hearty meal, meat and two vegetables, steamed pudding, custard or rice pudding, in the kitchen.

Sarah walked quickly along the street and on to the promenade, wondering why she had chosen this route since it was so exposed. '*It's me and Iain, it's me and Iain.*' She found herself mouthing the words like a drunken woman, and realised that she was staggering about the pavement like one. She must slow her pace a little, stare into shops, look like a lady of leisure out for her afternoon stroll.

When she came to the pier she stood at the railings and watched the bustle of the fishermen as they worked about their boats, shouting cheerfully at each other and overseen by the grey gulls who wheeled slowly overhead. She had a moment of unreality. Where was she? How did she get to this alien place with its white sweep of sky and the alien noises of gulls and fishermen swirling around her as if she were a rock?

'It's my heart, it's my heart that's going to break.' Her mouth shaped the words. 'I'll fall down here and there will be nobody who knows me, they'll leave me lying like a piece of driftwood . . .' She saw clearly her sister's face bent over her, a horrified hand held up as if to shield it. 'In the name of Heaven, Sarah, what kind of mess is this you've got yourself into?'

A youngish man with a soiled shirt collar came up to her and said, 'All right, missus?' She didn't like his familiar tone.

'Quite all right,' she said, and veered away from him across the street, scarcely looking at the traffic.

She went into a tearoom and sat down at one of the oak tables with a bunch of dried flowers in the centre. It was set with scones, pancakes, cups, saucers and plates, ready for afternoon tea. Two waitresses were chatting together, leaning against the panelled wall, and one nudged the other who straightened her apron and came towards Sarah. She looked down at her, taking a pencil from some secret place in her pleated white cap tied with a black velvet ribbon. 'Is it the afternoon tea for one?' The pencil was poised above her pad.

'Just tea, thank you,' Sarah said. The waitress stubbed her pencil into the pad as if she had received a shock.

'Scone, butter, jam and one fancy goes with the tea,' she said impassively. 'We don't do single teas.' Sarah looked up at the voice, only seeing a black and white blur.

'Just tea,' she said. 'I'll pay for the rest.'

'Oh, in that case!' The waitress made some rapid black hieroglyphics on the pad, jabbed her pencil in a decided dot underneath them and strode off. Sarah could see at the edge of her vision that she had stopped to make some remark to her fellow waitress.

Immediately the agitation which rose in her breast was not to be borne. There was no possibility that she could sit and wait until the tea came. Her heart would shatter into fragments. 'Iain and me,' she mouthed, getting up, 'just Iain and me . . .' She walked over to the other waitress, still propped up at the wall. 'Unfortunately,' she said, as if she were reading from a script, 'I suddenly feel unwell. Would you be kind enough to tell your friend to cancel my order.' She met her eyes and saw some kind of frightened sympathy there.

'Maybe the cup o' tea would help?'

'Nothing will help,' she said, and somehow found herself outside, standing in the shop doorway.

Along the promenade the snell wind blew at this time of the day as she struggled against it. The tall terraces were like aproned matrons, and the setting sun behind them gave them a halo, as if of righteousness. It was too righteous, this place, composed of people like Mrs MacIntyre. There would be no sympathy for a young woman whose lover had gone off with another man, one called Iain.

The grey sea licked greedily at the stone wall – why did everything seem menacing today, she wondered, as she went slowly along, holding on to her hat. And the waves were too venturesome – that one coming towards her had its tongue stretched out as it fell near her. Even the Great Cumbrae across the water seemed to be lying in wait, like her future, patiently, pitilessly. When an even bigger, stronger wave brushed her shoes, she was sorry it hadn't curled round them and dragged her into nothingness with it.

Glasgow would have been kinder than this. Glasgow had a soul, a warm soul. The soft rain was like tears. Mary had a warm soul too. Her anger at Barney would dull her shame at her sister's predicament. She would blame herself for not realising sooner, would make excuses for herself, the washing, cooking, the shops, the church, the weans, feeding John and his cronies.

And what about John? Would he say, 'Poor Sarah,' when he heard, but what could he do about it? He had his priorities too, his wife and family, the starving men and children he so constantly fought for. He had only so much pity left. Oh, she needed pity, to feel his strong arms round her as she had once felt them . . . 'It's just me and Iain.' The words were ringing round her head, making her feel like a crazy woman. She turned on her heel and made for Brisbane Street.

In Mrs MacIntyre's hall she knocked at the kitchen door and opened it slightly. 'No food, Mrs MacIntyre. I had a nice tea on the front.' She undressed in her cold room and crept into bed. Death, she thought, would be better than this.

Chapter Thirty

1926

The weather turned very cold after Christmas and remained so. Mrs MacIntyre said she had never known anything like it, and she sent Jimmy out to buy a 'wee paraffin stove' for Sarah's room. It was anxiety about her coal bill rather than kindness which prompted her. Had she known that Sarah kept the fire burning through the night she would have been even more worried.

Now the room was neither hot nor cold. It had a muggy paraffin-tinged atmosphere which nauseated Sarah. But she had a strong stomach. On the few occasions when she actually vomited she was careful not to retch. Mrs MacIntyre must be given no inkling of her condition (she was now seven months pregnant), or she would be out on her ear.

The cold weather had one overwhelming advantage for Sarah. Everyone bundled into as many clothes as they possessed regardless of appearance, and she was no exception. She now wore the heavy stays tightly laced on her swollen stomach, but in any case it was well concealed under her thick skirt and petticoats topped by a jersey and loose cardigan. She affected a long woollen scarf whose ends she arranged to hang down in front to her waist, and in the shop the voluminous apron was a further disguise.

What would they think of her at Charles et Cie if they could see her now? The elegant Miss Lane, Miss Frobisher's right-hand woman. What would Mrs de Vere think of her, the young woman she had taken a liking to originally because of her elegance, but later because they shared a friendship? Had she not buried herself in Largs she might have been visiting her in her picture-book cottage, being met at the train and driven back for tea in the inglenook of a chintz-covered room, perhaps going up to the Big House for dinner with Ronald and Elizabeth. 'This is my friend, Sarah Lane, from Glasgow.' She would wear her green chiffon for that and perhaps a white fur stole which she would buy for the occasion . . .

The shop itself was a failure. Hardly anyone came in for teas, although she paid half a crown every two or three days to Mrs Abernethy nearby to bake a few scones and cakes. Elderly women who had grown tired of baking for themselves were her only customers, and she got into the habit of eating what she didn't sell. On her way home she would stand at the railings of the pier and throw the left-overs to the raucous seagulls that swooped down from the grey sky.

The drapery side of the shop was no better. She was lucky if she sold more than a few articles each week, and the intensely cold weather prevented any visitors from coming from either Greenock or Glasgow to spend a day at the coast.

She could hardly afford to replace the goods she sold, but she made an effort to buy a few odds and ends from the packman who braved the elements every few weeks to call on her, a wisp of a man from the back streets of Greenock, scrawny, bandy-legged, who carried a huge battered suitcase of goods from the railway station, head down to the cruel wind blowing from the sea.

He was like a friendly whippet, unfailingly cheerful as they sipped their hot tea together, and he made short work of her pastries. 'The tide will turn, Missus. If you can just hold on to Easter, you'll have a good wee business on your hands. The Glesca folks aye have money to burn. They'll flock doon here in their thoosands. They've got a passion for shops, I mean the wummen, they hardly look at the waater! The men are different. They like the stir o' the boats at the pier, or goin' oot for a wee row. So keep your windows lively, and if I were you, a'd introduce a bit o' colour, and by gum,' he said, squinting up at her from his macaroon, 'you could dae wi' a bit o' colour yersel. A never seen ony yin sae peely-wally.'

She bought baby bootees and bonnets in crude pinks and blues in a sullen determination to keep the shop ticking over until she reached the 'end of the road'. On better days, she admitted to herself that it had been reached when Barney's letter came. There must be some explanation, some happening still to come. Most of the time, her mind dulled by cold and worry about the shop, she didn't think. Each day became a dreary dogged attempt at survival with the hope only of creeping into bed at the end of it.

Her money was beginning to run out, but to economise further she told Mrs MacIntyre that she would in future make her own tea in the shop. 'It sets me up for the walk home,' she said, 'the buses are so scarce.' Her landlady had been put out that her Friday plaice and chips, and her ham and egg teas were being spurned. She didn't approve of the five shilling reduction in the weekly bill that Sarah had suggested. The overheads were just the same, she pointed out. She would have been even more upset if she had seen how Sarah existed on endless cups of tea and Mrs Abernethy's stale residue.

The bad weather had yet another bonus. Mary and her family all had flu over Christmas and didn't want her to spend it with them. 'It's like a hospital here, Sarah,' she wrote. 'You'd be miserable, and you never were any good about a house. Any roads, I expect some of your fine friends you've made in Largs will give you an invite.' Sarah had spent money she could ill afford on presents for the four of them and posted them in good time.

In January there were heavy snowfalls in Glasgow and the trains were either running late or cancelled. No one was travelling about. They had dug themselves in for the winter, and there, as everywhere else in the country, the sword of Damocles was hanging over their heads, the prospect of a General Strike.

John, being one of the bulwarks of the Independent Labour Party, was away at meetings every night listening to the plans already being made for transport arrangements and routes. When he wasn't doing that, Mary wrote, he was sitting every night when he came home from Dixon's with his ear glued to the wireless.

'If I hear any more about the Samuel Report I'll leave him,' her letter said. 'We have meetings here during the week and he's on the Green most Sundays. Some housewives have even started laying in a bit more food when they can afford it. I've bought a few tins of salmon just in case.'

February came with the keen bitter winds which were even more trying to Sarah, now in her eighth month of pregnancy, perpetually tired, perpetually hungry. Survival took up all her energy. The walk along the front, morning and evening, to and from the shop, could have been a nightmare, but it was somehow reassuring. She would look at the grey swollen sea and think of it as a friend. 'When you're ready,' it seemed to say, slapping sullenly on the pebbly shore, 'I won't fail you when you reach the end of the road.' What that meant now she no longer knew nor cared. She had no energy left for thinking. Her brain seemed to be numbed by the cold.

In the middle of February she was beginning to find it difficult to walk with any semblance of lightness. The baby seemed to have settled low down, and that morning she had pulled the laces of her stays deliberately and cruelly over her distended stomach. She saw the child move under the stretched skin as if in protest. Somewhere at the back of her mind she knew it was wrong, but that it was the only thing to do. No one must know of this unwanted child she carried, Mrs MacIntyre with her flat stare, Mary, her shrewd sister, most of all, Barney in America.

She had never replied to his letter because she was afraid of what she might say. Because there was nothing to say. Even if she had had his address. She had tried. She had even gone to the local library and taken out '*The Great Gatsby*' so that America might come alive for her. She had even tried to imagine Iain. She had no one to base her imagination upon. Charles et Cie had been an all-female establishment. John's friends were steady married men. Their eyes were often alight with fervour, but not for her. They had wives and children to feed, jobs which were fast disappearing. Gus Carmichael, whom she had long ago played tennis with, had at least shown on their trip in his car that he was only partial to women.

She imagined Iain as slight and fair with fine hands, since he was an interior decorator. And he would wear fancy ties because he was interested in design. Would he and Barney dance together? Two men? Sometimes at the Plaza or the Albert ballrooms in Glasgow she had seen two women dancing together, the wallflowers. But never men. Maybe in America where things were different.

But it was no use. Whatever Iain's attractions, it was him and Barney, Barney and Iain. Some mornings, when her mind regained its usual sharpness for a little time, she admitted the truth to herself. It was over. Her dream of marriage and a home like her sister's was gone. There was nothing left for her but to finish it all.

It wouldn't be long now. Somehow or other she would work up the effort to do what she intended to do. The baby was filling every part of her body from beneath her heart to between her legs. It wanted to be admitted. Not yet, not yet, she would think, fighting with the terror. It struggled and kicked against the tight lacing, repaying her with a constant nausea which made her paler than ever.

Sarah met Mrs MacIntyre at the foot of the stairs one night when she came in.

'My goodness, you look wabbit,' she said. 'Could you no' get a bus the night?'

'No, they don't seem to run as regularly now. My brother-in-law in Glasgow thinks we're working up to a general strike. I thought of a taxi but I quite enjoy the walk. It keeps my circulation going.'

'I'm sure you've no need o' it. I don't like the look o' you at all. Folks'll be blaming me. Cutting out your tea. It was your idea, no' mine, don't forget. Look, I'll no' take no for an answer. Jimmy and I had a nice piece of fresh plaice the night. There's plenty left over. I'm going to send him up with some for your tea. I don't think you're feeding yourself properly in that shop.'

'I get plenty, Mrs MacIntyre, plenty.' The vision of a slice of plaice in its golden batter was too much for her. 'Well, just a taste, then, although I shouldn't if I want to keep my figure.' She watched the woman as she spoke. The recklessness was born of despair. Not long now till the end of the road.

'You're one of Pharaoh's lean cattle. I thought that when I first saw you.' Was there a gleam in the woman's eye? A slight emphasis on 'first'? 'Well, I'll away and put the fish in the pan while you get your things off.'

When Jimmy brought the tray there were chips with the plaice, a bottle of tomato sauce, and some trifle in a dish flanked by a jug of cream.

'What a spread, Mr MacIntyre,' she said. She tried to keep the greed out of her eyes.

'We've been thinking you didn't look so good those two or three weeks back. You aren't maybe used to the kind o' weather we get here. You've got to be a native of Largs to stand the snell winds.'

'I like the cold. It's . . . invigorating. I've never done with the heat. Those foreign places that people talk about . . .' Once she had dreams of she and Barney going somewhere exotic like Spain for their honeymoon. She had thought of a small white house, a *hacienda*, was that the name, perched on rocks above a deep blue sea, inviting, not like the dirty grey of the Clyde. And with cacti plants growing on the rocks, huge ones, quite different from the tiny things people collected on their windowsill. Her eyes filled with tears and ran down her face. She saw the man's eyes on her and whipped out her handkerchief. 'Me boasting about liking the cold and here I've got a real beauty today.' She blew her nose vigorously, surreptitiously wiping her cheeks. 'I maybe picked it up from one of my customers.'

'Well, I'll get away down and let you get on with your tea.' He still stood, looking down at her, and she saw some kind of pity in his mild face. 'Try some of the tomato sauce with it.' He turned and went out of the room. She could hear him stomping down the stairs, dot and carry one, on his bad leg. She could hardly wait to attack the food.

Satiated, she slowly stripped herself of all her layers, the cardigan, the scarf, woollen skirt, petticoat, woollen knickers, and, at last, the stays. When she took them off there were deep red weals on her stomach, and it ached so badly, a deep, low-down ache, that without washing, or cleaning her teeth, she pulled on her nightdress, tied on a grey shawl of her mother's round her shoulders, and crept into bed.

I feel like an animal, she thought, a heavy drowsy animal. What would Barney say if he could see me like this? He always liked me nice, scented, satin underwear, not without it . . . he hadn't liked her as much as Iain. What was it that Iain had to offer? She had loved him, her own dear boy. What did it matter? Nothing mattered now. She was nearing the end of the road.

In the middle of the night she wakened with a strong pain going through her like a sword blade. Sweat poured from her, more than sweat, her nightdress was wet and limp between her legs. The blade was turning in her insides, stirring them, sending out waves of referred pain, up her arms, down her legs, sending sickness up into her throat.

And then as quickly as the pain had come, it receded. It was that fried fish, she thought, and the rich cream. She lay like a beached whale on the shore. That was how she thought of herself, even to the unexplained wetness which was more than sweat. She was still lying, breathing easily, when the pain came again, strong, shooting through her, piercing right down to the pit of her, and with it a terrible desire to push, to rid herself of it.

It can't be, she thought. I've got a month to go yet, a month to plan . . . ah, there was another one, worse this time, squeezing the life out of her. *Squeezing the life out of her* . . . She rolled about in agony, stuffing her hands into her mouth to stop the screams. This is it! I'm having it! I'm at the end of the road, oh, God . . . her despair was not to be borne. She pushed her face into the pillows. Cruel, cruel . . . I wasn't ready to do it, to walk into the sea . . . the image of the grey cheated waves came back to her . . . I thought there would be time . . . she knew she was wailing into the pillow.

234

There was another searing pain, so great that it lifted her from where she rolled on the bed to sit on the side of it, her legs spread, head hanging, her teeth clenched over the groans which were being forced from her. 'I have to live . . . I never meant to . . . that cold sea . . . it was all a dream, rubbish, I was only *pretending* . . .' The last word was drawn from her in a long wail, and with it, for a moment, the pain.

It wouldn't last. The peace wouldn't last. She drew her hands downwards over her face, heaved herself to her feet, and just as she was, bedraggled, soaking nightdress, hair unkempt, staggered across the room to the door, wrenched it open, felt the bare cold boards of the landing under her feet. She lunged towards the door opposite, and raising her fist, knocked loudly, her head falling against it. She could hear the silence. Quick, quick, the pain would be back any minute, tearing her apart. She knocked again, fiercely, a hammer of blows. It wasn't Sarah Lane who was doing this, that elegant young woman trained by Miss Frobisher of Charles et Cie, it was some female beast who needed help, had to have it, no matter from whom, even from Mrs MacIntyre. She could hear scuffling, whispering, silence, then the man's voice, tremulous, fearful, 'Is it . . . is it Mrs Lane?'

'I'm ill. Help me, help me . . . for the love of God!'

'Just a minute.' More scuffling. Her hand was raised when the door opened. He stood there, thin hair spiky, trousers pulled on over his pyjamas. There was a piece of striped flannel sticking through his open fly in a peak.

'Help me . . .' The pain was there again, thrusting deep into her bowels, taking her legs from her, making her fall against him. She could see Mrs MacIntyre sitting up in bed, her horrified face beneath a pink boudoir cap with whorls of lace over her ears. She was saying something. Her mouth was open. Her hands were held up in front of her as if she was being attacked.

'It's . . . Mrs Thingummy, Martha . . .' Jimmy's terrified voice cut across his wife's. 'A think . . . a think she's havin' a wean . . .'

235

Chapter Thirty-one

Everything seemed like a long time ago, that nightmare of a night, the frightened face of Jimmy, the horrified face of his wife made more horrific by the bizarre boudoir cap, Jimmy half-dragging her back to her room (his wife still keening on the bed), the doctor's large hands on her with red hair which grew down his fingers, the sustained agony, at last, when it was no longer to be borne, the merciful nothingness.

The doctor had been matter of fact when it was all over, which was the only possible way to behave in a nightmare. 'Least said soonest mended. You've had a bad time and you've lost the baby. It was dead.'

'I'm sorry.' Sarah didn't know whether she was sorry or not. During those last months she had never even extracted from her mind the concept of the baby and looked at it as something apart from her. Why bother when she had no intention of having a life *with* it. She saw that now for the fallacy it was. It took courage to die. All the good arguments she had started off with, Barney wouldn't want it, didn't want to marry her anyhow, nobody wanted her, a pregnant, unmarried girl, 'damaged goods' were the words used by Mary for such people, hadn't meant a thing when she had found herself in labour. She had wanted to live.

But that had gone now. She was left only with a dull apathy in that cold room in Largs with the paraffin stove that still turned her stomach. 'You're not in a good state of health,' the doctor said. 'You've a bad chest as well. I don't like it.' He was impatient. 'Have you not been feeding yourself? You should have known you couldn't have a live baby if you didn't feed yourself.' Or give it room to breathe, she thought.

'I'm sorry.'

'I'm sending in the district nurse who'll attend to you twice a day till you feel better. I'm afraid we've no room at the Cottage Hospital for your type of case. Don't try to get up. Mr MacIntyre will bring up your food to you as before. I've given instructions about what you should get.'

'Mrs MacIntyre,' she began. 'Is she . . . ?'

'You gave that good lady the fright of her life.' His mouth twisted as if trying to hide a smile. 'I doubt if she'll ever get over it. "It's the deceit", she says.' He saw Sarah's face. 'You've got enough to worry about. She's never had a family. It makes a difference. You get set in your ways.'

'I'll clear out. I'll go tomorrow.'

'You're in no fit state to go anywhere yet, young lady. Unless you can afford a nursing home?'

'No,' she said dully, 'I can't. But I've got relations . . . in Glasgow.'

'I'm glad to hear it. Would you like me to let them know?'

'No, not yet.'

'They'll have to be told. Will you get Nurse Waddell to drop them a line, then?'

'There will be no need. I'll do it myself.'

'Would you like to have a talk with me?' He had a rough country face, but kind eyes. 'It might help.'

She turned her head away from him on the pillow. After a time she heard him go out.

The days passed and she didn't ask the bright-faced young nurse to write to Mary. The doctor let her be. She lay quietly in her bed, drained, and yet feeling conscious of some kind of relief. It was over. Her life was over. There would be no need to walk into the sea. All she had to do was to lie, and wait.

Strangely enough her mind went back to Ruth Crosbie. There had been no room for her for a long time. Now, she thought, I understand her agony. She had never found an Iain, or his equivalent. Had Ruth walked those dark streets around Minard Road as she herself had walked along the cold Largs shore, feeling she had reached the end of the road? Had there been some incident which had decided her to take her own life? She's gone and I'm still here. There was no pleasure in the thought, only a oneness, which was what Ruth had wanted, what everyone wanted.

'Ach, come away then, Mrs Lane,' Nurse Waddell would say each morning. 'Have you no' a smile for me? That's better. That didn't hurt, did it? Now you're just going to sit on that chair while I make the bed for you, and we'll see if you need a fresh nightie. Have you had any visitors yet?'

One morning Sarah said, 'Yes, one.'

'Who was that?' Brightly, rubbing Sarah's face briskly with a flannel, wringing it out in the basin, soaping it again. 'Lovely hands you've got. By Jove, you've taken good care of them.'

'The minister.'

'The Reverend Mr Gourlay himself? And what did he say to you?'

'Not much.' She saw the amused twist of the nurse's mouth, like the doctor's. She had given the whole of Largs something to talk about. The man had been embarrassed, had hummed and hawed and then suggested that they pray together. She presumed it was for her sins. He didn't mention the dead baby.

'And Mr MacIntyre's been a real brick bringing up these nice trays. She's been preparing them. The doctor gave her a diet sheet. You're lucky to have them both.'

'Yes, I'm lucky.' Sarah thought of saying to Nurse Waddell, 'She hates me, doesn't she?', but what was the point of involving the girl? What did it matter? 'Yes, I'm lucky,' she thought of saying, 'she throws the food at me like a sick cat that crept in when she wasn't looking.' 'She's a good cook.' The egg custards, the fine white fish, the nourishing vegetable broths, were like sawdust in her mouth.

When she had been up for a week but not out of her room, Mrs MacIntyre came upstairs. The resentment inside the woman filled the room. 'Rotten whore', her eyes said. She didn't ask how Sarah was. 'Ma man tells me you're up every day and Nurse Waddell's no' coming back. Is that right?'

'Yes.'

She folded her arms on her chest as if in a pulpit. A small gold brooch winked wickedly all the time she spoke, as if to

238

emphasise the words. 'I've done the Christian thing by you although you don't deserve it. My conscience is clear on that score. Oh, aye, I've nothing to reproach myself with, as I told the minister. But now that you're on your feet I'd be obliged if you would make arrangements to leave my house.'

'I've not written . . .'

'I daresay you've not written to anybody, least of all to the man who caused all the trouble. But it takes two for that sort of game. This is a decent house and I've done the decent thing. No stones will be thrown at me in Largs, I can assure you of that . . .' Sarah's mind drifted to the pebbly shore. There were plenty there . . . 'But enough's enough! I don't think, *Miss* Lane, you can have any idea of the shock you gave me, a decent body.' Her voice quivered in self-pity. 'One thing I know, I'll never be the same again.'

'I'm sorry.'

'It's too late to be sorry.' The big chin was thrust out, the mouth was like a petulant child's. 'The damage is done. You'll write, then, right away? Make arrangements?'

'Yes, I'll write.' She was very tired.

'This is Wednesday. I'll expect your sister to be here on Monday morning.'

'I'll write,' Sarah said again.

There was a pause. She knew the woman's flat gaze was on her, but her head was too heavy to lift. And her chest was dry and burning. She had kept that dark from Nurse Waddell when she had asked if everything was 'hunky-dory', her favourite expression. 'In that case I'll say cheerio, then, and you take my advice, dear, and get back as soon as you can to Glasgow. There's nothing like your own folk.'

'Have you nothing to say? No apologies for all the trouble you've caused in a decent house?' The harsh voice was in her ears, making her wince. 'When I think of how I was taken in by you, your fine manners, "Mrs MacIntyre this", "Mrs MacIntyre that", butter wouldn't have melted in your mouth.' The voice rose, strident, full of malice. 'Just deserts. It comes to everybody if they don't do what's right. The sleekitness of it, winklin' your way in here under false pretences . . .' Her

239

eyes, black in the thick-skinned face, fastened on Sarah with undisguised hate. 'Aye it's just deserts the wean died, you dirty bitch . . .' Sarah turned her head away from the woman and put her face in the pillow.

'I'm sorry . . . sorry . . . go away.' The woman's heavy breathing seemed to fill the room, and with it her malevolence. For a moment Sarah wondered if she would strike her, and then there was the heavy shuddering bang of the door and the heavy footsteps going downstairs.

When Jimmy came up with her teatray, a fine Fynan haddock swimming in rich yellow butter, fingers of white bread at the edge of the plate, there was an envelope lying beside it. 'She gave me the bill,' he said. 'A . . . had to take it. If it had been me . . .' His mild face expressed only mild regret.

'Would you pass me my bag?' Sarah said.

Mary arrived at eleven o'clock on Monday morning. Sarah heard her sharp voice downstairs, Mrs MacIntyre's strident one, then the sound of her sister's purposeful footsteps on the stairs. There was a pause, a knock, then she came into the room and stood with her back to the door, looking at Sarah. Her face was white with rage, her eyes were darting fire, either from her encounter with the landlady or shock at receiving Sarah's letter. Her black felt cloche was askew and her brown coat was all wrong with it. She never could match colours. She was breathing heavily. When she could bear it no longer, Sarah said, tears running down her cheeks, 'Are you going to give me a row as well, our Mary?'

'It's a good skelp I should be givin' you.' Her voice was a whisper and then suddenly she shouted, 'Oh, my God, Sarah, look at you! How did you let yourself get into a state like this?' She came half-running across the room and took Sarah in her arms. 'Why did you no' let on? The lies you've telt! I couldn't believe it when I read it, that you'd do that . . . thing, you always so nice brought up, the lady of the family. Look at me, greetin'. I haveny done that for years.' Her voice was choked with tears. 'Whit would our mother have said, and me promisin' to take care o' you? And that harridan down-stairs on top of it all. I've never heard such filth . . .'

'The baby died, Mary.' For the first time Sarah grieved bitterly for the child she hadn't seen. The tears streamed down her face.

'Aye, aye, I know. It never had a chance. I've seen the doctor. You're lucky you didn't go the same way. Poor wee mite, though. Never mind, you'll come back wi' me today and I'll get you fattened up in no time . . .'

'The shop. There's Mr MacPherson to tell.'

'John'll attend to all that. He's a dab hand at business affairs, Jimmy Maxton's right-hand man I tell him. There, there, don't cry like that, you'll only hurt yourself, wheesht, wheesht . . . we'll all take care o' you.' Mary rocked her against her breast as they both wept.

'What about Lachie and Bella?' Sarah said through her tears. 'I can't affront them.'

'They're too young. I just told them you'd been taken bad.'

'What did . . . John say?'

'D'you want to know?' She straightened to look at Sarah. 'He read your letter, and then he put it down on the table. "Whit are ye waitin' for?" he said. "You get your skates on and get that lass back here right away."'

'Did he? Did he say that?' Her tears would go on for ever. There was no way of stopping them. She cried her heart out while Mary held her. Pride in her husband had stopped hers. Out of the quietness, after a long time, Mary said, 'I could kill that Barney Turnbull for this.' Poor Barney, Sarah thought. It was kinder not to say anything. She heard her sister's voice again, no trace of tears in it now. 'I blame myself as well. I knew it wisny like you to bury yourself doon here.' She became brisk, her old self. 'Come on, give that up. It'll no' get you anywhere crying for something that's over and done with. Come on, now. I'll help you to pack your case. I wouldny stay in that she-devil's house a minute longer than need be.'

Sarah's tears dried.

Chapter Thirty-two

She thought that perhaps it was the happiest time in her life, being back with them all. Mary kept up her briskness, and John supplied the softer caring that she needed, 'cooterin', Mary called it. Every night when he came in from his endless meetings he would make straight for Sarah's room while Mary prepared his supper.

After the first week when she had pretended to be well, she had been glad to creep back to bed in her old room. It was as if she had never been away, the neatness of it, the clean, bright fire although it was May, the Paisley-patterned eiderdown with the pink inset border, the walnut-veneered furniture bought at the Co-op. But it was a young woman in love who had left it, not this sick creature who had no strength in her legs, who coughed all the time.

'And how's the patient been the day,' John would say, often putting a bunch of half-wilted flowers he had bought in the Barrows on the counterpane.

'Fine, John.'

'Well, you keep that shawl round you. It will help the cough.'

'It's one Mary knitted for Bella coming.'

'Well, it's no' lost what a freen gets.'

'Freen,' she repeated, smiling as she looked at him. 'Aye, wee Bella's my freen. How's Dixon's?'

'Shakin' in its shoes. If a General Strike happens, Glasgow, never mind Dixon's, will never recover from the blow.' She saw his careworn face, and felt his anxiety as if it were her own, recognised this rare feeling between John and her. Her eyelids grew heavy as if thinking tired her, and she knew he had slipped away. She was glad he hadn't seen the weak tears which had come.

One evening she said to him, 'I got a letter from my friend, Mrs de Vere.' She drew it out from under her pillow and handed it to him. 'Would you like to read it?'

'No, no, Sarah. It's private property.'

'I'd like you to read it. Out loud. Here.' He took it reluctantly. 'I couldn't believe my eyes when Mary brought it in. I thought she must have forgotten about me long ago.'

'You're no' easily forgotten.' His free hand covered hers, and she met his deep-set eyes with her own. They held, and she knew she could say things to him she could never say to Mary. All the understanding of the world was there.

'I think a lot lying here, John, about your concern for the workers. And your fair-mindedness. Never any reproaches when they let you down.'

'He that is without sin . . .' he said with the quirk so that it didn't seem sanctimonious.

'All kinds of things. Do you mind one Halloween when I came round to see you. Mary wasn't here?'

'I mind that fine. We were happy, eh?'

She nodded. 'Happy . . .' She thought of Bella nestling into her, the peace, with John across from her, Lachie on his knee. Her throat filled and the cough started. When she could speak, 'Aye, all kinds of things. Do you remember Ruth Crosbie?' She saw his surprise. 'I ran away from her flat? The poor soul died, you know. By her own hand.'

He nodded. 'Sad that she was driven to that. She gave you the scare of your life, all the same.'

'It wouldn't now.'

'Not a matter of life or death?' He smiled. John looked straight at things.

'And I think about Barney. He's never out of my mind. The good times we had . . .'

'You have to hold on to that.'

'You're not like Mary. She would like to wring his neck.'

'Mary sees only black and white.'

'Not the gradations. Ruth and Barney. There's room for all kinds in the world. I'm glad. She'll come to seeing that when she gets about a bit.'

'Or has a spell in bed.' The quirk was there. 'It does wonders for your thinking.'

'Space. He gave me so much, Barney. Such . . . joy.' She looked beyond John, seeing Barney doing one of his little tap-dancing routines in his twinkling nut-brown shoes. On the carpet at Grove Street, rolled up and damp now in the furniture repository. 'Jack Buchanan,' she said. She saw John's enquiring glance. 'I used to call him that . . .' Her voice broke. He leant forward and wiped her eyes with his handkerchief, put it in her hand.

'Crying's good for you. There's no bitterness where there's tears. Lie back, lass.'

'Will you read me my letter before you go ben, John? Out loud?'

'Out loud, then,' he said, lifting it from the side table where he had laid it. 'Dear Sarah,' he began.

'She called me Sarah after we got friendly. I should have told her how much that pleased me.'

'She would know.' He looked down again.

'Dear Sarah, I telephoned to Charles et Cie and was told you had left. What a forbidding woman Miss Frobisher is! She lacks your grace . . .'

'"She lacks your grace."' She repeated the words softly, then, her hand to her mouth to hide the smile, 'She should have said that to Mrs MacIntyre . . .' John grinned at her.

'I'm quite settled now in Barminster, the village near the Big House, as it's called here. The villagers are friendly, although quite different in style from Helensburgh. I had forgotten how carapaced the upper classes are in England . . .'

'That's a fine word, John, "carapaced". I learnt it in my reading.'

'Imprisoned in their shells. Yes, I've come across it.' He went on:

244

'However, I've made one or two friends, and I'm encouraged to call on Ronald and Elizabeth whenever I feel inclined.'

'I knew it would be called the Big House.' He nodded, his eyes on the letter.

'I never thought I would miss the sea, but I do. The countryside here, although pretty and neat, puts a limit on one's horizons. What pleasure I had sitting with you in that wide window of my old home, the calmness and peace, as if you were part of it. So different from Elizabeth, who is hearty and rumbustious, but not calming.

'My garden is going to be my principal joy, packed with old-fashioned flowers, hollyhocks, zinnias, pinks, rambling roses ... there are actually roses round the back door. How I'd like you to see it!

'Miss Frobisher was not at all forthcoming when I asked about you, but I hope there is some reasonable explanation, or even better, a joyous one, and that you are happily married somewhere. Perhaps if you are, your husband will spare you to come and visit me. I shall look forward to that. Do write and tell me when. Your friend, Violet.'

John looked up, folded the letter and handed it back to Sarah. 'That will be something to look forward to.' She placed it carefully beneath her pillow. The movement tired her, and she lay still, her eyes on him.

'I'll add it to Barney,' she said, 'I mean, the looking forward. Violet. She asked me to call her that.'

'Does she peep shyly from behind a mossy stone?' She knew he was trying to forget what he had seen in her eyes.

'You're a caution, John Gibson,' she said. Her heart was heavy with foreboding.

'John!' Mary called from the kitchen. 'Come away ben and get your supper.'

'On you go.' She drew her eyes away from him.

He stood up slowly and fished in his pocket. 'I forgot this. I got it in Grant's Educational for you. Second-hand. A wee book of Burns' poems. "A man's a man for aw that."' He bent down and placed the small book between her hands on the counterpane. She was too tired to grasp it.

'John!' Mary shouted.

'"O, my luve's like a red, red rose . . ."'

Her lids dropped over her eyes. They were burning hot. She thought he bent down and kissed them, one after the other. She wasn't sure.

Chapter Thirty-three

At least they won't have me to feed, she thought. She knew she was going to die. The first time she spat bright blood she hid it from Mary, staggering to the kitchen sink when she was out to wash her handkerchief, but the next time there was no concealment. The sheets had to be stripped and soaked in cold water. The doctor was sent for. He has death in his face, she thought, because he sees it in mine.

Lachie visited each night with wee Bella by the hand, pushed in by their mother, but after Lachie had got over the strangeness of seeing his smart auny so white and thin in bed, he chattered away about his school, his teachers, and how he might be allowed to be a conductor on the trams when the strike came.

'Mr Thompson, my teacher, is going to drive one!' he said, his eyes shining with pride. 'And he might get the chance of a train as well.' He laughed, his eyes on Sarah. Bella giggled, a look of worship on her face. She was shyer than her brother, and she sat primly in a chair at the side of the bed, holding Sarah's hand. The little fingers curling round her own made Sarah's eyes fill.

I might have had a wee girl like Bella, she thought, if I hadn't . . . did what I did. She shied away from the word. She hadn't been able to mention it to Mary, but once when John was sitting quietly beside her she said to him, 'Do you think folks will say I murdered my baby, John?'

His eyes turned towards her, deep with understanding. She tried to smile. 'I wouldn't like to go with that on my conscience.'

'Nobody's ever blamed for loving too much,' he said. 'If there's any blame it rests with Mary and me, too busy, she with her household cares, me working for the men. It's too easy sometimes to neglect what's near you and more important. And there's such a thing as recognising a person's responsibility to themselves, letting them dree their own weird. You know I've always been an advocate of that.'

'Mrs MacIntyre said it was just deserts, my baby dying.'

'I'm sorry for people who think like that. You can afford to ignore them.'

'You've made me feel much better.' She turned her head into the pillow. It was too late to wish she had done things differently. All you had to do was to accept everything, the good and the bad.

She knew he sat for a long time. Once she felt him touch her shoulder, heard him say softly, 'Sarah.' It wasn't a question, just a naming, and with infinite tenderness. She didn't know when he went away.

A few weeks later the children were debarred from the sick room. 'Where are the weans, Mary?' she asked her. 'They cheer me up.'

'The doctor says they're too noisy for you.'

'Oh, no! I liked them coming. Lachie chatting away, and Bella sitting there, her big eyes on me, like John's . . .'

She knew the doctor was right. Her chest was still burning, and she knew she had a constant fever because Mary came in at intervals to bathe her face and arms. Her briskness was forced. Sarah could see through her.

'Mary,' she said, and was surprised to hear she could only whisper. 'Mother couldn't have had a better deputy. I don't know how to tell you . . .' She put up her hand and Mary clasped it in hers.

'Oh, I'm a rough soul,' she said, 'no good to you.'

'Aye, you're good to me, that good . . .' She had to stop trying to speak.

When she had the next haemorrhage she knew it wouldn't be long. She had strange light-headed thoughts that she might see her baby where she was going. Since she had lost it, it had become an entity, something to be constantly grieved over. The regrets would be back, if only she had done it differently, looked after herself, decided to keep it instead of not giving the poor wee thing room to breathe.

Sarah couldn't speak about Barney to Mary, who wouldn't have let his name sully her lips. She had always known he was no good, him and that chum of his. He wouldn't have taken her in, by God, but Sarah had always been shy, impressionable, too romantic by half. It never did you any good in this world, being romantic. It was as if Mary had spoken.

The day the General Strike started it was strangely quiet. 'And behold, peace fell on the land,' she said to Mary, and saw fear come into her eyes.

'Well, there's nothing in the streets, that's why. Everything's stopped. John'll be in the thick of it. I'll send someone . . .' She held up her hand, waved it feebly.

'No . . .' She could only whisper. 'He's needed.' And then, because she had to say it, 'I've leant on your John. Maybe too much.'

Mary sat down beside her, which was rare enough. 'I know that, Sarah,' she said. 'And I know he's gey fond o' you. A special fondness he doesn't give me. He's no' sleepin' at nights. Thinkin' of you . . .'

Her mind was wandering. 'Mary . . .' She could feel her sister's strong grasp as she took her hand. 'Mary, what did you call . . . that woman . . . in Largs?'

'Mrs MacIntyre.'

'She said . . . I'd got . . . my just deserts.'

'The cheek o' it!' Her voice was dismissive. 'Well, what would you expect? They're all the same, they Coast landladies. Hard as nails.'

'Oh, Mary . . .' Her lips moved in a smile. Poor Mrs MacIntyre. She felt kindly towards her, kindly towards herself. John had taught her that.

What did it matter? She would soon see the baby, see its wee face. She knew Mary was stroking her hand, helping her, understanding. She could feel the rasp of the work-roughened skin, backwards and forwards, backwards and forwards. How important the touch of hands was . . . she thought of wee Bella sitting primly on the chair, her childish fingers curling round her own. 'What lovely hands you have,' Nurse Waddell had said. All Miss Frobisher's young ladies had nice hands. It was to be expected at a Court Dressmakers.

And there was the clasp of John's, steadying her, night after night, sometimes late, sometimes when Mary was asleep.

'Is there anything I can get you, hen?' Mary asked.

How quiet it was. Like Sunday before the bells rang, or in a graveyard. The whole world had stopped to watch her die.

She nodded. 'The wee box in my case . . . if you would.'

Mary got up and in the quietness the hasps of the suitcase snapped loudly. Sarah heard the rustle of tissue paper (you always used plenty of tissue paper at Charles et Cie), and then Mary was at her side again.

'It's here, Sarah. I've opened it. There's a wee green Buddha kind o' thing, and the . . .' Her voice broke. 'Do you want me . . . to put it on for you?'

'Yes. The third finger . . . of my left . . .' She felt the coldness of the gold.

'It's that big.'

'Never mind. And give me the wee Buddha to hold, Mary. It was Barney's first present to me.' Her hands closed round the smooth soapy surface. It felt green. 'He was my boy, Mary . . .' She couldn't see now. 'He was my . . .' It was so heavy, too heavy to hold. She could feel it slipping out of her grasp, then Mary's rough hands closing over hers. 'I never could fathom . . . why . . . he liked his chum . . . better . . .'

The room was very quiet.